Now
You
See
Her

Books by Linda Howard

A LADY OF THE WEST

ANGEL CREEK

THE TOUCH OF FIRE

HEART OF FIRE

DREAM MAN

AFTER THE NIGHT

SHADES OF TWILIGHT

SON OF THE MORNING

KILL AND TELL

NOW YOU SEE HER

Published by POCKET BOOKS

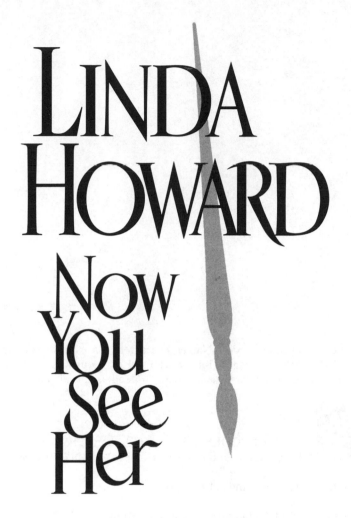

LINDA HOWARD

Now You See Her

 POCKET BOOKS

New York London Toronto Sydney Tokyo Singapore

POCKET BOOKS, a division of Simon & Schuster Inc.
1230 Avenue of the Americas, New York, NY 10020

ISBN: 0-671-56882-5

First Pocket Books hardcover printing September 1998

10 9 8 7 6 5 4 3

Designed by C. Linda Dingler

PROLOGUE

Clayton, New York

It was the third of September, one of those cloudless, perfect days nestled between the heat of summer and the approaching winter chill. The sky was so blue that Sweeney, getting out of her car in the supermarket parking lot, went stock-still and gawked upward at that amazing blue bowl as if she had never seen sky before. She hadn't—not like this.

If there was one thing in life she knew, it was colors, and she had never before seen that particular shade of blue. It was incredible, deeper and darker, richer than any sky had the right to be. Just for today, this perfect day, the haze of atmosphere between heaven and earth had thinned, and she stood closer to the edge of the universe than she ever had before, so close that she felt almost as if she might be sucked into that blue, right away from earth.

Could she reproduce it? Mentally she mixed the pigments, automatically discarding some as her internal eye judged the results. No, that touch of white would make the shade too baby-ish. This wasn't a wimpy blue—it was the most kick-ass blue she had ever seen. This was pure and dramatic, pulling her in and overwhelming her with the richness of its beauty. She stood with her face upturned, errand forgotten, and felt exalted by color, filled to overflowing, her heart swollen and aching with ecstasy.

When she finally remembered to drag her gaze back to earth, her eyes were dazzled. She saw a flash of . . . something, and though she hadn't been looking at the sun, she thought the sky must be brighter than she'd thought, because her eyes needed to adjust. She blinked, then squinted. It was something solid, and yet not quite. . . . It was a child, oddly two-dimensional.

She looked at the child, blinked, then looked again. Shock hit her like a sledgehammer, congealing her blood, numbing her fingertips.

The child was dead. She had attended his funeral a month before. But on this perfect day, while performing a perfectly ordi-nary errand, she saw a dead child walking across the parking lot.

Speechless, Sweeney darted her gaze to the woman the boy was following: his mother. Sue Beresford was carrying a bag of groceries in one arm, her other hand clutching the little paw of her rambunctious four-year-old, Corbin. Her face was drawn, her eyes shadowed with the sharp grief of a mother who had lost her older son to leukemia only a month before.

But there was little Sam, dead a month, following along behind her.

Sweeney's feet were frozen to the pavement, her entire body numb and incapable of movement as she watched the little boy desperately trailing behind his mother, trying to get her attention. "Mom," ten-year-old Samuel Beresford kept saying, his voice thin with anxiety. "Mom!" But Sue didn't respond, just kept walking, towing little Corbin behind her. Sam tried to catch her shirt, but the fabric slipped through his insubstantial grasp. He looked at Sweeney and she plainly saw his frustration, his bewilderment and fear. "She can't hear me," he said, the words wavering as if she heard them through an imperfect sound system. He hurried to catch up, his thin legs flashing under the loud plaid of his baggy shorts.

Sweeney swayed with shock and put her hand on the hood of the car to brace herself. The sun-warmed metal felt slightly gritty under her fingers. The blue bowl of the sky pressed down as if it would swallow her, and she stared mutely after the dead child.

The thin figure clambered into the backseat beside Corbin, moving quickly before his mother could shut the door. Sue got behind the steering wheel and drove out of the parking lot. Sam's pale, translucent face shone briefly in the rear window as he looked back at Sweeney; his hand lifted in a forlorn little wave. Automatically she waved back.

Her mind formed one word:
Ghost.

CHAPTER ONE

It was one thing to believe in ghosts, another to actually see them. Sweeney had discovered, though, that the kicker was whether or not she *knew* the ghost. In the small village of Clayton, New York, where she had lived until almost a year ago, she'd had at least a nodding acquaintance with most of the inhabitants, including the dead ones. In New York City, she didn't know any of them, so she could look past the translucent faces in the crowd and pretend not to see them. Back in Clayton, after she had seen the ghost of Sam Beresford, she had never known when another ghost would stop and speak, and she had never been sharp enough to play it cool and pretend nothing had happened. No, she'd just *had* to react, and before long people were giving her those looks that said they suspected she was losing her marbles. She had packed up and moved before they began pointing at her on the street.

Yeah, the city was better. Warmer, too. About the time she began seeing the ghosts, her internal heat regulator seemed to go on the fritz, too. She always felt chilled these days, had for the past year. Maybe the cold had started even before she saw little Sam Beresford; she couldn't remember, because who paid attention to things like that? It wasn't exactly something anyone would mark on their calendars: *August 29: Felt cold.* Yeah, sure.

Sweeney didn't know what had brought the ghosts to mind this bright September morning, but they were the first things she thought of when she woke. That, and the cold, which seemed worse. She got out of bed, hurriedly changed her pajamas for sweats, and went into the kitchen to get that first cup of coffee, thanking God for automatic timers as she went. It was so nice to have the coffee waiting for her when she got up, because she thought she'd probably freeze to death if she had to wait for it to brew.

The first sip warmed her insides on the way down, and she sighed with relief. She actually tasted the second sip, and was going back for the third when the phone rang.

Phones were a necessary nuisance, but a nuisance still. Who the hell would be calling her at—she checked the clock—seven-forty-three in the morning? Irritably, she set her cup down and walked over to snag the receiver off the wall.

"Candra here," a warm voice replied to her cautious greeting. "I'm sorry to call you so early, but I don't know your schedule and wanted to be certain I caught you."

"You got me on the first cast," Sweeney replied, her irritation fading. Candra Worth owned the gallery where Sweeney sold her work.

"Beg pardon?"

"Never mind. It's a fishing term. I don't suppose you've ever been fishing?"

"God, no." Like her voice, Candra's laugh was warm and intimate. "The reason I called was to ask if you could be here at about one to meet some potential clients. We were talking at a party last night and they mentioned they're thinking of having their portraits done. I immediately thought of you, of course. Mrs. McMillan wanted to come by the gallery to look at a particular piece I've just gotten in, so I thought it would be convenient for them to meet you while they're here."

"I'll be there," Sweeney promised, though she had looked forward to a day of uninterrupted work.

"Good. See you then."

Sweeney shivered as she hung up and hurried back to her coffee. She didn't like meeting prospective clients, but she did like doing portraits—and she needed the work. About the time she had started seeing ghosts, her work had gone to hell in a handbasket. The trademark delicacy of her landscapes and still-life studies had given way to an uncharacteristic boisterousness, and she didn't like it. Her colors had always been transparent, as if they were watercolors instead of oils, but now, no matter how hard she tried, she found herself gravitating toward deep, passionate, unrealistic shades. She hadn't carried anything to Candra's gallery in months, and though her old pieces were still selling, there couldn't be many left.

She owed it to Candra to take the job, if the couple liked her work. Sweeney was aware that she was not now and probably would never be a hot commodity, because her art was considered too traditional, but nevertheless Candra had always steered her way those customers who preferred the traditional approach, thereby providing Sweeney with a fairly steady, moderately lucrative income. Above that, last year when Sweeney had announced her intention of leaving Clayton, it was Candra who had scouted out this apartment for her.

Not that New York City would have been Sweeney's first choice; she had been thinking of someplace warmer. Of course, New York was warmer than Clayton, which sat on the St. Lawrence River, just east of Lake Ontario, and every winter was the recipient of lake-effect snows. New York City was coastal; it snowed during the winter, but not as often and not as much, and the temperatures were more moderate. Not moderate enough; Sweeney had been thinking more along the lines of Miami, but Candra had talked her into coming to the city and Sweeney didn't regret it. There was always something going on, which provided her with plenty of distraction whenever she thought she was going to scream from frustration.

Above all, New York was big enough that she didn't know any of the dead people, didn't feel compelled by good manners to acknowledge them. The city also provided a steady supply of faces—live ones. She loved faces, loved studying them, which was why her portrait work was steadily increasing—thank God, because otherwise her bank account would have been in serious trouble, instead of just in trouble.

The city suited her, for now, and by New York standards the rent was reasonable. Candra had known about the apartment because her husband, Richard Worth, owned the building. He was some sort of Wall Street whiz, a self-made market millionaire; Sweeney had met him a couple of times, and tried to stay as far away from him as possible. He had an interesting but intimidating face, and she thought he must be the type of man who steamrollered over everyone in his path. She made it a point not to be in his way.

The neighborhood wasn't the best, nor was the building,

but the apartment was a corner one, with huge windows. She could happily have lived in a barn, if it had as good a light—and central heat.

The coffee had stopped her shivering. She always felt a little chilled now, but mornings were the worst. She would have gone to a doctor, but whenever she imagined talking to someone about what as going on, her common sense stopped her. *"About a year ago I started seeing ghosts, Doctor, and that's when I got cold. Oh, by the way, traffic signals turn green whenever I approach, too. And my plants bloom out of season. So what's wrong with me?"* Sure. Not in this lifetime. She'd been pointed at enough when she was a kid. Being an artist was uncommon enough; she wasn't about to let herself be labeled as wacko, too.

The past year had been trying for more reasons than just seeing ghosts. Sweeney resisted change with a stubborn determination that was no less unyielding for its lack of ferocity. She wasn't ferocious about anything but painting. Still, over the years those who knew her well had learned how tenacious she was. She liked routine, liked her life to have an even tenor. She could get along just fine without drama, despair, and excitement, having had a surfeit of it in her childhood. For her, sameness and normality equaled security. But how could she feel secure when *she* had changed, when *she* knew she was no longer normal, even if she had managed to hide it from the rest of the world? And now she seemed to have lost her direction, if not her talent; but what good was talent if she didn't know what she was doing with it?

She turned on the television to keep her company while she rustled up breakfast, though cereal didn't require much rustling. She ate the corn flakes dry, without milk, because the milk was cold and she had just gotten rid of the chill, so she wasn't eager to reacquire it. As she ate, the sexy Diet Coke commercial came on, and she paused, spoon halfway to her mouth, eyes widening as her lips formed a silent "wow."

By the time the commercial ended, she felt almost sweaty. Maybe watching more television ads was the key to feeling warm.

After putting in several hours of work in the studio, Sweeney realized it was almost one o'clock and she had to get ready to go over to the gallery. She hated dressing up, but she found herself reaching for a skirt and top instead of her usual jeans and sweatshirt. A flash of scarlet caught her eye, and she slid clothes hangers to the side to extract a red sweater she had never worn that someone had given her for Christmas several years before. The tags were still on it. Studying the bright, rich color, she decided that was just what she wanted today.

She supposed she should take some pains with her hair, too. Standing in front of the mirror, she frowned. She had been blessed, or cursed, with very curly, very unruly hair, and she kept it longer than shoulder length because the weight helped hold it down. Her options were limited; she could pull it back and look like a schoolgirl, try to pin it up and hope she didn't end up with stray curls sticking out like corkscrews, or leave it loose. She opted for loose; the possibility of humiliation was less.

She took a comb and tidied the more unruly parts. When she was little, she had hated her hair. She had inherited the wild curls from her mother, only her mother had gloried in having an untamable mane of hair, bringing even more attention to it by coloring it every shade of red imaginable. She had wanted to color Sweeney's hair, too, but even as a child Sweeney had clung to the small bits of normalcy in her life. Her hair was brown, and she was going to keep it brown. Not red, not black, not platinum. Brown. The color was ordinary, even if the curls were a bit flamboyant.

Putting down the comb, she critically surveyed herself. There. Except for the hair, there was nothing about her that would draw attention. Trim, medium height—well, almost. She would have liked another inch or two. Blue eyes, curly brown hair. Good skin. She was thirty-one, and still no wrinkles had appeared. The black skirt stopped right above her knees, her shoes were sensible enough to walk to the gallery in but didn't look seriously grandmotherly, and the scarlet sweater was . . . great. She almost took it off, but was too beguiled by the color.

Some makeup seemed called for. She was never certain she knew what she was doing with the stuff, so she limited herself to the most basic: mascara and lipstick. This was her insurance against looking like a clown. *Or Mom,* her almost-subconscious jibed. Sweeney always made a real effort to avoid looking or acting like her mother. Being an artist was already enough of a family resemblance.

Because she was fairly certain that all Candra had left of her paintings at the gallery were a couple of landscapes, she sorted through the stack of sketches she'd made of people, selecting the ones that were closest to being finished and put them in a portfolio to show to the McMillans. She didn't have any finished portraits to show, because they were all commissioned and went to the subject as soon as they were completed.

Portfolio tucked under her arm, she left the apartment for the walk to the gallery. The warm September sun beamed down on her as soon as she stepped onto the sidewalk, and she drew a deep sigh of pleasure at the heat. Most of the people she passed, except for the business types who probably wore suits and ties to bed, were in short sleeves. A sign alternating with the time and temperature announced that the temperature was eighty-four degrees.

It was a nice day, the kind of day when walking was a joy.

She came to the corner where her favorite hot dog vendor worked his stand and stopped.

The old man had one of the sweetest faces she had ever seen. He was always smiling, his teeth bright and even in his dark-skinned face. Dentures, probably; people his age seldom had their own teeth. He was sixty-eight, he'd once told her; time to retire. Old folks like him needed to get out of the way and let some youngster make a living. He'd laughed when he said that, and Sweeney knew he had no intention of retiring. He kept selling his hot dogs and smiling his sweet smile at his customers. She had noticed him the first week she'd been in New York and made it a point to pass by his stand as often as possible so she could study his face.

His expression fascinated her. She had sketched it a few times, the work quick and rudimentary because she didn't want him to notice what she was doing and become self-conscious. She hadn't quite gotten it right yet, the look of a man who had no quarrel with the world. He simply enjoyed life. It was that, the total lack of cynicism in his eyes, like a child's, that made her fingers itch to capture him on paper and canvas.

"Here ya go, Sweeney." He swapped the hot dog for the money in her hand, and she tucked the portfolio safely between her calves while she slathered a ton of mustard on the dog. "You look all spiffy today. Hot date?"

Yeah, sure. She hadn't had a date in . . . in so long she couldn't remember exactly how long it *had* been. At least a couple of years. Probably several. She hadn't missed it. "Business," she said, and took a bite of the dog.

"That's a shame, lookin' as hot as you do today." He winked at her and Sweeney winked back, though she was a bit startled by the compliment. Hot? Her? She was the least hot person she knew, in any sense of the word. She would rather work any day, lose herself in color and form, light and texture, than waste time worrying what some man thought about her hair or if he was dating others, too.

During college she had gone through the motions because it had seemed to be expected of her, but aside from a couple of rare crushes in high school she had never cared much about any guy. She hadn't felt even a frisson of lasciviousness since . . . well, since that morning, come to think of it. She was more than a little surprised at herself, letting the Diet Coke commercial get to her like that. This late-blooming lust took her aback. She had thought herself safe from the insane hormonal urges that wrecked the creative careers of so many women, or at least diluted them.

"You'll knock 'em dead in that outfit," the vendor said, winking at her again.

Funny, she hadn't thought the simple skirt and sweater that fetching. It had to be the color, she thought. New Yorkers always wore black; sometimes she thought no one in the city owned a single bright-colored garment. She must look like a cardinal among crows, decked out in her scarlet sweater. And combing her hair had been a definite plus. Hell, she was even wearing earrings.

She retrieved the portfolio from between her legs and continued down the sidewalk, hot dog in hand. The gallery was four more blocks, plenty of time to finish the dog and wipe the mustard from her mouth. Greeting the McMillans with goo smeared on her face wouldn't leave a good impression.

It had been nice of Candra to set up the meeting. Other gallery owners probably wouldn't have overly concerned themselves with her. The big bucks were in primitive and modern art, not in the traditional style she preferred, but Candra was always looking out for Sweeney's interests, guiding business her way. She did that for all the artists whose work she displayed, from the lowest seller to the highest, with a natural warmth that attracted customers, probably making the gallery a ton of money every year. Not that Candra had to worry about money; Richard's wealth made the gallery's profit, or lack of one, unimportant.

At the thought of Richard Worth, his face sprang to her mind, accompanied by the usual uneasiness. She would have liked to paint him, but couldn't see herself asking. His face was all hard angles and sharp eyes. She would never portray him in one of the double-breasted, three-thousand dollar Italian silk suits he liked, though; she would put that face on the docks, or behind the wheel of a big truck. Richard Worth looked like a sweaty T-shirt kinda guy, not a Wall Street wizard.

He and Candra seemed like such opposites. Candra was lovely, aristocratic, with her sleek dark hair and chocolate eyes, but it was a bland sort of loveliness, the type possessed by thousands of women: attractive, but not remarkable. Her true charm lay in her friendly personality, which, like the vendor's sweetness, came from what lay behind the face. Richard's nature seemed molded in his bones, his tough, angled face a testament to the man. As a couple they seemed mismatched, though their marriage had lasted ten years. The times Sweeney had seen them together, she had gotten the impression that though they were standing side by side, it was merely by chance. Richard seemed too cold, too much a workaholic, to appeal to a woman of Candra's warmth, but who knew what went on between a couple in their private moments? Maybe he sometimes actually relaxed.

As Sweeney approached a corner, the traffic signal changed and the Walk sign lit. She had become accustomed to the convenience of never having to linger on any corners waiting for the signals to change. A few drivers seemed bewildered by the brevity of the green light, but that wasn't her problem. She almost smirked at them as she crossed the street. She hated wasting time, and standing around on a street corner sure qualified as wasted time. She begrudged every moment away from her painting, so much so that even eating almost qualified as wasted time.

Not sleeping, though. She loved to sleep. One of her favorite things was to work late into the night, until she was exhausted, then to fall into bed, feeling that delicious heaviness as she lost consciousness, like falling into a hole. The only thing that made it better was if it was raining, too. The pleasure of going to sleep while listening to the rain was almost sensual.

These days, sleeping was an adventure, because with sleep came dreams. She had always dreamed in color, but now her dreams were almost painfully vivid, in lush, brilliant Technicolor. She was fascinated by the hues of her dreams, so intense and vibrant. When she woke she tried to reproduce those colors, only to find they didn't fit her work and she could never get them quite right anyway. They were wrong for the delicacy of her technique, for the precise brushwork that was her trademark. She loved the colors, though, and was disappointed on those mornings when her memory failed to dredge up any dreams at all.

She finished the hot dog, tossed the paper in the trash can, and ran a finger around her mouth to remove any leftover mustard. She didn't much like hot dogs, so she had to smother the taste with a lot of mustard. She supposed she could eat something she *did* like, but, well, the vendor was always there and she enjoyed his face, and she didn't have to go out of her way, so getting a hot dog saved time. Not only that, now she wouldn't have to waste time eating once she got home.

People marched along the sidewalks, not talking—unless it was on their cell phones—and seldom making eye contact. Sweeney openly studied their faces, knowing they weren't likely to look at her and thus catch her looking at them. She ignored the occasional face that was too transparent. It was easy; being New Yorkers, even the ghosts tended to avoid eye contact.

The huge variety of faces in the city was a constant source of wonder and inspiration to her. Paris . . . well, Paris was okay, but even its name made her uncomfortable. She had seen too many pretentious artists, like her mother, make a big deal about painting in Paris, and Sweeney just didn't fit in with the art crowd there. Not that she fit in with the art crowd here, either, she reflected, but somehow in New York, she had more room, more a sense of being unseen. Candra's idea to relocate to the city had been brilliant. Though Sweeney could foresee a day when she would leave, for now she loved it.

Someday, the city would pall; all the places she had lived in had eventually bored her. She had never done any tropical landscapes and figured one day she'd feel the urge to go to Bora Bora, though on her budget she'd probably settle for Florida. After all, a palm tree was a palm tree. But for now she was still fascinated with faces, and right here was the best place to be.

The gallery was discreetly ensconced behind two double sets of glass doors, the outside set the bulletproof variety, at Richard's insistence. The lettering on the door was small and plain, announcing "Worth Gallery" and leaving it at that. There wasn't a curlicue in sight, which Sweeney appreciated. Ornate gilt lettering would have turned her stomach.

As usual, the first sight to greet anyone entering the gallery was Kai, which in Sweeney's opinion was a sight indeed. He was beautiful; that was the only word for him. She supposed he filled the function of a receptionist, but she wasn't quite certain what his official title was, or if he even had one. Judging from the way some of the female customers stared at him, it was enough for him just to be there; no other function was required. He had glossy, shoulder-length black hair and narrow dark eyes set above chiseled cheekbones, with lush lips that made her think he must have a Polynesian heritage, and strengthened her urge to paint palm trees. He did some modeling on the side and took art classes at night, which made Kai a very busy boy.

She suspected Kai and Candra had had, if not a full-fledged affair, at least a fling. Sweeney could be amazingly oblivious to everything around her when she was working, but painting portraits had made her acutely observant of faces and expressions, and a few times there had been a hint of intimacy between him and Candra. Nothing overt, just a flicker of expression, a brief meeting of gazes, a momentary possessiveness in Kai's manner. Candra would never wear her heart on her sleeve, but Kai wasn't as sophisticated. Sweeney hoped he wasn't emotionally involved, because Candra would certainly never allow herself to reciprocate those feelings. Richard's bucks far outweighed Kai's beauty.

Kai left his seat behind the elegant Queen Anne desk from which he oversaw all entrées, coming toward her with a white smile and raised dark eyebrows. "Sweeney. Wow." His gaze slid down her. "You're looking hot." He had a faint accent, a melodious singsong quality that had to be Hawaiian. His expression was openly admiring.

A bit concerned, Sweeney glanced down at herself. This made two men who had, within the space of ten minutes, told her she looked "hot." The simple scarlet sweater must pack more punch than she had realized. From now on, she would be more careful about wearing it. On the other hand, she adored the color.

"The McMillans aren't here yet," Kai said, touching her elbow, his fingertips lingering on the inside of her arm. "Would you like a cup of tea while you wait?"

This was the treatment he gave customers. Her concern edged toward alarm. Whatever mysterious power the color scarlet had, she didn't like all this male attention. Men were trouble, capital *T,* italicized, underlined. She didn't have time for men, especially not a smooth, twenty-four-year-old high-maintenance boy toy like Kai. She hadn't lived seven years longer than he had without learning a few things about herself, namely that she was one of those people who function better alone.

The tea sounded good, though.

"Earl Grey, one lump of brown." Candra used the European custom of offering both brown and white lumps of sugar with the tea she kept brewed for her customers. Sweeney considered it an immensely civilized thing for her to do.

"Coming right up." Kai flashed his brilliant smile at her again and disappeared into the small alcove where the tea service was kept. Sweeney looked around, wondering where Candra was. If the McMillans were due, then Candra should already be here; she was extremely punctual, always there to greet the customers with whom she had appointments.

Standing where she was, Sweeney could see most of the gallery. It was two stories high, with regal, curving stairs arching like ribbons up both sides of the room, but the space was mostly open and wonderfully lit, which gave her an excellent overall view, and Candra wasn't in sight.

Kai returned, bearing tea fragrantly steaming in a translucent china cup. "Is Candra here?" Sweeney asked, taking the cup from him and inhaling the steam with unconscious delight.

"She's in her office, with Richard." He glanced over his shoulder at the closed door. "I gather the amicable proceedings aren't proceeding very amicably."

Sweeney frowned into her cup, pondering that opaque statement. "What proceedings?"

Kai blinked at her. "The divorce, of course."

"Divorce?" Sweeney was startled, and disappointed. She had suspected Candra's marriage wasn't perfect, but still, she hated to see people she knew break up. It always distressed her, reminding her of how many divorces she had lived through as a child.

"My God, don't tell me you didn't know. It's been in the works for almost a year, since right after you moved to the city. I can't believe you haven't heard anything about it."

Despite her shock, Sweeney almost snorted. She had lost track of *national elections* when she was working; why would a divorce blip on her radar? She didn't move in Candra's circles, and though they were friendly acquaintances and had a mutually profitable arrangement—usually profitable, that is—they weren't ex-actly bosom buddies. Or maybe Candra didn't think the divorce was important; it was so common in the art world Sweeney wondered why people bothered going through the motions of getting married.

Her own parents had each been married four times, twice to each other. Sweeney had one younger brother, after whose birth her mother had decided motherhood distracted her from her devotion to her art and had herself spayed. Her father, though, just kept on begetting with his various wives and had produced two half-brothers and three half-sisters for Sweeney, none of whom she saw more than once every couple of years. There had never been any question of fatherhood being allowed to distract him from *his* art, which was filmmaking. The last Sweeney had heard, he was about to take wife number five, but that had been at least two years ago, so he might well be on number six by now. Or maybe he had gone back to number four. For all she knew, he might be back with her mother. Sweeney didn't exactly stay in touch.

"Candra moved out of the town house just after last Thanksgiving, I think." Kai's eyes shone with the joy of gossip. "I know it was before Christmas, because she had a Twelve Days of Christmas party in her new apartment on the Upper East Side. It's totally swank. She called the party her Twelve Days of Free-dom. Don't you remember?"

"I don't do parties," she said, as politely as possible. The last party she had attended had been her own eighth birthday party. She had escaped to her room before the ice cream was served, leaving the little hooligans her mother had invited to scream and fight without her. The ice cream had been Neapolitan, anyway, which she hated, but which her mother always served on the theory that this was the easiest way to satisfy all the children's ice cream preferences.

The truth was, Sweeney didn't do well in crowds, period. Socializing wasn't her strong point, and she was acutely aware of her shortcomings. She never relaxed, and she was always afraid of doing something totally stupid. Her mother, a great ego-builder, was fond of saying Sweeney had the social grace of a Tibetan goatherd.

"You should have done this one." Kai moved closer to her, his fingertips once again touching the inside of her elbow. "The food was fantastic, the champagne never ran out, and so many people were there you couldn't *move*. It was great."

Kai's idea of great differed considerably from hers. She was deeply grateful she hadn't been invited, though she had to admit that she might have been and promptly forgotten about it. Parties were her idea of hell—and speaking of which, what the *hell* was Kai doing to her elbow?

Scowling, she lifted her arm away from his touch. She knew Kai was a lover-boy, but he'd never before turned his attentions to her, and she didn't like it. She made a mental note to return the damn sweater to the back of the closet when she got home.

"Sorry." He was astute enough to know his subtle attentions weren't having the desired effect. He smiled down at her. "Like I said, you look hot. It was worth a try."

"Thanks," she growled. "I've always wanted to be worth a try."

He laughed, his amusement genuine. "Sure. That's why your 'Don't Touch Me' sign is high, wide, and flashing bright neon. Ah, well, if you're ever lonely, give me a call." He shrugged. "So, what've you been up to? Come to think of it, I don't think I've seen you at all for a few months. How's the work going?"

She shrugged. "I don't know. I'm producing, but I'm not sure *what* I'm producing. I'm trying some techniques." That wasn't the truth, but she wasn't about to cry on Kai's shoulder. He didn't need to know how deeply disturbed she was by the direction her painting had been taking or that she was helpless to stop it. She tried to do the same delicate, almost ethereal work she had done before, but she seemed to have lost the knack. Those damn vivid colors kept getting in her way, and even though she cursed them, she was losing herself in them. And not only were her colors changing, but it seemed as if her perspective was, too. She didn't know what was going on, but the result was jarring, somehow discordant. She had always been confident about her talent, if nothing else, but now she was so paralyzed by insecurity about her new work that she hadn't been able to show it to anyone.

"Oh, really." He looked interested. Of course, he was paid to look interested, so she didn't read a whole lot into his expression. "Do you have anything ready to hang? I'd like to see what you're doing."

"I have several canvases ready to hang, but I'm not sure *I'm* ready."

"I think you have only one piece left on display; everything else has sold. You need to bring something in."

"I will." She had to, reluctant though she was. If her new work didn't sell, she didn't eat; it was that simple. And they couldn't sell if she never allowed anyone else to see them.

Kai glanced at his watch. "The McMillans should be here

soon. I hope Richard leaves before then. Candra doesn't like him coming here at all; she prefers to meet him in the lawyer's office, so she'll be furious if he delays her. She's furious anyway, because he keeps balking."

"He doesn't want the divorce?"

Kai gave another graceful shrug. "Who knows what Richard wants? All I know is, he isn't being very conciliatory. Candra seems to have two moods these days: worried or infuriated."

Infuriated sounded like normal behavior during a divorce; *worried* didn't. "Maybe she's changed her mind and wants to back out of the divorce, but doesn't know how to smooth things over."

"Oh, she didn't want it at all." His eyes sparkled with the glee of delivering juicy gossip. "From what I gather, Richard's the one who filed. Candra's putting a good face on things, acting as if the decision was mutual, but she isn't at all happy with the split."

Abruptly Sweeney felt ashamed of herself, and irritated, too. Candra had supported her professionally, promoted her, steered clients her way. It went against her grain to gossip like this. If only gossip weren't so titillating. Sweeney tried to control an avid desire to know more, to dig for all the dirty details.

The temptation was great. Dirt was like fat; it made life more delicious.

She was saved from herself by the opening of Candra's office door. She turned and for a brief moment found herself looking directly into Richard Worth's eyes. It was like being touched with a cattle prod, an unwanted but electric connection. Then Candra appeared, her face pale with fury, gripping his arm and pulling him around as the door slammed shut again, closing out the sight and sound of marital disintegration.

"Uh-oh," Kai said with malicious satisfaction. "There's gonna be murder."

CHAPTER
TWO

S weeney was numb with shock. She wasn't certain what had just happened, but she knew something had. For a moment, just a split second, it had been as if she and Richard Worth were linked. She didn't like the sensation, didn't want that uncomfortable intimacy. She had always enjoyed her sense of being alone, envisioning herself as a ball that rolled through life, bumping into other lives but not stopping. For a moment, just for a moment, the roll had been halted, and she didn't know why. He was only an acquaintance, little more than a stranger. There was no reason for him to look at her as if he knew her. There was no reason for her to feel that funny jolt in her stomach, akin to the pleasure she had gotten from the Diet Coke commercial.

If this was another one of the weird changes that had been going on in her life for the past year, she didn't like this one any more than she did all the others. Damn it, she wanted things back the way they had been!

Before she could gather herself, the front doors opened behind her. Kai's face lit with the smile he reserved for buyers. To her surprise, he didn't seem to have noticed anything unusual. "Senator and Mrs. McMillan," he exclaimed, strolling toward them. "How nice to see you. May I get you anything? Tea, coffee? Something stronger?"

Sweeney swung around as a tall, thin, impossibly stylish woman said, "Tea," in a languid tone that was almost drowned by her husband's stronger voice as he said, "Coffee, black." His tone was as forceful as hers had been die-away.

To her surprise, Sweeney recognized him. She was notoriously oblivious to current events, but even so, this face had been on television often enough that she knew who he was. If Kai had said "Senator McMillan" before, instead of "the McMillans," she would have known. Senator Carson McMillan had a charisma that had carried him from city government to the state house, and from there to Washington, where he was in his second term. He had money, charm, intelligence, and ambition—in short, the qualities expected to eventually carry him to the presidency.

She disliked him on sight.

Maybe it was the career politician's practiced suavity that put her off. It wasn't the ruthlessness she read in him; she understood ruthlessness, having her share of it when it came to clearing out the space and time for her painting. It could have been the hint of disdain that seeped through his charm like the occasional whiff of sewer gas coming from a drainage grate. He was the type of politician who secretly thought his constituents were either dim-witted or hayseeds, or both.

On the other hand, he was undeniably striking in looks: about six feet tall, with a certain beefiness through the chest and shoulders that nevertheless struck her as muscular rather than fat, and gave him the impression of power. His brown hair was still thick, and attractively grayed at the temples. His hair stylist did a good job with that. His eyes were a clear hazel, his facial structure strong and almost classical, though his jaw and chin were too pugnacious for true classic beauty.

She immediately knew she didn't want to paint his portrait. She didn't want to spend another minute in his presence. But still . . . what a challenge. Could she portray the essential good looks and still catch that expression of condescending superiority, like a transparent overlay? The expression was everything. Senator McMillan had learned, for the most part, to put on a congenial face for the benefit of the public. In this situation, with only Kai and herself as witnesses and with both of them in what he would consider a subservient position, the public face slipped a bit. Sweeney didn't doubt that if she had been dressed in designer clothes and expensive jewelry, rather than a simple skirt and sweater, the reaction she had gotten from him would have been something other than the glance that was both dismissive and insulting, lingering on her breasts as it did.

She almost sniffed her own disdain, but caught herself in time. Candra had put herself out for this, so the least Sweeney could do was be polite. She switched her gaze to Mrs. McMillan, already inclined to feel sorry for the woman.

Her inclination was wasted. Mrs. McMillan obviously considered herself so superior that sympathy from lesser beings was unthinkable. The senator had worked on his public persona; his wife hadn't bothered. She was utterly secure in her position;

there wouldn't be any young trophy wife taking *her* place, unless her husband wanted to risk losing his career. Any divorce proceedings involving this woman, Sweeney thought, would be messy, bitter, and extremely public. Mrs. McMillan would personally see to it.

The senator's wife was fashionably thin, stylish, bored. Her hair was champagne blond, at least this week, and cut in a classic bob that dipped just short of her shoulders and was swept back from her face to reveal ornate gold earrings studded with tiny diamonds. A good New Yorker, she wore a simple black sheath that made her seem thin to the point of emaciation, and which probably cost more than Sweeney's entire wardrobe as well as part of her furniture.

Kai returned with a tray bearing tea and coffee, and noticed Sweeney standing there, joining the McMillans in silence. "I'm sorry, I didn't introduce you," he exclaimed. "Senator, Mrs. McMillan, this is Sweeney, the portrait artist Candra wanted you to meet. Sweeney, Senator Carson McMillan and his wife, Margo."

Sweeney held out her hand to Mrs. McMillan, feeling like a dog offering its paw, and from the look the senator's wife gave her, she might as well have been. Mrs. McMillan offered only her fingertips, probably to lessen the risk of contagion. If the senator ever did run for the presidency, his handlers would have to do some heavy-duty work with his wife to make her constituent-friendly and keep her from being a hindrance to the campaign.

The senator's handshake, on the other hand, was both brisk and firm without being crushing. He had a very nice handshake. It was probably one of the first things a career politician worked to achieve. She had a sudden vision of a classroom full of deadly earnest young politicians, with a sign on the door saying "Handshakes 101." He ruined the effect, however, by eyeing her breasts again. She was beginning to think the scarlet sweater was more than just dangerous; the damn thing was cursed. Maybe she shouldn't have combed her hair or put on lipstick, either, though the lipstick probably hadn't survived the hot dog.

Candra's office door opened once more, and Sweeney turned, glad of the interruption. Candra swept out, her face tight with fury, but the expression in her eyes, oddly, was almost frightened. The expression was fleeting; as soon as she saw the McMillans, her face changed into its usual warm, friendly lines.

Richard loomed in the doorway behind her. Sweeney didn't want to look at him, in case that odd thing happened again, but curiosity and compulsion switched her gaze to him. To her relief, this time he didn't return her gaze. His face was much more controlled, as if Candra's upset in no way touched him. His eyes were hooded as he took in the small group with one glance, then leisurely walked toward them. He was a tall man, but he didn't shamble; like an athlete, he was in control of his height and his body. Remembering the Diet Coke commercial, Sweeney wondered how Richard would look without his shirt.

That funny little jolt tightened her stomach again. She wasn't in the least hungry, but her mouth began watering as if she hadn't eaten at all that day and had just caught the scent of fresh-baked bread. A woman could feast all day on Richard. *Don't go there,* she silently warned herself, both alarmed and embarrassed, but she had taken too many art classes not to be able to accurately picture him without his clothes. From the way his clothes fit, she could tell he was a muscular man who hadn't let himself get soft. In her mind's eye she saw him naked and flat on his back, and it was a fine sight indeed. The disturbing part was seeing herself crawling over him, intent on kissing him from head to toe and not missing an inch in between. He would have several very interesting inches that would require a lot of attention—

"Carson, Margo, how good of you to come." Candra's voice jerked Sweeney out of her lascivious little daydream. Hastily she looked away from Richard, aware that she had been staring at him. She felt her cheeks heat and hoped her entire face wasn't red, to match the accursed sweater.

Candra came toward them, her lovely legs showcased by the short skirt of a tailored suit in a beautiful shade of coppery beige that made her complexion glow. Distracting herself, Sweeney studied the color, noting the richness of the material. She couldn't tell one designer's clothes from another's, but she never forgot a color.

Candra and Margo exchanged air kisses, then Candra turned her megawatt charm on the senator. He took both her hands and leaned forward to kiss her cheek, and there was nothing airish about it. Standing where she was, Sweeney saw the senator's hands tighten on Candra's before she subtly freed herself and turned to Sweeney.

"I see Kai has already offered refreshments—"

"Richard," the senator said heartily, his rounded, speech-therapist moderated tones completely overpowering Candra's lighter voice, just as they had his wife's. Sweeney wondered if he made a habit of interrupting women. He held out his hand; she saw the flicker of Richard's eyes that said he was reluctant to stop and chat, but good manners compelled him to accept the senator's hand.

Senator McMillan put everything he had into the handshake, even covering their clasped hands with his free one in a gesture his handlers had no doubt told him imparted a sense of empathy. It didn't work with Richard. If anything, his face became even more impassive. "You're looking great."

"Senator." The one-word greeting, if it could be called that, was terse. No great friendship there, Sweeney surmised. Watching them as closely as she was, she saw the senator's knuckles whiten, and an instant later Richard's knuckles did the same.

A pissing contest, she thought, fascinated. For whatever reason, dislike or competition or simple male aggression, the senator had tried to crush Richard's hand. It wasn't a smart move. He quickly became the crushee when Richard turned the tables.

"How's business?" the senator asked, trying to keep his expression neutral as he continued to grip Richard's hand, or maybe he simply couldn't let go now even if he wanted. "It has to be good, with this economy. Amazing, isn't it?"

"I don't have any complaints."

A bead of sweat appeared on the senator's forehead. Tiring of the game, Richard abruptly ended the handshake. Senator McMillan gamely managed not to massage his aching hand, though the impulse must have been strong.

Well, Sweeney thought. She wouldn't have been surprised if the senator had challenged Richard to an arm-wrestling contest. She wondered if the animosity existed because of what she had seen in the senator's eyes when he kissed Candra, or if he just didn't like it because Richard could piss farther than he could. Richard, she thought, didn't much give a damn one way or the other, which was very adult of him. In any contest between him and the senator, she was on his side; she might not like Richard, exactly—she didn't know him well enough one way or the other—but she had detested the senator on sight.

"I hear you're off to Rome." Candra turned to Margo, her voice as easy as if it didn't bother her at all that they had witnessed the discord between her and Richard, but Sweeney knew better. Her habit of studying faces made her alert to the most fleeting expression, and the tension around Candra's eyes was as telling as a neon sign.

"No, that's been delayed. Carson has an emergency meeting

in the morning, with the president." *Top that,* said the smugness of her tone. "We've postponed the trip—"

The senator began speaking to Richard again, his voice overriding his wife's, so that Candra had to lean closer to Margo to hear her. Maybe the senator deliberately interrupted women as a way of showing his dominance, or perhaps he simply didn't notice when they were talking, which was even more insulting.

Sweeney tuned out, hearing the four clashing voices but not the individual words. She wasn't interested in the McMillans' trip to Rome, or in stock options, whatever they were. She shifted restlessly, bored, ready to dispense with the business at hand and get back to her apartment and her painting. Why was Richard hanging around, anyway? He couldn't give two hoots in hell about the senator's opinions on the stock market. Surely he knew Candra would feel more relaxed if he left. And so would she, Sweeney admitted. She deliberately kept her gaze away from him, afraid of triggering that weird connection again.

"I'm so glad you had this chance to meet Sweeney," Candra said. The mention of her name brought Sweeney's attention back with a rush, and she found Candra smiling warmly at her. "I have an example of her work here if you'd like to see it, but unfortunately not any of her portrait work, as that's done only on commission."

Sweeney kept her mouth shut, and the portfolio firmly under her arm. She had no intention of showing any of her work now.

"It isn't important," Margo said, bored. "I'm sure she'll do, if you recommend her. What I'm really interested in is the new VanDern you mentioned. I'm sure the colors will go marvelously in the living room."

Sweeney refrained from rolling her eyes, but it was difficult. She couldn't fault the woman for wanting her wall decor to complement the room, because color was vital to Sweeney's own sense of well-being, but . . . a *VanDern?* He was a hot commodity right now, but he was a sly, talentless clod who daubed huge clumps of color on a canvas and called it art.

"I'm sure they will," Candra agreed, indicating with a graceful wave of her hand the direction of the VanDern.

Sweeney had no intention of trailing along behind them. "I have to go," she said, gripping her portfolio. She needed the job, she really, really needed the job, and she steeled herself to say something polite and make arrangements to begin after the couple returned from Rome. She opened her mouth and heard, "I'm sorry, but I can't do your portraits, Mrs. McMillan. I'm booked."

The words surprised even herself. So much for good intentions, but at least she had given a polite lie instead of saying she had despised the couple on sight and the only way she would paint them would be if she could add horns, goatees, and pitchforks. She was a little proud of herself; a Tibetan goatherd couldn't have come up with such a good lie.

"What?" Margo looked startled. Candra's lovely face looked first amazed, then alarmed, as if she had begun imagining all the responses Sweeney could make to Margo's incredulous question. Sweeney didn't give herself time to think of any. She had to get out of there before her thin layer of tolerance for fools and jerks was worn through and she said something that would really embarrass Candra. She swung around and headed for the door, going as fast as she could without actually running.

She switched the portfolio to her left hand and reached out with her right to grab the door handle, but a tall body was suddenly right next to her and a dark-clad arm shot out in front of her, blocking her way. Over her head a deep voice said, "Allow me. I was just leaving, too. Good-bye, Senator, Mrs. McMillan. Kai."

Startled by the novelty of having a door opened for her,

Sweeney didn't think to call her own good-byes. To be honest, it wasn't just Richard's courtesy that had startled her, but his closeness. Her stomach jittered again. It was unsettling to have him right next to her when only moments before she had been mentally stripping him.

Richard let the door close behind them and for a moment they were enclosed in the silence of the small vestibule, the smoked glass of the outer door dimming the sunshine outside. Then he stepped past her and opened that door, too, his movement bringing him so close that his suit jacket brushed her arm and the quiet scent of expensive cologne drifted to her nose. Another jolt hit her, accompanied by a sudden wave of physical awareness.

This wouldn't do. This wouldn't do at all. Bemused, she stepped out onto the sidewalk. First the Diet Coke commercial this morning and now *Richard,* of all people. Maybe there was a full moon or something, though lunar cycles had never before affected her hormones. Not much of anything had. Maybe she should make a doctor's appointment, make sure her ovaries hadn't suddenly gone into overdrive, flooding her with an overdose of unruly hormones. If they were going to do that, they should have done it when she was a teenager and didn't know any better. She was thirty-one now and didn't have either the time or the inclination to indulge in any hormonal frivolity.

"Sweeney?" Richard waved his hand in front of her face, and she snapped back to the present, flushing as she realized she had been staring at him while she pondered the state of her ovaries.

"Sorry," she muttered. "What did you say?"

The corners of his mouth curled a little, as if he was suppressing a smile. "I asked if you wanted a lift home. It's starting to rain."

So it was. It hadn't been just the smoked glass of the doors making the day look dreary; the bright sunshine was gone and the sky had turned cloudy while she was in the gallery. She looked up as raindrops began to spatter on the sidewalk.

Instantly she hugged the portfolio closer to her, as if she could protect it with her body. There was no decision to it, not when the choice was between keeping her drawings dry or letting the rain ruin them. "Thanks, I would. Where's your car?" she asked, looking around.

"Right here." He raised his hand, and a dark gray Mercedes rolled forward to stop at the curb in front of him. That struck her as a lot handier than standing on the curb waving frantically at passing cabs, as she knew hundreds of people had started doing as soon as the first raindrop fell.

He put his hand on her back as he leaned forward to open the car door. The contact was so unexpected, and so unexpectedly pleasurable, that she almost stumbled. Recovering, she juggled the portfolio out of the way as she bent down to slide into the car, continuing across the buttery leather seats to give him room to get in. Her insides were doing the rumba: heart pounding, lungs heaving, stomach clenching. It was the most amazing thing she'd ever felt. Too bad it undoubtedly meant she was losing her mind.

Richard folded his tall body into the seat beside her. "We're giving Sweeney a lift home, Edward," he said to his driver.

"Very good, sir." The accent was faintly British, the word choice even more so. "What is Miss Sweeney's address?"

Richard gave it, and Sweeney stared at him in surprise for a moment before remembering that he owned the building where she lived. She was surprised he had remembered, but probably stock-market geniuses had to be able to remember the tiniest detail. Forcing herself to relax, she settled back into the ultracomfortable embrace of dead cows' hides. She stroked the seat, delighted in the smooth, soft texture of the leather, and the delicious smell. Nothing rivaled good-quality leather in its richness, its utter luxury.

Then temptation got the better of her, and she glanced at Richard, to find him watching her and smiling slightly. Funny, she had never associated him with smiles; he was too controlled, even remote, but this smile looked as natural as if he'd had a lot of practice. She felt a moment of kinship, and her lips curved upward, too. "I guess your tolerance for bullshit is as low as mine," she said, her smile widening into a grin, and he laughed. It was an honest-to-God, throw-your-head-back laugh, and damn it, even that made her insides start jumping around again.

"I thought you were going to run right through the glass, you were in such a hurry to get out of there."

"I don't know who is worse, the senator or his wife. They both gave me the creeps."

"That was pretty obvious, to everyone but them. Kai was trying to make himself invisible, but at the same time he didn't want to leave in case he missed some fireworks." Richard's tone turned neutral when he mentioned Kai, and Sweeney wondered if he knew about Candra's affair with her assistant. That could certainly be the reason for the divorce; Richard didn't look like a man who would tolerate infidelity or try to "work through it" with marriage counseling sessions.

The first warning sprinkles of rain abruptly turned into a downpour, sending pedestrians scurrying for doorways or taxis; umbrellas bloomed like mushrooms. Sweeney loved the sound of rain anyway, but today it was particularly evocative, making her heart pound the way it did whenever she heard cello music or taps. A delicious chill suddenly prickled her skin, and she hugged herself.

"Edward, turn on the heat, please. Sweeney is cold."

"Of course, sir."

"I'm not really cold," Sweeney denied, without knowing why. Her constant coldness was somehow embarrassing, a weakness she didn't want to acknowledge. "Listening to the rain gave me goose bumps."

"You were shivering. Do you want to put my coat around you?"

There it was again, shaking her insides as if the San Andreas Fault ran right through her. He had been watching her closely enough to notice a small shiver. She didn't know which was more disturbing, that realization or the flood of warmth she felt at the thought of being draped in his coat, his body heat being transferred to her, his scent surrounding her. The warmth was welcome, but the reason behind it wasn't. At least her fascination with the commercial had ended when the ad was over. This strange awareness would end, surely, as soon as she got out of the car and away from Richard, but until then she had to guard against doing something stupid, like throwing herself into his arms. Wouldn't *that* raise Edward's eyebrows! It would probably raise her own, because if anything was out of character for her, throwing herself at a man ranked at the top of the list.

"Sweeney?" Richard prompted, waving his hand in front of her again. He was smiling again, too. She wished he would stop doing both. One was annoying, and the other was downright disturbing.

"What?"

"Do you want my coat?" He was already shrugging out of it.

"Oh—no, thank you. I'm sorry, my thoughts wandered."

"I noticed." He smiled again, his dark eyes slightly heavy-lidded. Despite her refusal, he draped the coat over her.

She almost moaned in delight. It was just as she had imagined, so toasty warm she thought she might melt. She snuggled into the coat, pulling the fabric high around her face and unconsciously inhaling, drawing his scent into her lungs like a smoker taking the morning's first drag.

"I had to do something to cover up that sweater," he said by way of explanation, his tone amused.

"It's cursed. I'm going to burn it when I get home."

"Don't bother. It's what's underneath that's doing the damage."

Oh, God. He felt it, too.

The realization was like a punch in the stomach. She froze, unable to look at him, afraid of what she would see in his eyes. This wasn't just an aberration inspired by the red sweater. This wasn't a strange moon cycle. She couldn't say how she knew; it certainly couldn't be experience telling her, because she had made it a point through the years to avoid letting messy relationships clutter her life. Richard was the third man in an hour to look at her with appreciation—well, the fourth, if she counted the senator, but his look had been more insulting than appreciative—but in Richard's case, it was something more. Not even Kai's knee-jerk attempt at casual seduction had been like this, but then Kai was a lightweight, and Richard . . . Richard was not.

Still, she would have been tempted, if he hadn't been embroiled in a divorce; a divorce, moreover, from a woman very much involved in Sweeney's career. No, be honest. She *was* tempted, beyond a doubt, and against every grain of common sense in her body. But being tempted didn't mean she had to act on that temptation; a woman who could see ghosts and make traffic lights change when she approached sure didn't need a man in her life to complicate things. She could handle the ghosts; she couldn't handle a man, especially not Richard. Just why she thought he was more trouble than any other man was an issue she didn't want to explore.

Still, the urge to look at him, watch him, study him, was almost overpowering. To keep her gaze away from those intense, knowing dark eyes, she looked down, and found herself staring at his hands. They were rather elegant hands, she thought in surprise, in a rough way. She had always thought of him as an expensively dressed dockworker, but she had never before noticed his hands, and now she wondered why. Their shape was beautiful, with the beauty of strength, like Michelangelo's *David*, long-fingered and sinewy. She saw the roughness of calluses, a few scars, manicured nails. Senator McMillan had been a fool to pit his strength against this man's.

She chuckled at the memory. "I'll bet the senator won't try to squeeze *your* hand again," she said with relish.

Bold dark eyebrows slanted upward. "You saw that juvenile stunt?"

"Um. It was fun. His knuckles turned white, then yours did, and he broke out in a sweat. I almost cheered."

He laughed. "You wear your civilization very lightly, don't you? I never noticed before."

"I wasn't the one in the pissing contest," she pointed out, a little irritated that he obviously thought she was a savage. She considered herself a very civilized person. She'd never squeezed anyone's hand, because she was afraid of hurting her own hands. Maybe that wasn't the same as not wanting to hurt someone else, but the outcome was the same, so surely she got points for that.

"No, you weren't." He was smiling again, very faintly. Glancing up, he saw that they were almost at her apartment building. "The trip didn't take very long," he noted, and didn't sound pleased.

She didn't tell him why all the traffic lights had turned green or traffic mysteriously detoured out of their way.

"Will you have dinner with me tonight?" He turned back to her, and somehow he was closer than he had been before, his shoulder touching hers, his left leg against her right one. She felt his body heat like a lodestone all down her right side, triggering an insane impulse to get closer and see just how warm he could get her. Plenty warm, she bet. On fire. Melting.

"Good God, no!"

He laughed. "Please, don't spare my feelings."

Sweeney blushed like a teenager. One day, maybe when she was ninety years old, she might learn the art of the polite lie. She had done well enough with the McMillans, but obviously that was her quota for about a year.

"I didn't mean . . . It's just that you'd be a big complication, demanding time and sex and things like that, and I have all I can handle right now." Great. He was laughing again, and when she realized what she had just said, she wanted to bury her face in her hands. Instead she doggedly plowed on. "And then there's Candra. She's been good to me, promoting me when a lot of other gallery owners wouldn't. Even though you've been separated for almost a year . . . Anyway, I don't think it would be a good idea."

He didn't say anything for a long time, just watched her with a completely unreadable expression on his face. "I'll ask again," he finally said.

She wasn't sure how those three words could sound almost like a threat, but they did. Richard Worth wasn't a man who was used to being turned down "You do that," she said, as the Mercedes slid to a stop in front of her apartment building. "And I'll turn you down again." She removed his coat and gave it back to him, and reached for the door handle.

"Don't be ridiculous," he said, staying her hand. "There's no point in getting wet. I have an umbrella, and I'll walk you to the door."

"I can manage, thanks."

"What about your portfolio?"

There was that, damn it. The rain was really coming down. She scowled at him. "You don't have to look so satisfied," she growled, knowing he had her.

His mouth quirked as he reached for the umbrella. "Honey, you don't have any idea how I look when I'm satisfied."

No, but she could imagine, and her mental image knotted her stomach. He bent his head and kissed her sulky mouth, the contact light and warm and devastating. "Think about it," he whispered, then opened the door and extended the umbrella out, opening it so it provided a circle of protection. He climbed out and held it for her as she slid from the car.

"Think about it," she mimicked savagely, making him laugh. "Damn you." She was so annoyed she didn't care that sliding across the seat made her skirt ride high on her thighs. Let him look; that was all he was going to do.

Together they dashed across the sidewalk to the sheltered doorway. He took care that her portfolio didn't get splashed, and she appreciated his concern, even though she wanted to give him a good swift kick. He left her there and strode quickly back to the waiting car. She didn't wait until he left, but went inside immediately. He didn't need any ego stroking, and she definitely needed to get back to her safe, isolated world, away from temptation.

She needed order, not disorder; peace, not excitement. Most of all, she needed to paint. With a brush in her hand, she could shut out the world.

CHAPTER THREE

Think about it. Well, she had. Despite her best efforts, and to the point where she was about to have a screaming fit, she had. With hours stretching before her in which she could paint, instead she continually found herself standing in front of the canvas with an idle brush in her hand while she stared off into space like some giddy adolescent. The problem, of course, wasn't so much Richard's attraction to her as her attraction to him. What disturbed her most was her inability to stop thinking about him. Other men had been distinguished by their total lack of distinction; she could put them out of her mind, if indeed they had ever entered it, and go on with her life as usual. None of them had ever tempted her. She couldn't say that about Richard.

She felt silly, obsessing about a man. Nothing was ever going to come of her attraction, she would see to that, so it was stupid to waste time mooning over him. Not that any other man would have had a better chance, but the fact that this was *Richard* kept stunning her over and over again, hitting her right between the eyes. Of all the men in the world she might have expected to appeal to her hitherto nonexistent libido, Richard wasn't even on the list. Richard was married, he was married to a business associate of hers, and now the two were involved in an acrimonious divorce, which was an even better reason to stay the hell away from him.

Okay. Her mind got the message. Now, if the word would just seep farther down, she might be able to get some work done.

The rain had stopped but the day remained cloudy, and though she had installed bright lights in her studio, it wasn't the same as sunlight. Normally that wouldn't have bothered her, but today it did. She wanted bright sunlight. She had been working from a photo she'd taken of the St. Lawrence, which remained one of her favorite subjects, but without sunlight she couldn't get the colors right. Disgusted, she thrust the brush into the can of turpentine and swished it around. Who was she kidding? She couldn't get the colors right anyway. She hadn't been able to get the colors right for a year.

She wished she could put her finger on any one event that had obviously triggered the change, but she couldn't. Nothing stood out in her mind. Why would she have noticed Clayton's lone traffic light turning green? It did on a regular basis. She had noticed that her plants looked unusually happy, but at first had simply written that off as acclimation or her having stumbled across some hardy plants that could withstand her haphazard care. Maybe that was still all it was. Before, though, she had had to replace them on a fairly regular basis, but now, no matter what she did, they were thriving. Not even the move to the city had disturbed them. The Christmas cactus was blooming merrily as it already had several times this year, her bromeliads were fat and succulent, her ferns lush, and the finicky ficus kept its leaves no matter how often she moved it around the apartment.

She didn't want to be different. She had seen her parents use their talent as an excuse for all sorts of god-awful, selfish, self-aggrandizing behavior, and seen the havoc they had wrought in other people's lives. She didn't want to be like that. She wanted to be a perfectly normal person who happened to have a talent for painting; that was different enough, but she could handle that. But an artist who screwed up electronic timers, affected nature, and saw ghosts—whoa, that was way out there. Not even her mother had gone that far, though she had gone through a period when she sought inspiration in the metaphysical. As Sweeney remembered it, that had consisted mostly of toking on a joint. Excuses were where you found them.

She sighed as she cleaned her brushes. The St. Lawrence was out of the question today, not that she had been making much progress anyway. The river didn't fascinate her the way it once had, didn't hold the lure of even the most ordinary face.

The hot dog vendor's face popped into her mind, complete with sweet smile. Sweeney cocked her head, considering the image. He looked so young in her mind, despite the gray hair. How had he looked when he was twenty? Or ten? She thought of him as a six-year-old with here-and-there teeth, beaming at the world.

Absently whistling through her teeth, Sweeney reached for her sketch pad. It would be interesting to do him at different ages, a collage of faces on the same canvas and all of them his.

Some artists only did rough blocking to get the right proportions, but Sweeney was a good sketch artist, too. She usually spent more time than she should on the preliminary sketches because she couldn't resist adding in shadings and details. To her delight, the vendor's sweet expression didn't elude her pencil this time. Everything fell into place, in a way it hadn't done in a long time.

The vendor's name was Elijah Stokes. Today he closed his stand at the usual time, counted the day's take, and made out a deposit slip, then walked to the bank and stood in line for maybe fifteen minutes. He could have dropped the deposit in the overnight slot, but he liked to deal with humans, not holes. He liked to walk away with the stamped deposit receipt in his pocket, and the first thing he did when he got home was put the receipt in a file. He was real careful with his paperwork, partly because his mama had been that way, but mostly because, as he grew older, he saw that being careful with the details always saved him some trouble on down the line.

Elijah had been married to the same woman for forty-four years, until her death five years before. They had raised two fine boys, put them through college, and had the pleasure of seeing them become fine men, get good jobs, marry, and begin raising their own families as they had been raised. There was a lot of satisfaction in knowing you had done something right, and Elijah knew he had done right by his boys.

He could have closed his stand a long time ago; he had saved his money, made some small but careful investments, and seen them prosper. He didn't need the money; with Social Security and his dividends, he could live just as he was living now, because most of what he made still went into savings. But every time he thought about retiring, he'd think about his boys, and the five beautiful grandchildren he had, and how every penny he saved now would help pay for their education later. It wouldn't hurt him to work a couple of more years; seventy seemed like a good age to retire.

The rain began again as he walked home, driving people off the sidewalks. He just pulled his cap down more snugly on his head and trudged on. A little rain never hurt nobody. The clouds had brought on an early twilight, making the streetlights wink on. Summer was leaving in a hurry; he could smell the crispness of fall in the rain, as if it had come straight down from Canada. Spring and fall were his favorite seasons, because the weather was better, not too hot and not too cold. He hated winter; the cold made his bones ache. Sometimes he thought about going south to retire, but he knew he wouldn't leave his boys and those grandkids.

He was still three blocks from home when the neighborhood began to deteriorate. Some rough characters hung around the streets these days. His kids wanted him to move, but he had lived there since the oldest was only a year old, and it was hard to leave all those memories. His wife had cooked thousands of mouth-watering meals in that old kitchen, and he had listened to his kids running across those worn floors. His wife had fixed the place up nice over the years, though he hadn't done anything to it since she died and everything was beginning to look shabby. He just hadn't wanted to make any changes. Somehow he could remember her better if he left things just the way she'd wanted.

Normally he paid more attention when he was walking, but this time, this one time, he let his guard down. A punk slid out of an alley to block his way, feral eyes gleaming. Elijah barely had time to notice the pimply complexion and bad teeth before the left side of his head exploded with pain.

The force of the blow knocked Elijah to the ground. The punk leaned down and grabbed the old man, dragged him back into the shadows. Maybe four seconds had lapsed since he had stepped out of the alley. He swung the club two more times, just because it felt good, even though the old man hadn't struggled at all. Then he leaned down and grabbed the wallet from the old guy's pocket and fumbled the money out, shoving it into his own pocket without bothering to count it. There weren't any credit cards. Shit. In disgust he tossed the wallet aside and pelted out of the alley, head down. The whole operation, refined by practice, took about twenty seconds.

Elijah Stokes, a careful man, never carried much cash on him. The punk's take was twenty-seven dollars. Elijah lay in the twilight shadows of the alley and felt the light rain on his face, but the sensation was oddly distant. In a brief flash of clarity he knew he was dying, and he wanted to think about his kids, but his brain felt funny and their faces just wouldn't form. His wife, though . . . ah, there she was, smiling her angel's smile, and that was good enough for Elijah.

"This is *Jeopardy!*" the announcer crowed, dragging out each word. Sweeney sat down in her ultracomfortable, overstuffed chair and curled up with a big bowl of popcorn in her lap. The three contestants were identified, and as usual she watched their faces, not even hearing their names. The one in the middle, she thought. He would win. He looked quick, his eyes lively with intelligence. She liked to play a game with herself, trying to guess beforehand which contestant would win. Lately it hadn't been much of a challenge.

The streak of luck was getting on her nerves. Traffic signals were one thing, but if the weird stuff started affecting *Jeopardy!*, she was going to get testy. She loved the show.

Alex Trebek came out and began the game by reading the categories. *"Mystery Writers."*

"Dick Francis," said Sweeney, popping a salty kernel in her mouth.

"Potent Potables."

"Absinthe," she responded.

"British Royalty."

"Charles the Second. This is too easy."

"Science."

"Cold fusion—you wish."

"The States."

"Delaware. Try not to be so obvious."

"And finally, *Deep Space.*"

"Quasars, of course." It was another little game she played, trying to guess what the questions would be before she heard the clues. Lately she had been doing really well at that, too.

The defending champion began with Potent Potables. Alex read the clue. Stumped, the contestant stared at the board as if he could force it to give him the answer. The buzzer sounded, and the contestant in the middle rang in. "What is absinthe," he said.

Sweeney reached for the remote control and turned off the television without waiting to hear Alex confirm that was the correct question. She knew it was right. These days she was always right.

She felt jittery, more unsettled than she could remember ever feeling before. Getting to her feet, she walked to the window and stared out at the rain. She loved rain; normally it soothed her. Tonight the magic wasn't working.

Surely falling in lust with Richard hadn't upset her to this extent. She was surprised, sure, because such a thing normally didn't happen to her, but after all it wasn't such a big deal. Women lusted after men all the time. She chose not to act on it, and that was that. The excitement had been heady, though. She could understand how people came to act irrationally while they were under the influence, so to speak. Hormones were as potent as whiskey, and twice as sneaky.

No, she thought, it wasn't Richard and her unusually strong reaction to him. She had made her decision on that and put it out of her mind, sort of. This was something else, a bone-deep uneasiness that had nothing to do with the state of her ovaries. She felt sad, almost grief-stricken, and she didn't know why.

She tried to do some more sketches, but couldn't concentrate. Television held no appeal, but finally she settled down with a book, wrapped up in a blanket, and managed to get in a good hour of reading before she became so sleepy her head kept drooping. It was only nine o'clock, but Sweeney figured if she was that sleepy, then she needed to be in bed.

The on-and-off rain was on again, and she crawled under the covers with a sigh of pure pleasure. The electric blanket had her bed nice and warm; crawling into it was like crawling into a cocoon. It wasn't as nice as Richard's coat, but it was still wonderful. She stretched out, wriggling her cold toes against the warm blanket, and in minutes was asleep.

A little after midnight she began to toss restlessly under the covers, making pushing motions with her hands. She muttered sounds that weren't quite words. Her head moved back and forth on the pillow, and her eyelids fluttered. Her breath rushed in and out of her lungs as if she had been running.

Then she stilled. Even her breathing stopped for a long moment.

Her breathing started again. Her eyes opened, the expression in them was distant. She got out of bed and silently, without turning on any lights, walked barefoot through the apartment to her studio. She didn't turn on any lights, but the wash of colorless light from the street was enough for her to make her way through the big, cluttered room without bumping into anything.

Several easels stood around the room, all wearing canvases in varying stages of completion. She took one canvas down and laid it on a table, then put a blank one in its place on the easel.

Her movements were precise as she took a tube and squeezed a glob of bright red onto her palette. The first brushstroke on the blank expanse of canvas left behind a violent streak of red. Next she reached for the black. There was a lot of black.

She stood there for two hours, her brush moving with silent skill. She didn't hear the sirens as a fire truck raced down the street beneath her window. She didn't feel the chill on her bare feet. Not once did she shiver.

Suddenly she sagged, like a balloon going flat. She dipped a brush into the black one more time and added a touch down at the bottom. Then she carefully placed the brushes in the turpentine and left the studio as silently as she had entered it, retracing her steps through the dark apartment, a slim, barefoot woman in pajamas, with curly hair rioting around her shoulders. She moved as quietly as a ghost, back to her bedroom and the warm nest of her bed.

The alarm went off at six-thirty. Sweeney fumbled a hand out from under the cover and swatted the clock, stopping the obnoxious noise. The smell of coffee teased her out of bed. Dragging on a pair of thick socks, she lumbered like Frankenstein's monster into the kitchen. As she did every morning, she sent up a silent thank-you to God for electronic miracles and waiting coffee. With the first cup in hand, the first too-hot sip warming her on its way down her throat, she was sufficiently awake not to spill any of it on her way to the shower.

Ten minutes later, awake and warm, dressed in sweats, and with the now-drinkable coffee in her hand, she went into the studio, her most favorite place in the world. The room was in a corner of the building, which meant it had windows on two walls. Actually, the two walls *were* windows, great big tall ones that looked like factory windows, though she didn't think the building had ever been used for manufacturing. On sunny days, the light was fantastic.

It was still too early for that, though, so she flipped the light switch, flooding the room with almost blinding light. The lights she had installed were huge round metal fixtures that hung from the ceiling and beamed down an incredible amount of wattage. Shadows were nonexistent in the room, which was great, but she preferred natural light.

She knew her studio intimately. The first thing she noticed was the canvas on the table. Frowning, she walked over. It was the St. Lawrence canvas, and she knew she hadn't put it on the table; she had left it on the easel. A chill went through her. Who had moved the canvas, and when? Another canvas stood in its place now, and Sweeney stared at it for a moment, strangely uneasy, before walking around the easel to see what it was.

She went very still, blue eyes wide as she stared at the canvas. Her lips were white, her fingers clenched on the coffee cup.

It was ugly. It was the ugliest thing she had ever seen. A man sprawled in the dirty, garbage-filled space between two buildings. She knew exactly what she was looking at, even though the buildings were nothing more than black hulks on either side that somehow gave the appearance of height. Something was wrong with the man's head. There was a little blood pooled around his nostrils, and a thin line of it ran from his left ear, curving under the ear to drip into his gray hair.

For a moment she stared at the painted face without recognition. The eyes were open, blank, glazed with the film of death.

But then she saw the facial structure she knew so well, having sketched it so often.

It was the old hot dog vendor.

Her first irrational thought, rushing through her brain on a flood of rage, was that someone had broken into her apartment and painted the disturbing picture. Logic pointed out the idiocy of that scenario. For one thing, the style, though not as detailed as usual, was her own. That, and her signature scribbled in the lower right corner of the canvas, told her she had done the painting.

The only problem was, she didn't remember any of it.

CHAPTER FOUR

At nine, the telephone rang. Sweeney was still numb with shock, and so cold she couldn't seem to get warm no matter how much coffee she drank. She'd kept edging the thermostat upward until it was sitting on eighty, and she refused to turn it higher. The local weather forecast, delivered by a woman so chirpy Sweeney felt like smacking her, had told her the day would be *beautiful,* with highs in the mid-seventies. People outside were walking around in short sleeves, children were still wearing shorts, and she was freezing. She felt as if her inner core was pure ice, the cold coming from inside rather than out.

She couldn't settle down to paint anything, not even something unsatisfactory. Every time she saw that ugly painting of the old hot dog vendor, she wanted to weep, and she wasn't a leaky-eye type of woman. But she felt so sad, almost as if she were in mourning, and when the phone rang, she grabbed it up, glad for a change, for the distraction.

"Candra here. Is this a good time?" Candra's warm voice sounded in her ear.

"As good as any." Sweeney pushed an unruly curl out of her eyes. "About yesterday—"

"Don't apologize," Candra interrupted, laughing. "I should be apologizing to you. If I had stopped to think, I would have known immediately you wouldn't be able to stand them. A little of Margo goes a long way, though in her defense, Carson is enough to give a saint a bad attitude."

"He has the hots for you." Damn, she hadn't meant to say that. She liked Candra, but they had never crossed the line between friendly business associates and *friends*. Intimate conversation wasn't her strong point, anyway.

Candra evidently had no such hang-ups. She laughed dismissively. "Carson has the hots for anything female. To say he's like a dog would insult the dog community. He has his uses, though, which is why Margo stays with him."

Sweeney didn't say anything, because she knew anything that came out of her mouth would be uncomplimentary, and the McMillans were not only in Candra's social circle, they were her clients. Insulting them wouldn't be diplomatic. Keeping silent was a strain, but she managed.

"I saw you get in the car with Richard yesterday," Candra said after a slight pause, and there was a faint hesitancy in her tone.

Oh, boy. Sweeney's radar began beeping an alarm. "It was starting to rain and I had the portfolio, so he gave me a lift home." She clutched the phone, hoping Candra would leave it there and go on to another subject.

No such luck. "He can be very courteous. It's that country-boy Virginia upbringing."

"I didn't know he was from Virginia." That seemed like a safe thing to say.

"He still has the accent. No matter how I begged, he absolutely refused to have speech lessons to help him get rid of it."

Sweeney didn't think she had ever noticed his accent, though now that she thought about it, his speech did have a certain lazy quality about it. Virginia wasn't exactly the Deep South, though Candra made it sound as if Richard talked like the Beverly Hillbillies. Sweeney didn't want to talk about him; just thinking about him made her uncomfortable. She especially didn't want to talk about him with his soon-to-be ex-wife.

"You know we're getting divorced," Candra said casually. "It's a mutual decision. Richard and I had been drifting apart for some time, and shortly after you moved to the city last year, we separated and filed for divorce. He's being a bastard about the settlement, but I suppose that's to be expected. A divorce isn't exactly a friendly proceeding, is it?"

"Not usually." Maybe if her responses gave Candra no encouragement, the other woman would tire of the subject and move on.

"Ah . . . did Richard say anything yesterday?"

The hesitancy was back in Candra's tone. Sweeney got the feeling this was the real reason behind the call. "About what?" She actually managed to sound blank. She was proud of herself, and irritated at the same time. She had no reason to feel guilty, because even though Richard had asked her to dinner, she had turned him down, but evidently logic had nothing to do with guilt.

"About the divorce."

"No, he didn't mention it." Relief crawled through Sweeney at being able to say something that was totally, one hundred percent true. She wasn't good at this subterfuge stuff, even though everything she had said was accurate in letter, if not in spirit.

"I didn't really think he would, he's so damn discreet." The words sounded bitter. Candra paused again. "I noticed when we were in the gallery, he barely took his eyes off you."

The uncomfortable feeling intensified as it inched like a worm up Sweeney's back. She didn't want this. She didn't want to get caught in the middle during their divorce. All she wanted was to forget she had been bushwhacked by some malfunctioning hormones and for a moment responded to his attractiveness.

"He's been so damn careful since we separated that if he's had any lovers, I haven't been able to find out about it," Candra continued. "When I saw the way he watched you yesterday . . . well, I was curious."

Yeah, sure. There was definite bitterness there, Sweeney thought. And she definitely wanted to end this conversation. "Maybe there haven't been any."

Candra laughed. "What, Richard go without sex? Not likely. Anyway, what I wanted to say is, if you and Richard have something going, I wouldn't mind. We've been separated for almost a year, so of course I've gotten on with my life. I've met someone I'm very fond of, and he's far more comfortable to be with than Richard ever was."

Sweeney couldn't think of anything appropriate to say. *Thank you* was out of the question. Why on earth would Candra call about this, anyway? Was she concerned that if Sweeney actually did begin seeing Richard, she would try to find another art dealer to handle her sales? That didn't make sense, because Sweeney had no illusions about her worth to Candra; the gallery handled artists who made a lot more sales than she. No, this call was prompted by sheer nosiness, the curious inability of estranged couples to let go even though they were embroiled in the legal surgery that would sever them.

Well, she didn't want any part of it. She shivered and reached for a blanket to wrap around her while she tried to think of a way to tiptoe through this conversational minefield. But a response seemed called for, so at last she said, "I hope you'll be very happy." There! That was innocuous enough.

Candra laughed, and sounded genuinely amused. "Oh, I doubt this is anything permanent. Life's too short and too full of men to chance making another mistake. But I admit I was hoping Richard was interested in you."

"What?" The word was faint with surprise.

Candra laughed again. "Don't sound so shocked. I don't care if he has a lover, or ten lovers. I don't hate him; I don't wish him ill. I just want him to stop being so stubborn about the settlement so we can be finished with this and move on. If he were interested in someone, he might want to get the divorce finalized and out of the way so he would be free. I know Richard, I know how he is when he focuses on one woman." For a moment Candra's voice softened, warmed with memory, and then she gave a little chuckle. "I had some *very* good times."

Sweeney almost said Richard *had* asked her out. She wanted to ask exactly how good a time Richard showed a woman. For a moment the words lay on her tongue like ball bearings, ready to roll out. Caution made her swallow them. She had turned Richard down, so there was no point now in putting herself in the middle of this situation. Nor did she want to exchange girly talk on how good a lover Richard was, not that she knew or had any intention of knowing. She couldn't bear any more of this weird conversation, so she subtly changed the subject.

"I thought I would bring some new pieces to the gallery." Then she grimaced; damn, why had she blurted that out? Why couldn't she have come up with something else? She didn't want anyone to see the mess her work had turned into.

Candra laughed. "Enough of Richard, huh?" She shifted into business mode. "I'd love to see your new work. I've been so worried about you; you haven't been producing the way you were before."

"Oh, I've been producing," Sweeney muttered.

"I know, you think it's crap. I admit, I've been consumed by curiosity, but I didn't want to push you. When can you bring them by? I want to be certain I'm here."

She was committed, damn it. She glanced out the window to check the weather. "If it doesn't start raining again, how about this afternoon?"

"Wonderful. I don't have any appointments, so I'll be here. See you then."

Sweeney hung up the phone, then hugged the blanket tighter around her. Damn it, damn it, damn it. This was it, then. She had to take some canvases in, let someone else see them. She cringed at the thought, but at least now she would know if what she was doing was awful, or salable. This uncertainty about her work was dreadful, paralyzing.

She shivered violently and swore under her breath. Damn, why couldn't she get warm?

Candra stretched to hang up the phone, then lay with her head pillowed on her arms. A large warm hand stroked her naked bottom. "No luck, huh?" Kai said. "I told you." He bent to press kisses down her spine, more interested in his libido than her financial worries.

Normally she loved having sex with Kai. He was young enough to still be obsessed with sex, but old enough to have acquired some skill. There was a certain freedom in being with him, because he was so innately self-centered she had no qualms about focusing totally on herself, which intensified her pleasure. Now, however, she felt annoyed that he couldn't seem to grasp how important it was that Richard stop being such a hard-ass about the divorce settlement. She shrugged away from his kisses and buried her face in the pillow.

He merely shifted closer, pushing the damp head of his erection against her leg. The hand on her bottom curved downward, fingers probing.

"Stop it," she said irritably, shaking her ass to dislodge his hand. "I don't feel like doing it again. You should be worried, too," she added spitefully. "If Richard doesn't back down on the money, you'll be out of a job."

"There are other jobs," he said, so blissfully unworried she wanted to slap him. He slipped his hand back between her legs, this time sliding two fingers right in. Despite herself she couldn't stop her indrawn breath or the automatic arch of her back.

"Not at what I'm paying you."

"I'll get by." Slowly he began moving his fingers in and out, and Candra bit the pillow to hold back her moan. His ego was big enough as it was.

Because she was so irritated with him, she wriggled once more, dislodging him again. "You were staring at Sweeney yesterday, too. I thought she wasn't your type."

A slow smile curved his lush mouth. "I'm not *her* type. Sweeney's cool, and all that hair gives a man ideas. Besides, the way that red sweater hugged her tits was something else."

"I didn't notice," Candra said frigidly.

"That relieves me, darling." Kai leaned over and began kissing her spine again, this time down close to the twin dimples set high on her buttocks. He liked the idea of Candra being jealous, and that was what he was hearing in her voice. "But take it from me, her tits are fine." Candra went rigid with rage, and he chose that moment to push his fingers into her again, knowing her stiffness would make her less receptive, make the penetration rougher. Sometimes Candra liked being handled a little roughly. She stifled a moan, and he knew he had her.

The bedroom was silent for several minutes, except for her heavier breathing and the rustle of the sheets from their movements. Kai continued to work her with his fingers, until her thighs loosened and spread. "Do it," she ordered angrily, and immediately he moved behind her. She raised up a little on her knees, lifting her buttocks and giving him better access. His fingers were replaced by the hard, smooth thrust of his dick. She sighed and pushed her worries away to better concentrate on the physical pleasure. Kai wouldn't stay around if she went out of business, damn his shallow hide, but for now he was here, so she might as well use him while she had him.

As soon as they had finished and she got her breath back, however, all her worries returned with a rush. She had so hoped she hadn't misread Richard yesterday afternoon. If he were involved with Sweeney, he might be more amenable to meeting her terms, just to get the divorce out of the way so he could concentrate on his new relationship.

She sighed. It had been a long shot, but at this point she was desperate enough to grasp at straws. Unfortunately, Sweeney was so oblivious to everything but her work, she probably wouldn't notice that a man was attracted to her until he took off his clothes, and even then she might think he wanted her to sketch him. Richard wasn't a man who would play second fiddle in a woman's life, not even to talent, and Sweeney was undeniably talented.

Worry gnawed at her insides. If only Richard would back down—no, there was no sense in fretting about *if onlys*. That was like planning your future if you won the lottery: useless.

She knew she hadn't managed her money well; she had never had to. There had always been plenty of it, first her father's money, and by the time that was gone, there had been Richard's. But she wasn't stupid, she had learned from her mistakes. With the profit from the gallery and the lump-sum alimony Richard had agreed to pay, she would be able to manage—not as well as she would like, but she could manage—if she could pay off the mountain of debt hanging over her.

That was the real problem. When she thought of what she owed, she broke out in a sweat. The amount was staggering to her now that she was on her own. After the split she had gone on a spending binge, furnishing her apartment with top-of-the-line everything, and she had taken several very expensive trips and bought new clothes. Somehow she hadn't thought Richard was serious about the divorce, and she'd spent all that money as a means of punishing him for scaring her so. But he was deadly serious about the divorce and had no intention of covering her new debts, even though he could probably pay them out of petty cash and never know the difference, if he just would.

Candra squashed a tinge of regret. There was no point in rehashing the past, and Richard was irretrievably in the past. All her attempts to smooth things over with him had been rebuffed. She imagined a tiny part of her would always miss him. It wasn't just the sex, though God knows that had been hot, at least for the first five years. None of her other lovers had ever matched Richard in bed.

What she missed most, though, was the security. Richard was a very secure man, a rock on which she could always depend. His attributes sounded like an ad in a singles column: reliable, intelligent, good sense of humor, great lover, honorable. By all means, don't forget "honorable." His damn standards were so high you'd think he'd been born in Buckingham Palace instead of on some little dirt farm in western Virginia.

It was her fault, though. She'd always known how he would react if he found out about the abortion. She had been so careful, paying for it in cash so there was no chance of him finding a canceled check or a credit card slip. She hadn't *liked* having an abortion, but she hadn't seen another option. She didn't want a child; she had never wanted children, not even when she was young and just married and wildly in love with him. Nor was having the child and giving it up for adoption a possibility, because Richard would have died before he let that happen. And it wasn't so much raising a child that she found so distasteful as actually being pregnant, having it wriggling around inside her like some larva, distorting her body and wrecking her life.

No, abortion had been the only answer. The bloom had long since been off their marriage, had been ever since Richard discovered that little fling with . . . what was his name? He hadn't been important, just a moment's entertainment. It had taken all her persuasiveness to keep their marriage together then, and she had been extremely cautious about her affairs after that; they weren't serious to *her,* but she had known Richard wouldn't see it that way. Still, she had no doubt they would have made the best of things and continued to rock along if she hadn't had too much to drink, if they hadn't been arguing, if she hadn't gotten so angry she had thrown the words at him like rocks, just for the satisfaction of hurting him. If, if, if. The mistake had been final.

Their marriage, in all but the legal sense of the word, had ended on the spot.

She accepted the blame. That didn't mean she would meekly accept whatever Richard deigned to give her. She had hoped he would become involved with Sweeney, because Sweeney, for all her quirkiness, had a soft heart. Moreover, Candra genuinely liked Sweeney and thought the regard was returned. Richard would do a lot to please a woman he wanted, as she had reason to know. If he wanted Sweeney, and she thought he did, and Sweeney urged him to generosity, there was a good chance he would do as she asked.

After speaking with Sweeney, though, Candra thought that scenario was shot. Her thoughts jumped to the other plan she had formulated. She didn't like it, it wasn't without risk, but at this point it looked as if her best bet was Carson McMillan.

When you danced with the devil, or slept with him, it was a good idea to find out all you could about him and take steps to protect yourself. She knew a lot about Carson, things he wouldn't want known, though maybe she wouldn't have to use them. Perhaps she could get him to believe the child had been his; the timing made it roughly possible, though of course she had no doubt Richard was the father. Yes, that might work. Tell him about the abortion, that it had been his, but when Richard found out about the child, he had assumed it was his and that was why they were being divorced. That would obligate Carson to cover some of her financial obligations. Yes, she would prefer doing it that way.

If he balked, then she would bring out the big guns.

CHAPTER
FIVE

The chill was worse. Sweeney sat huddled in the blanket, shivering continually. She felt as if she might die from the cold and had some fun imagining the medical examiner's perplexity at someone's dying of hypothermia in an eighty-degree apartment on a warm September day. She thought of going back to bed and getting under the electric blanket, but if she did that, she would have to admit she was sick, and she didn't want to do that. When the doorbell rang, she ignored it, because by staying huddled she could conserve what little heat she generated, and moving around made her even colder.

But it rang again, and again, and at last she struggled to her feet. "What!" she snapped as she neared the door.

There was a curiously muffled sound, and she stopped in her tracks, sufficiently city-smart not to go any closer. "Who is it?"

"Richard."

Stunned, she stared at the wood panels. "Richard?"

"Richard Worth," he added helpfully. She thought she could hear laughter in his voice.

She thought of not opening the door. She thought of simply walking away and pretending she hadn't said anything. The thing was, he owned the building, and even though it wasn't the ritziest place in the world, she suspected he could get a lot more in rent than what she had been paying. And right now, she couldn't afford to pay more, so it behooved her to be polite to the landlord. That was the excuse she gave herself as she fumbled with the locks, and of course it was the cold that made her fingers tremble.

He stood in the hallway with its dingy, worn carpeting. He would have looked totally out of place, in his expensive Italian suit, if it hadn't been for those stevedore shoulders and that hard, almost-craggy face. Her artist's eye noted every detail, almost hungrily drinking them in; if she had hoped yesterday had been an aberration, the sight of him disillusioned her. Her stomach fluttered, her mouth watered just as it did when she saw cheese-cake. This couldn't be a good sign.

He was smiling, but the smile quickly faded at the sight of her standing there swaddled in a blanket. His dark gaze went swiftly down her, then returned to her face. "Are you sick?" he asked in a brusque tone, stepping forward so that he crowded her back, and that easily he was inside her apartment. He closed the door and reset the locks.

"No, just cold." She moved away from the dangerously close

proximity to him, scowling. "What are you doing here?" She felt terribly off-balance; she wasn't prepared to see Richard at all, much less be alone with him in her apartment. This was her sanctuary, where she could let down the guard she always kept between herself and the rest of the world, where she could relax and paint and be herself. Closing the door behind her often felt as if she had left a ton of chains in the hallway. Here she was free, but she could be free only if she was alone.

"I came to take you to lunch."

"I told you no yesterday afternoon." She hugged the blanket around her, suddenly self-conscious about how she must look. She was still wearing sweats, and she hadn't brushed her hair, so she knew it was bushed around her head in a wild tangle. A long curl hung in her eyes; she pushed it back and blushed, then scowled. She didn't like the feeling of embarrassment. She couldn't remember the last time she had cared what someone thought of how she looked, but . . . but Richard was different. She didn't want him to be, but he was.

"That was for dinner." He eyed her critically, moving forward even more, frowning as he registered the heat in the apartment. "Why do you have it so hot in here?"

"I told you, I'm cold." Despite herself, her voice sounded querulous. He reached out and placed a warm hand on her forehead. She would have jerked back, but the warmth felt so good she felt herself lean a little into his hand.

A slight frown knit his forehead. "You don't seem to be feverish."

"Of course I'm not. I just told you, I'm cold."

"Then something is wrong, because it's hot in here."

"Says the man wearing a jacket." She sniffed in disdain and moved away from him to reclaim her seat in the corner of the couch, curling into herself for warmth.

He wasn't the least put off by her snappishness. "It's called a suit," he said, sitting down beside her. "Do you feel ill in any other way?"

"I don't feel ill at all. I'm just cold."

He regarded her stubbornly set face for a moment. "You know that isn't normal."

"Maybe my internal thermostat's messed up," she muttered, though she didn't really think so. The coldness had begun with the change, so she had thought there was nothing she could do about it. On the other hand, the thought that she might actually be ill wasn't any more welcome. She didn't have time for illness, so she refused to be ill. It was that simple.

His dark eyes were sharp and probing as he continued to study her. "How long has this been going on?"

If she hadn't been so cold, she could have asserted herself, but it was difficult to sound assertive when anything she said was filtered through chattering teeth. Rather than appear ridiculous, she said, "I stay cold, most of the time, but this is the worst it's been."

"You need to see a doctor," he said decisively. "Come on, get dressed and I'll take you."

"Forget it." Pulling the blanket closer, Sweeney rested her head on her knees. Deciding to turn the pressure on him, she said, "You should have called before you came over."

"So you could tell me not to come? That's why I didn't call." He touched her hand and frowned at the iciness of her fingers.

"Well, I can't go out, and you can bet your last penny I'm not going to cook for you."

"I don't expect you to." He was still frowning as he watched her, half turned toward her with one arm resting along the back of the couch. She clenched her teeth to keep them from chattering, wishing he would go. He was too close, and she was too cold. A woman couldn't muster her defenses when she had to concentrate on shivering.

"Okay," he said, getting to his feet as if he had made a decision. He unbuttoned his suit jacket and shrugged out of it.

"What are you doing?" Sweeney demanded, sitting up in alarm. Even as she said it, the question struck her as stupid, since obviously she could see what he was doing. It was the *why* that alarmed her.

"Getting you warm." He plucked the blanket from her grasp and pulled it away. Before she could protest, he settled his jacket around her shoulders.

The warmth was almost shocking. She inhaled sharply in relief as the heat sank into her spine. My God, the man must be like a furnace, for his jacket to absorb that much of his body heat. The sensation was so delicious she didn't notice him sitting down again until he scooped her onto his lap.

She went rigid with a brief moment of panic, then pushed hard at him as she swung one foot to the floor so she could stand. To her astonishment, he simply wrapped his arms around her and gathered her in as if she were a child, lifting her feet onto the couch and holding her close. He tucked the blanket around both of them, making sure her feet were covered.

"Body heat," he said calmly. "That's one of the first things they taught us in army survival courses, to huddle together when we got cold."

Sweeney stilled, lured both by the incredible warmth wrapping around her and by the image his words brought up in her mind. She couldn't help smiling. "I can just see all you tough young soldiers cuddling together."

"Not cuddling, huddling. There's a difference." He laid his

hand over her feet; she was struck by the fact that his hand was big enough to cover both of her feet. Heat began seeping through her socks to her icy toes.

Convulsive shivering suddenly shook her, despite the warmth of coat, blanket, and body, and Richard gathered her closer, tucking her head under his chin and pulling the blanket up so that her nose was covered, warming the air she breathed. "You're going to smother me," she protested.

"Not for a while yet." There was that note of laughter in his voice again, though when she rolled her head back to see, his mouth was perfectly straight. No, not straight; she paused, mesmerized by the clear cut of his lips. He had a good mouth, not too thin, not too full. Not so wide that a woman would feel as if she might fall in, and not so small it looked as if he'd just sucked a lemon like Ronald Trump's, or whatever his name was. All in all, Richard's lips looked just right.

"You're staring," he said.

Over the years she had been caught staring at people more times than she could remember, and usually it didn't bother her, but this time she blushed. "I do that," she mumbled. "Stare at people. I'm sorry."

"It doesn't bother me. Stare away."

There was a warm, soft, indulgent tone in his voice that gave her another one of those alarming, exciting stomach flutters. It occurred to her that sitting in a man's lap was not a good way to discourage his attentions, or flatten her own interest. On the other hand, not only did she doubt he would let her get up, the warmth was so marvelous she didn't *want* to get up, at least not now. Though she still shivered, she could tell the body heat thing was working, because the shivers were lessening in intensity.

"When were you in the army?" She felt she had to say something, because just sitting there was awkward, and if you couldn't talk to a man when you were in his lap, then when could you?

"A long time ago, when I was young and macho."

"Why did you join? Or were you drafted?" She had no idea when the draft had been abolished.

"I joined. I didn't have any money for college, so that seemed like the best way to get an education. Turned out I had a knack for things military. I would probably still be in if I hadn't stumbled on a knack for the stock market, too. The stock market is a lot more lucrative, and I wanted money."

"Well, you have it now."

"Yes, I do."

His body heat was seductive, melting her bones, leaching strength from her muscles. She felt herself sinking into him, molding to him like soft gelatin. The departing chill left her limp and sleepy, utterly relaxed. Not even the hard ridge forming under her bottom could alarm her. She yawned and stuck her cold nose into the warm curve where jaw joined neck. She felt him give a little jump, but then his arms tightened.

She should get up. She knew she should. This was asking for trouble. She wasn't a child, and she knew how sexual this situation was, and how much more sexual it could become. But the warmth . . . ah, God, the warmth! She was comfortable for the first time since getting out of bed that morning, more comfortable, truly, than she had been in a long time, at least a year. An electric blanket didn't provide the same kind of heat as another body, didn't reach all the way down to the marrow of her bones. The army knew what it was about, making its young soldiers cuddle.

She yawned again and felt a chuckle rumble in his chest, his throat, though it never actually made it out. "Go to sleep," he murmured, deep voice soothing. "I'll take care of you."

Sweeney wasn't a trusting soul; a solitary woman couldn't afford to be. But she didn't have a moment's doubt that Richard was a man of his word. She could feel sleep coming, heavy and delicious, and she gave herself up to it with a little sigh. "Don't let me sleep past one o'clock," she said, the words slurred, and closed her eyes.

One o'clock? Richard stifled his laughter. A glance at his wristwatch told him the time wasn't yet eleven-thirty. Sweeney evidently saw nothing wrong in expecting him to hold her in his lap for an hour and a half and let her sleep, disregarding all concern for any cramps he might develop or appointments he might have. The thing was, she was right. He would rather be right where he was than any other place he could think of.

His cell phone was in his coat pocket. Using his free hand, he carefully reached inside the jacket without disturbing her, though the back of his hand brushed her breast, which disturbed *him.* He ignored his aching erection and flipped open the flat little phone, pressing the buttons with his thumb. "I won't be going out to lunch," he said quietly when Edward answered. "Pick me up at one-fifteen."

"Very good, sir."

Richard ended the call and folded the phone. Sweeney stirred and nudged her nose against his neck, but didn't open her eyes. She was truly, deeply, asleep.

He shifted into a more comfortable position, settling his shoulders and easing his head back against the couch. He was going to be here awhile, so he might as well relax and enjoy it. Holding Sweeney on his lap was definitely enjoyable. He had a sneaking idea she had no clue how appealing she was, with her big blue eyes and curly mass of hair, but he had always thought she was one of the most attractive women he'd ever met. Not beautiful—attractive. People liked to look at her, talk to her. Men would have been swarming all over her if she had ever given any indication she was aware of them as *men,* not just sexless acquaintances. She was an expert at keeping people at a distance, blocking any but the most superficial contact.

Until yesterday. He didn't know what had happened, but suddenly he had known her blinders were gone and she was aware of him personally, emotionally, sexually. God knows he had been aware of her, standing there with that red sweater molded to her breasts and those blue eyes getting wider and wider as she listened to the McMillans. He had almost been able to see some irrepressibly scathing comment welling up in her throat, because she was known for saying what was on her mind. In the world he moved in, such spontaneous honesty was so rare as to be almost nonexistent. People guarded their words and stuck to the polite, the politically correct, the inane. He knew Sweeney tried to be polite, but as she had said yesterday, her tolerance level for bullshit was really low.

She made him grin. Hell, she made him laugh. He had the feeling he could spend every day with her for twenty years and not know all of her quirks or exactly how her mind worked.

He liked her. He had dated other women since he and Candra had separated, but he had been careful to keep any relationships casual, and in fact hadn't really *liked* any of the women. Enjoyed them, yes, even been aroused by them, but he had never felt any of them could be a friend. Maybe that was why he hadn't slept with any of them, which Candra would never believe, and in fact he astonished himself with his reticence. He missed sex. He wanted sex. He was so horny he was going through the torments of the damned, holding Sweeney on his lap, but the truth was he had turned down a lot of opportunities.

Legally, he was still married. He couldn't forget that. The

marriage was over—he could barely tolerate being in the same room with Candra—but until a judge ruled the marriage was dissolved, he wasn't a free man. It wouldn't be fair to any woman to start a sexual relationship with her knowing he wasn't able to offer more. Until yesterday, when he had met Sweeney's eyes and felt that zing of attraction, it hadn't mattered. Now it did.

Gently he touched one of her curls, picking it up and stretching it out, marveling at its length. Straightened, her hair would reach over halfway down her back. He released the tension on the strand and it wrapped around his finger like a loose spring.

The chill she'd had worried him. The apartment's heat, added to the warmth of both her and the blanket draped over him, had sweat running down his face. Her face had been pale, her skin clammy. She had looked shocky, as if she had lost a lot of blood. Since that obviously wasn't the case, something else was wrong. Glancing down at her now, though, he saw a tinge of delicate color in her cheeks, and her face had lost the drawn look of hypothermia.

One unrestrained breast pressed against his rib cage. She was definitely braless, a detail he had immediately noted, with her chill pinching her nipples into tight little points. They had plumped out now, though, because he couldn't feel them pushing at him.

Not today, but one day soon, he would hold her naked breasts in his hands and rub his thumbs over her nipples and watch them pucker. He closed his eyes as he let himself imagine how it would feel to hold her beneath him and push deep into her. Making love to Sweeney would be a challenge; despite the startled awareness in her eyes, she was resisting doing anything about it. Part of it was scruples, yes; he understood that. But part of it was sheer stubbornness, an unwillingness to open herself up to him. She wanted her life just the way it was, without a man around to distract her. She was good at keeping it that way, too, because judging from the comments Candra had dropped over the years, Sweeney was practically a nun.

Not for much longer, though.

He closed his eyes and forced himself to relax, but as he began to doze, he remembered her charge—he would demand time and sex and things like that, he thought was the way she'd put it. She was right on the money. He went to sleep with a slight smile on his face.

In the army, he had trained himself to sleep for a specified length of time, no matter how brief, and wake up when he wanted. Now they were called power naps, but then he had called it staying alive. He shut out of his mind the uncomfortable heat, ignored it as if it didn't exist, another trick he had learned in training. When he woke half an hour later, he felt rested despite the fact that his shirt was wet with sweat. Sweeney was warm, too; she had pushed the blanket down from around her face, and her fingertips were pink. As he had expected, she began stirring just a few moments later, rather than the hour and a half she had given herself; sleep was the body's reaction to cold, and once warmth was restored, the sleepiness was gone.

He was looking down at her, so he saw her eyes pop open. Like flashes of lightning, her expression was startled, then flickered to alarm. She sat up suddenly, catching his balls beneath her and pinning them. He barely restrained a yelp and swiftly shifted her weight in his lap.

"Oh, God, I can't believe I did that," she muttered, scrambling off his lap in a tangle of blanket and coat.

"I can." Wincing, he eased into a different position.

She looked down, and her eyes widened. "I didn't mean that," she blurted. "I was talking about going to sleep in your lap. I'm so sorry." She bit her lip. "Are you all right?"

A chuckle burst through his clenched teeth. Gingerly he moved again, and the pain began to fade. "I don't know," he said, deliberately pitching his voice high.

She threw herself back against the couch, shrieking with laughter.

Richard bent over her, framed her face with his hands, and kissed her laughing mouth.

She went still, like a small animal trying to hide from a predator. Her hands came up to clasp his wrists, clever hands, the skin soft and sensitive over delicate bones. He wanted to crush her mouth with his, but he gentled his kiss, treasuring rather than taking. Her lips trembled, just a little. He opened them and sought her tongue with his. Heat roared through him, white-hot and urgent. His entire body tightened with the need to cover and enter. Ruthlessly he restrained himself, knowing she was far from acceptance.

Then she kissed him back. The movement of her lips and tongue were tentative, almost shy at first, and then a low moan vibrated in her throat and her grip tightened on his wrists. He felt tension invade her body, felt her strain upward even though she never left her seat beside him. He deepened the kiss, his tongue slow and sure, both taking and inviting.

She tore away from him, launching herself to her feet and stomping several feet away. When she whirled to face him, her expression was tight with anger. "No," she said, voice clipped. "You're married."

He got to his feet, gaze locked on her face. "Not for much longer."

She made an abrupt motion. "You're married *now*, and that's what counts. You're in the middle of an unfriendly divorce—"

"Is there any other kind?" he interrupted, tone as mild as if he were asking the time.

"You know what I mean. Candra's my business associate, and on top of that I like her."

"Most people do."

"Getting involved with you would be messy. It wouldn't be right."

His dark eyes narrowed. "Okay."

Her eyebrows arched in surprise. "Okay?"

"For now. Until the divorce is final. Then . . ." He shrugged, letting the word trail off, but from the way he still watched her, she could figure out what "then" entailed. "One question: What's your first name?"

She gaped at him. "What?"

"Your first name. What is it? I refuse to call a woman I've slept with by her last name."

"We didn't—" she began, then scowled, because sleeping together was exactly what they had done. "You have to call me by my last name," she snapped. "Because it's the only name I'll answer to."

"Maybe. You might as well tell me," he said maddeningly. "You had to fill out an application when you moved into the apartment. I can find out from that."

Her scowl deepened. "Paris," she said abruptly.

He didn't follow. "What about it?"

"That's my name," she growled. "Paris. With one *r*. Like the city. Like the dead Greek guy. Paris Samille, if you want the whole enchilada. And if you ever—*ever*—call me either one, I'll hurt you."

Richard checked the time as he stood and picked up his jacket. He wasn't an idiot, so he didn't so much as smile. "All right," he agreed. "I promise I'll never call you anything you don't like." Before she could evade him, he bent and kissed her again.

"I'll lay off," he said softly. "For now. But when this divorce is final, I'll be back."

Sweeney didn't say anything, just watched silently as he let himself out of the apartment. Was that a promise, or a threat? The decision was up to her, and she had no idea which it would be. The only thing she knew for certain was that when he kissed her, she had left safety far behind.

Sweeney picked up first one canvas and then another, trying to decide which she should take to the gallery. She didn't like any of them, and the thought of anyone else seeing them embarrassed her. The bright colors looked childish to her, garish. Twice she started to call Candra and tell her she wouldn't be bringing anything over after all, but both times she stopped herself. If what she was doing was crap, she needed to find out for certain now before she wasted any more time. She didn't know what she would do if it *was* crap; therapy, maybe? If writers could have writer's block, the equivalent had to be possible for artists.

She could just hear it now; a therapist would solemnly tell her she was trying to resolve her childhood issues by *becoming* a child again, seeing things through a child's eyes. Uh-huh. She had resolved her childhood issues a long time ago. She had resolved never to be like her parents, never to use her talent as an excuse for selfish, juvenile behavior, never to have children and then shunt them aside while she pursued her art. Her mother advocated free love and went through a period of trying to "free" Sweeney from her inhibitions by openly making love with her various lovers in front of her young daughter. These days, she would have been arrested. She should have been then, too.

The wonder, Sweeney thought grimly, was that she had had the courage to paint at all, that she hadn't gone into something like data processing or accounting, to get as far away from the art world as possible. But she had never considered not painting; it had been too much a part of her for as long as she could remember. As a little girl she had eschewed dolls, choosing colored pencils and sketch pads as her favorite toys. By the time she was six, she had been using oils, snitching the tubes from her mother whenever she could. She could lose herself in color for hours, stand enraptured staring not just at rainbows but at rain, seeing clouds as well as sky, individual blades of grass, the sheen of a ripe red apple.

No, there had never been any question about her talent, or her obsession. So she had tried to be the best artist she could, and at the same time to be normal. Okay, so she sometimes slipped and forgot to comb her hair, and sometimes when she was working, she forgot and shoved her hands through said hair, leaving bright streaks of paint behind. That was minor. She wasn't promiscuous; she paid her bills on time; she didn't do drugs even on a recreational basis; she didn't smoke; she didn't drink. There wasn't a swag of beads anywhere in her apartment, and she was a regular June Cleaver in her personal life.

The most abnormal thing about her was that she saw ghosts, which really wasn't so bad, was it? Like maybe a sixty-seven on a scale of one to ten.

Sweeney snorted. She could stand there and philosophize all day, or she could pack up some canvases and get them over to the gallery.

Because she had said she would, and because it didn't matter which she chose, finally she just picked three at random. She thought they were all equally bad, so what difference did it make?

As an afterthought, she picked up the sketch she had done of the hot dog vendor. She was pleased with that, at least. She had just guessed at how he would have looked at six years of age, as a teenager, as a young man, but she had kept that same sweetness of expression in all the sketches in the collage. She hoped he would like it.

Her mind made up, she left the apartment before she could talk herself into dithering further. The rain the day before had left the air fresh and sweet; after a moment, surprised, Sweeney had to admit the weather forecast had been accurate: it *was* a beautiful day. That weird chill was gone, chased away by Richard's body heat, and she felt warmer than she had in a long time. If it wasn't for the anxiety that kept gnawing at her, she would have felt great. She decided to enjoy being warm and forget about how she had gotten that way.

The hot dog vendor wasn't in his usual spot. Sweeney stopped, disappointed and unaccountably uneasy. As if she could will it into appearing, she stared at the location where the cart was usually parked. He must be sick, because she had never before walked down this street without seeing him.

Worried, she walked on to the gallery. Kai rose from his desk and came forward to take the wrapped canvases from her. "Great! Candra and I have been talking about you. I can't wait to see what you're doing now."

"Neither can I," Candra said, coming out of her office and smiling warmly at Sweeney. "Don't look so worried. I don't think you're capable of doing a bad painting."

"You'd be surprised what I can do," Sweeney muttered.

"Oh, I don't know," drawled a thin, black-clad man with stringy blond hair, sauntering out of Candra's office. "I don't think you've surprised any of us in a long time, darling."

Sweeney stifled a disgusted groan. VanDern. Just the person she least wanted to see.

"Leo, behave yourself," Candra admonished, giving him a stern look.

At least, Sweeney thought, seeing VanDern chased away her anxiety. Hostility overrode anxiety any day of the week. Her eyes narrowed warningly as she looked at him.

Like her mother, he epitomized what she despised most, dramatizing himself by wearing black leather pants, black turtle-neck, black Cossack boots. Instead of a belt, a hammered silver chain was draped around his skinny waist. He wore three studs in one ear and a hoop in the other. He was never clean-shaven, but cultivated the three-day-stubble look, expending more energy on appearing not to shave than he would have on shaving. She suspected he went months, certainly weeks, without washing his hair. He could go on for hours about symbolism and the hopelessness of modern society, about how man had raped the universe and how his single glob of paint on a canvas captured the pain and despair of all mankind. In his own opinion, he was as profound as the Dalai Lama. In hers, he was as profound as a turd.

Candra unwrapped the canvases and in silence set them on some empty easels. Sweeney deliberately didn't look at them, though her stomach knotted.

"Wow," Kai said softly. He had said the same thing about her red sweater the day before, but this time the tone was different.

Candra was silent, tilting her head a little as she studied the paintings.

VanDern stepped forward, glancing at the paintings and dismissing them with a sneer. "Trite," he pronounced. "Landscapes.

How original. I've never seen trees and water before." He examined his nails. "I may faint from the excitement."

"Leo," Candra said in warning. She was still looking at the canvases.

"Don't tell me you like this stuff," he scoffed. "You can buy 'pitchers' like this in any discount store in the country. Oh, I know there's a market for it, people who don't know anything about art and just want something that's 'purty,' but let's be honest, shall we?"

"By all means," Sweeney said in a low, dangerous voice, stepping closer to him. Hearing that tone, Candra snapped her head around, but she was too late to preserve the peace. Sweeney poked VanDern in the middle of his sunken chest. "If we're being honest, any monkey can throw a glob of paint on a canvas, and any idiot can call it art, but the fact is, it doesn't take any talent to do either one. It takes talent and *skill* to reproduce an object so the observer actually recognizes it."

He rolled his eyes. "What it *takes*, darling, is a total lack of imagination and interpretive skills to do the same old thing over and over again."

He had underestimated his target. Sweeney had been raised in the art world and by the queen of sly, savage remarks. She gave him a sweet smile. "What it *takes*, darling"—her tone was an almost exact mimicry of his—"is a lot of gall to pass your kind of con off on the public. Of course, I guess you have to have something to offset your total lack of talent."

"There's no point in this," Candra interjected, trying to pour oil on the waters.

"Oh, let her talk," VanDern said, languidly waving a dismissive hand. "If she could do what I do, she would be doing it, making real money instead of peddling her stuff to the Wal-Mart crowd."

Candra stiffened. Her gallery was her pride, and she resented the implication that her clientele was anything but the crème de la crème.

"I can do what you do," Sweeney said, lifting her eyebrows in exaggerated surprise. "But I outgrew it somewhere around the age of three. Would you like to make a small bet? I bet I can duplicate any of your works you choose, but you can't duplicate any of mine, and the loser has to kiss the winner's ass."

A low rumble sounded in Kai's throat. He turned his head, pretending to cough.

VanDern gave him a furious look, then turned his attention back to Sweeney. "How childish," he sneered.

"Afraid to take the bet, huh?" she said.

"Of course not!"

"Then do it. I tell you what: I won't limit you to just my work. Pick a classic; duplicate a Whistler, a Monet, a van Gogh. I'm sure they would be worthy of your great talent."

His cheeks turned a dull red. He glared at her, unable to win the argument and equally unable to think of a graceful way of getting out of the bet. He glanced at Candra. "I'll come back later," he said stiffly, "when you have more time."

"Do that," she said, her tone clipped. Her annoyance was obvious. When the doors closed behind him, she turned to Sweeney. "I'm sorry. He can be an arrogant jerk sometimes."

"Without straining," Sweeney agreed.

Candra smiled. "You more than held your own. He'll think twice before he challenges you again. He's hot right now, but fads pass, and I'm sure he knows his day in the sun won't last very long."

In Sweeney's opinion, VanDern thought he was the center of the universe, but she shrugged and let the subject drop.

Candra returned her attention to the paintings, tapping one

elegant nail on her bottom lip as she considered them. Sweeney's stomach knotted again.

"They're almost surreal," Candra murmured, talking to herself. "Your use of color is striking. Several shades seem to glow, like light coming through stained glass. A river, a mountain, flowers, but not like any you've done before."

Sweeney was silent. She had spent hours, days, staring worriedly at those canvases; she knew every brushstroke on them. But she looked at them again, wondering what she had missed, and saw that nothing had changed. The colors still looked strangely intense, the composition was a little off in some way she couldn't explain, the brushstrokes were a touch blurred. She couldn't tell if it was surreal, as Candra said, or exuberant. Maybe both. Maybe neither.

"I want more," Candra said. "If this is an example of what you've been doing, I want every canvas you've completed. I'm doubling your prices. I may have to come down in price, but I think I'm judging it right."

Kai nodded in agreement. "There's energy here, a lot more than I've ever seen in your work. People will go nuts over these."

Sweeney dismissed the bit about energy; that was just a buzzword. His last statement was more honest, an assessment of their marketability. Relief swamped her. Maybe she hadn't lost her talent, just her ability to judge it.

"What's that?" Candra said, indicating the folder holding the sketch of the hot dog vendor.

"A sketch I made of a street vendor," Sweeney said. "I want to give it to him." She shivered suddenly, a chill roughening her skin. Damn it, she had been enjoying feeling warm, but the warmth hadn't lasted long.

"I'll have these framed immediately," Candra said, turning back to the paintings. "And bring the others. I'd like to make a full display of them, place them close to the front so the light is better and they're the first thing clients see when they come in. I promise, these are going to fly out the door."

Walking back home, Sweeney hugged herself against the cold. She was relieved at Candra's reaction to the paintings, but for some reason she couldn't enjoy her relief. The uneasy feeling was growing stronger.

She reached the corner where the old vendor had always been, but it was still empty. She stopped, a great sadness welling in her as she wondered if she would ever see him again. She wanted to give him the sketch, wanted to know if she had accurately deduced his childhood features from the facial structure of an old man. She wanted to see that sweet smile.

"Hi, Sweeney," said a soft voice at her elbow.

She looked around, and delight speared through her. "There you are," she said joyfully. "I thought you must be sick—" She halted, shock replacing delight. He was faintly translucent, oddly two-dimensional.

He shook his head. "I'm all right. Don't be worryin' about me." The sweet smile bloomed in his dark face. "You got it right, Sweeney. That's just how I used to look."

She didn't say anything else. She couldn't. She wanted to weep, she wanted to say she was sorry she hadn't gotten it right sooner, so she could have given him the sketch.

"Do me a favor," he said. "Send it to my boys. Daniel and Jacob Stokes. They're lawyers, my boys, both of them. Fine men. Send it to them."

"I will," she whispered, and he nodded.

"Go on now," he said. "I'll be fine. I just had some loose ends needed takin' care of."

"I'll miss you," she managed to say. She was aware of people giving her a wide berth, but they were New Yorkers; no one stopped, or even slowed.

"I'll miss you, too. You always brought the sunshine with you. Smile now, and let me see how pretty you are. My, my, your eyes are as blue as heaven. That's a mighty nice sight . . ."

His voice became gradually fainter, as if he were walking away from her. Sweeney watched him fade, becoming more and more transparent until there was nothing left except a faint glow where he had stood.

The chill was gone. She felt warm again, but frightened and sad. She wanted to be held the way Richard had held her that morning, but he wasn't here, and he wasn't hers. She didn't have him. She was alone, and for the first time in her life she didn't like it.

CHAPTER SIX

Candra took the early shuttle from New York to D.C. the next morning. The capital suited her purposes better, so she didn't mind the inconvenience. For one, seeing him in D.C. was easier than seeing him in New York, where he was seldom in his office. She would have had to either go to his house or call him there for an outside meeting, and she preferred not to.

Perhaps Margo knew about her affair with the senator, but perhaps not. Despite her own stupidity in telling Richard about the abortion when she should have kept her mouth shut, Candra didn't believe in unnecessarily hurting or humiliating anyone.

Margo might not care how many women Carson banged, but she definitely wouldn't want him banging them in her house. Knowing what she knew about him, Candra wouldn't be surprised if he insisted on having sex right there in the office, before he even knew why she was there. She smiled thinly, humorlessly. First he would fuck her, then she would fuck him; she thought that was fair.

She had taken extra pains with her appearance that morning, not to attract attention but to avoid it. On went the black business suit, the staid black pumps with one-and-a-half-inch heels. Her earrings were plain gold hoops; she left off all rings and exchanged her wafer-thin, impossibly elegant Piaget wristwatch for an old Rolex, one her father had given her when she was sixteen. She doubted it had cost more than a couple of thousand. A Rolex wouldn't stand out in the capital, where status was everything and Rolexes were as common as embassy plates.

She brushed her hair more severely and toned down her makeup. She wouldn't stand out; she would look like thousands of businesswomen or lobbyists. She didn't want to be memorable, should anyone see her. It was, perhaps, a foolish precaution on her part, but then she had never before blackmailed anyone and she thought some discretion was needed.

Today was Margo's regular day at Elizabeth Arden; since the trip to Rome had been postponed, she would go about her normal routine, and Margo was a fanatic about pampering her looks. With Margo safely in New York, Candra didn't worry that Carson had told her to come to his town house in the capital. Doing so actually suited her better, because she wouldn't have enjoyed the crassness, the utter distastefulness, of being screwed on an office desk with a troop of aides just outside the door.

At the airport, she hailed a taxi and sat quietly in the backseat, not encouraging the driver's occasional attempts at conversation. To her surprise, she felt the beginning flutters of excitement and anticipation she normally felt when she knew she was going to have sex. Until now her mind had been completely on what she would say afterward, but now she began to think about the act itself. Carson had little technique but a lot of vigor, and sometimes, when she was feeling a little nasty, that was just what she wanted.

He had to be in his office at ten-thirty. She would have an hour with him. That would be sufficient.

Carson met her at the door himself, smiling and saying all the inane social things in case anyone was listening. He had staff here, of course, at least a cook and a housekeeper. He was very good looking, Candra thought, smiling up into that almost classical face. How odd that she actually preferred Richard's more rugged looks. Richard was one of those men who was so overtly *male* a woman couldn't help looking at him. She gave herself a small mental shake; she had to stop thinking about him, because she had lost him. That part of her life was over, and she had to make a success of this new chapter or lose everything.

"You said there was something urgent you needed to discuss with me," Carson said for the benefit of anyone listening, smiling smugly as he escorted her into his office and shut the door, locking it behind him. He thought he was being smooth about it, but Candra was listening for that small click. She was glad he was taking care they wouldn't be interrupted, and if he hadn't locked the door, she would have done it herself.

He grabbed her breasts the moment he turned around, and maneuvered her toward the large sofa. She barely had time to place her bag on the floor before he bore her down on the expensively upholstered cushions, already tugging her skirt up and his zipper down. "We have to hurry," he panted, shoving into her and immediately moving into a fast, pounding rhythm. "Before Margo comes down."

"*What?*" Candra gasped, instinctively pushing against his shoulders. All her initial excitement was gone. Ugly scenes didn't appeal to her, and she had no doubt Margo could enact the ugliest of ugly scenes.

The senator pulled her hands away from his shoulders and pinned them to the sofa, his face set. He didn't intend to let a little thing like his wife's presence in the house keep him from doing what he wanted. Candra held herself still and silent, not wanting to either slow him down or draw attention to the office. Mentally she urged him to hurry. God, the stupid arrogance of the man! Regardless of how much Margo enjoyed the status of being a senator's wife, or how much she looked forward to the White House, there was a limit to what she would turn a blind eye to. Knowing about Carson's indiscretions was one thing; seeing them for herself was very different.

Clinically she watched as his face turned red from effort, and the veins in his neck stood out. He hadn't even loosened his tie. His thrusts moved her back and forth on the sofa.

If he noticed her lack of response, he didn't care. Within two minutes he stiffened, his pelvis jerking and his face twisting into a carnal parody of pain. Odd, she thought, how something that was exciting when she was turned on was distasteful when she wasn't.

He pulled out of her, panting, and took out a handkerchief to wipe himself clean. "Do you have another of those?" she murmured, and seeing his blank look, added, "The handker-chief."

"No, this is the only one." He started to fold it and return it to his pocket—disgusting—but Candra took it from him and folded it herself, touching it as little as possible, and tucked it between her legs.

He looked uneasy. "It's monogrammed."

"I'll give it back to you," she said impatiently. "Or would you rather I destroy it?"

"Burn it," he said, but he still looked unhappy about her having his handkerchief. Too bad he didn't apply that caution to the rest of his behavior, she thought.

She sat up and straightened her clothing, within moments looking as if nothing had happened. Nothing *had,* for her, she thought.

"Sit down," she said. "I *do* have something to discuss with you."

"Of course, anything I can do to help." His own clothing restored to respectability, he sat down behind his desk, made of good old American oak. He was always careful not to flaunt his wealth where his constituents might see, here in his D.C. home and in his office. His home in New York, however, was as luxuri-ous as a palace, with imported everything.

He smiled at her now, the smooth, urbane smile of a man who knows he has power. In coming to him like this, he thought she was going to ask him for a favor. His hazel eyes glit-tered; during their sporadic relationship, Candra had firmly refused to do anything more than occasionally accommodate him. Carson was accustomed to calling the shots, accustomed to having women do his bidding, and her cool distance both annoyed and challenged him. Of course, she had further annoyed him by making their encounters as memorable as possible.

"Two years ago," she said, "I had an abortion."

"I trust you had good care. I've always supported legislation to—"

"I'm not interested in what you've supported," she interrupted. "Carson, the child was yours. But when Richard found out I'd had the abortion, he thought it was his. That's the basis of the trouble between us."

"Really." He leaned back in his huge leather chair, steepling his fingertips together. "How interesting. But why are you telling me this?"

His expression hadn't even flickered at the news that she had supposedly aborted his child. That wasn't the reaction she had hoped for. "Richard is being difficult about the settlements, and without going into detail, he's in a position to win. I could use some financial help, just this one time."

"To the tune of how much?" he asked mildly.

Unease prickled her spine. This wasn't going quite as she had imagined. A million would take care of all her debts, letting her start fresh, but because she was uneasy she said, "Half a million."

"That's a lot of money." He shrugged. "Your pussy isn't that good."

She didn't react to the crudity. She was aware, after all, of just how crude he could be.

"I wonder just how you managed to get pregnant," he mused. "You always told me you were on birth control pills."

"An accident. I had a respiratory illness, and the antibiotic I took affected the pills."

"Unfortunate. However, I sincerely doubt the child was mine. I had a vasectomy some years ago."

Anger curled in her stomach, but she controlled it. He

thought he had just played her for a fool. If, however, he thought that was her only approach, he would be unpleasantly surprised. "Did you? You never mentioned it to me."

"Why would I? You were on the pill anyway, and I've never been fool enough to think I was the only man fucking you. The vasectomy was insurance against this kind of blackmail."

"Now, that's interesting," she said smoothly. "I took out a form of insurance, too. I've never underestimated you, Carson, but I do believe you've underestimated me."

"In what way?" To her gratification, he did look a little wary.

She leaned over and took an envelope and a tiny tape player from the large bag she had carried. His face went stony when he saw the tape player.

"Oh, it isn't on," she said. "It doesn't record, anyway; it's just a player. Our little tryst was private. Others, however, weren't." She punched the "play" button and sat back.

With satisfaction she watched his face blanch as voices filled the room, scratchy but recognizable. She had made the tape at a raunchy little orgy she had staged at the beginning of their relationship, while Richard was in Europe for several days and she had plenty of time. She had done it deliberately, of course, because she had never had any illusions about Carson and suspected that one day she might need a club with which to bludgeon him.

She turned the tape player off, ejected the cassette, and tossed it to him, then placed the envelope on his desk. "Keep it," she said. "It's your personal copy. The accompanying pictures are in the envelope."

His jaw bulged with rage, and he flushed a dark red. "You bitch." The words were low, as if he couldn't manage anything more.

"I don't suppose I have to tell you I have the originals, in a very safe place."

"You're incriminated by these tapes, too." He was breathing hard.

"Yes, but I don't have a career to lose. Of course, your constituents are pretty liberal, they might say live and let live. I don't think the other senators would agree, though, especially those you've fucked over the years. They would enjoy having evidence of their esteemed colleague's illegal behavior." Her tone was rich with irony.

Murderous hatred was in his eyes. Candra controlled a shiver. It was a risk, crossing Carson like this, and she had walked in here knowing it. That was why she had made certain her weapon against him was so powerful he couldn't ignore it.

"This won't be an ongoing thing," she said impatiently. "Just this once. You can afford the money, and I need it."

"Sure," he said sarcastically. "I'm supposed to take your word for it."

"I'll send you the originals as soon as I have the money." She meant it. What she wouldn't send him was the videotape she hadn't mentioned. She would use that only if he tried to get revenge.

Of course, he had no way of being positive anything she gave him was the original, no way of ever being sure there were no more copies in existence. Blackmail was forever.

She placed a small piece of paper on his desk. "This is my bank and account number. Wire the money into it. I opened the account just for this, and I'll close it after I get the money. I trust I won't be audited by the IRS either, so you really should hope the random audits miss me."

He didn't pick up the paper. Candra got to her feet and looped her purse strap on her shoulder. "I had the cab wait.

Don't bother seeing me out." When she got to the door, she unlocked it, then paused and looked over her shoulder at him. "By the way . . . make it a million."

The front door had barely closed behind Candra when Margo entered Carson's office. Her face was white and rigid. "You fool," she said scathingly. "You stupid, goddamn fool, always thinking with your dick instead of your head."

"Shut up," he snarled, erupting from his chair. "What were you doing, listening at the door?"

She walked over and punched a button on the intercom console. "I opened the intercom when I found out she was coming here. You think you're so damn smart, but you never check to see if the intercom is open."

He grabbed her by the arm, his powerful fingers biting into her flesh. "Don't take that tone with me," he warned.

"Or you'll what? Divorce me? I don't think so." She jerked her arm free and picked up the envelope Candra had left. Carson made a move for it, but Margo stepped away and opened it, removing the pictures.

She looked at them, and ugly red color splotched her cheeks. She flipped through the photographs, and her mouth contorted. She whirled, her hand lashing out with all the strength in her arm behind it, catching him full across the face. His head jerked around under the impact.

Slowly he looked at her. His face was white except for the imprint of her hand. His eyes burned like coals.

Margo was shaking. "You're worse than a fool; you're the most imbecilic egomaniac I've ever known, and it takes some doing to top my father. I haven't put up with you all these years to let you fuck things up now, with everything in place for the next election. You have to do something."

"I'll pay the goddamn money. I don't have any choice."

"What if she wants more?"

"I'll handle it. Just shut the fuck up. I'm not in any mood for your shit."

"Tough." She threw the pictures at him. They hit him in the face and fluttered to the floor, eight-by-ten glossies. "I hope you've had an AIDS test."

"Don't be stupid. How long do you think that would stay confidential?"

She almost screamed with rage. "You'd risk my life rather than risk having someone find out you'd taken an AIDS test," she said, her voice trembling. "You fret about a stupid handkerchief. How in *hell* can you be careful about a handkerchief but let yourself be photographed having sex with a man? Those are great pictures, by the way. The only thing more ridiculous than your expression while you screw him is the look on your face while he's screwing you! Face red, mouth open—"

He backhanded her, knocking her against the desk. The contact was so satisfying he wanted to hit her again. "Shut up," he said between clenched teeth. "We had snorted some coke, or it never would have happened!"

Slowly Margo straightened, hand to her aching cheek. Her hip throbbed where she had hit the desk. Hatred and disgust congealed in her stomach. "I don't suppose it ever occurred to you not to take illegal drugs. There's a picture of that, too. Won't that look lovely on the evening news?"

"She won't release the pictures. If she does, she won't have any means of getting more money from me." He was confident of that, at least. You never went wrong betting that someone would protect their own interests.

"You don't know what she'll do," Margo said sharply. "Your track record so far isn't anything to brag about. You have to take care of this, and you have to do it now. Offer her two million for the originals."

"And you call me a fool," he sneered. "There's no way to tell if she gave me the originals. And even if there were, she could have any number of copies made."

"Then you'd better think of something." She was breathing hard, her nostrils flared. "And you'd better think fast."

CHAPTER SEVEN

Richard didn't have a downtown office. Instead he had converted the bottom floor of his town house into a small office complex: an office for him, with the state-of-the-art computer with which he worked his market magic; small offices for his two assistants; a tiny kitchen; two bathrooms, one connecting to his office and the other shared by his assistants; and two rooms for storage and files. The arrangement was extremely convenient should he want to work late into the night or even all night.

Every day, he had one objective: to make as much money as possible.

He had spent most of his adult life amassing wealth. He

enjoyed the challenge of anticipating and outguessing the market, but the pleasure was only moderate. He had known poverty and he hadn't liked it, so when he was old enough to do something about it, he left home, joined the army, and set about learning skills that would enable him to make money. He hadn't learned quite fast enough. Pops, his grandfather, had died before Richard could do much to alleviate the grinding poverty of the little farm in western Virginia where he had been born and raised. At least his mother's last years had been better; if she planted a garden, it was because she wanted to, not because she had to in order to eat.

Poverty ground you down, turned you into a social parasite, or it made you tough. Pops had eschewed welfare as charity, and instead worked his small acreage as well as taking any other work he could find. Richard's mother had taken in sewing and ironing. When he himself was old enough he had not only helped with the farming chores but hired himself out for small jobs such as cutting the grass, helping cut and haul hay, the odd carpentry job where function mattered more than appearance.

He had only a vague, maybe wishful image of his father, and a grave in the small country graveyard to visit a few times a year, but from his grandfather he had learned that men didn't lie around all day drinking beer and collecting what the old man called "damn government handouts" once a month, men got out and worked. So Richard worked, and worked hard. Survival of the fittest. You either surrendered, or you fought like hell to better your position.

He'd never been ashamed of his poor country roots, the roots that made him strong, though Candra was embarrassed enough by his origins to insist he say only that he was "from Virginia." If he had let her, she would have invented an antebellum mansion in his background and had one of his ancestors signing the Declaration of Independence.

He had taken steps to ensure he was never poor again. His investments were varied, to weather the hiccups and burps of the market, and he had put money into gems and precious metals as a hedge against a market crash. It was a high, a challenge, a game, to gather tiny details of information and decide which stocks would increase in value and which were in trouble. He seemed to have a sixth sense for it, and he had long ago gained the amount he had set in his mind as "enough," but he kept playing the market, and kept getting richer.

It was eating at Candra's soul that she couldn't get a bigger share of his wealth.

The thought of her brought a bitter taste to his mouth. He supposed he had loved her, in the beginning, though she might have been just a challenge, like the market. From a distance of over ten years he couldn't remember exactly how he had felt about her, though he knew what had attracted him. Candra had been—still was—very attractive, with impeccable social credentials backed by old money, and blessed with an outgoing, friendly personality. If anything, she was *too* friendly, especially with other men.

Their marriage had already been in trouble when he first learned about her affairs, and by that time he simply hadn't cared enough about her infidelities to do anything about them. She thought he knew about only one lover, but he was far from a fool. He had made it his business, over the years, to find out about all her lovers. He knew about Kai. He knew about Carson McMillan. He knew about all the artists she slept with, which social acquaintances found their way into her bed. After he stopped caring, he used her occasionally for sex, and used a condom, even though she was on birth control pills. She had never asked why. He supposed she knew.

Unfortunately, condoms sometimes tore. Two years ago, one had, and combined with some antibiotics she had been taking, that had been enough for her to get pregnant. Not that she had told him, not at the time. Instead she had gotten an abortion.

He wanted children, had always wanted them. When they were first married, Candra had wanted to wait, and he had agreed because his financial position hadn't been as strong as he wanted it to be before he had any children. By the time he felt prosperous enough, Candra had already begun taking lovers and he had lost all desire to have any children with her. But when she told him what she had done, threw the words at him like weapons, everything inside him had hurt at the thought of that small lost life, and from that second on he hated her.

He hadn't spent another night under the same roof with her, but packed her bags and carried her to a hotel, with her crying and cursing, and swearing that she hadn't really done it, that she had only said so because she wanted to hurt him. And he had rousted a locksmith out in the middle of the night and had the locks changed on the town house. Candra had been forced to make appointments to pick up the rest of her belongings, a humiliation that had galled her soul.

He knew she had told all her friends and acquaintances that the decision to divorce was mutual. He didn't care what she said. All he wanted was to get the divorce finalized and never see her again. This was something he should have done years ago, rather than burying himself in the pursuit of wealth. He had known for quite a while, in the back of his mind, that the time would come when he would look at her and realize he couldn't bear living in their sham of a marriage a moment longer. He had stayed with her for his own reasons, using her sexually with little emotion, as if she were a stranger, and because of that his child had died. He should have left her long before that tiny lost life had been conceived.

Lately he had been restless, consumed by the sense it was time to move on. He had made his millions sifting through stock information, but he sure as hell didn't want to spend the rest of his life staring at a computer screen analyzing profit margins and product demand. There was no challenge in it any longer, and he was a man who thrived on challenge. He had enjoyed his army years because of the sheer challenge of the specialized training in the rangers, the sense of testing himself in life-and-death situations. He could have made a career of the military, if he hadn't been driven by the need to make a lot of money, enough so his mother and grandfather would never have to worry about money again.

Mission accomplished. It was time to move on.

Sweeney's face flashed in his mind, and he leaned back in his chair, grinning. Now, there was a challenge.

After Candra's laxity in the morals department, Sweeney's refusal to go out with him because the divorce wasn't final and he was still legally married gave him the feeling of having held something clean and fresh in his arms. His mother and grandfather had possessed that same stringent attitude, seeing behaviors as black and white. The concept of doing whatever you wanted, because you wanted, was foreign to them. That was common enough in their generations, in that part of the country. How had Sweeney come by those standards?

Because he wanted to know everything about her, he'd had a copy of her application for the apartment faxed to him. *Paris Samille Sweeney, age thirty-one, artist.* She hadn't lied about her name, though he bet she cringed at the pretentiousness of being an artist and having Paris as a first name. Anyone else would have played it up for all it was worth, but instead she ignored her given names, to the extent that she was known exclusively by her surname.

Her mother's occupation was also listed as artist, but he didn't recognize her name, and after ten years of marriage to Candra he was very familiar with the art world. He did recognize Sweeney's father's name; the man was moderately successful in Hollywood. A brother was down as next of kin. Richard wondered why she hadn't listed either of her parents.

Bare facts weren't enough. He wanted to know her, what she liked to eat for breakfast, her favorite books and movies, whether she slept sprawled out or curled in a ball. He wanted to strip her naked and spend all night on top of her, inside her. He knew she wanted him, too, though she seemed surprised by her own lust. He grinned again, remembering the look on her face when she jumped away from him as if he were a lit stick of dynamite. This was going to be fun, and frustrating as hell. He'd had a hard-on for two days, and it didn't show any signs of going away soon. All he had to do was think about Sweeney and his dick started throbbing, and he hadn't been able to think about anything else. The abstinence of the past year had been a bitch anyway, and now it was becoming unbearable.

In attitude, she was Candra's polar opposite. Candra was very conscious of her beauty, her appearance, and dressed according to the image she wanted to project. Sweeney had no idea how pretty she was, and from what he could tell, she threw on whatever was closest to hand. Candra was socially adept; Sweeney was constitutionally unable to play social games, assuming she even recognized them. Candra was social, period; Sweeney was a loner. Getting her to admit him into her life was going to take perseverance and careful planning—perseverance more than anything else. Most of all, Candra's attitude toward sex was casual and permissive, while Sweeney was so exclusive she was startled by a kiss.

He wanted her. In bed, out of bed, it didn't matter. If he couldn't coax her into a relationship so he could seduce her, then he would have to seduce her in order to coax her into a relationship. He didn't want her just for sex; he wanted to spend time with her; she was the only woman with whom he had ever wanted to watch the evening news, just to get her take on things. Sweeney might be in the same parade, but she was definitely marching along to a different rhythm.

And Candra was in the way.

He picked up the phone and called his lawyer, Gavin Welles. He was put through immediately. "This has been going on long enough," he said without preamble. "Get it finished."

"Considering the amount of your assets, a year isn't a long time. Be patient," Gavin advised. "Your position is strong, and sooner or later Candra will realize she's throwing away a fortune in legal fees. She'll cut her losses."

"I'm going to make her losses bigger every day she delays. Call her lawyer and tell her I'm reducing the settlement offer by ten thousand every day. After five days, if she hasn't signed the papers, I'm rescinding my offer to sign over the gallery to her."

Gavin was silent a moment. "She'll fight to the bitter end for the gallery, and you know it."

"And *she* knows that in the bitter end she'll lose. I want her out of my life. This isn't a bluff, Gavin. I should have forced her hand months ago, but I wanted to do what I thought was right. That's over. Give her lawyer the message." He hung up and sat back, his expression grim.

In his downtown office, Gavin Welles shrugged and placed a

call to Olivia Yu, Candra's attorney. When she heard Richard's ultimatum, her responding blast nearly ruined Gavin's eardrums. "That bastard! Was he serious?"

"Serious as a heart attack," Gavin said.

"What the hell brought this on? I could have eventually convinced Candra she had the best offer she was likely to get, but she's going to hit the ceiling over this. He must have her replacement waiting in the wings."

Gavin had already thought of that possibility, but he was too discreet to say so. "Not to my knowledge."

"Bullshit. He has a little honey lined up and you know it."

"So what if he does?" Richard could have slept with a different woman every night, in the middle of Times Square, and his position wouldn't have been weakened.

Olivia knew it. Only Candra's reluctance to settle for what she thought was an unfairly minuscule amount had kept her from signing the papers before now. Olivia had tried to make her see she couldn't hope for anything more, but Candra had seemed almost desperate for more money. "All right, I'll call her. You'd better take cover under your desk."

"What?"

Contrary to Olivia's expectations, Candra's reaction was a horrified whisper, not an outraged shriek. Olivia repeated the terms.

"He can't do that! We've already agreed—"

"You haven't signed the papers," Olivia said pointedly. "Legally, he isn't bound by his offer because you refused it. He can do anything he likes."

"But the gallery is *mine.* I'm the one who searched out artists, who built their reputations and made the gallery profitable. He can't take it!"

"His money bought the building. His money backed the gallery, got it started. His name is on all the checks paying all the bills. A smart lawyer—and believe me, Gavin Welles is smart—could make the argument that Richard is the driving force behind the gallery and you were little more than window dressing. You should have incorporated the gallery in your name, but that's hindsight." In Olivia's profession, she saw incredible financial stupidity every day.

"I would have if I'd had any warning," Candra said. Her voice was wretched. "One day we were fine, then we had that argument and the next day he filed for divorce. I didn't have time to do anything to protect myself."

The time to protect yourself, in Olivia's opinion, was while everything was still fine. The point was moot, the water long since passed under the bridge. She wondered what the argument had been about; Candra had never said, but it must have been total war, to have triggered such an abrupt and final break. Whatever the reason, in their meetings Richard had been cold, ruthlessly controlled, and absolutely unyielding. He hadn't compromised on a single issue, and now he was taking an even more hard-ass position.

"I'll talk to him," Candra said. She sounded on the verge of tears.

"Candra . . ." Olivia sighed. "What good can it do? Name one tiny detail he's budged on. Sign the papers, before you lose another ten thousand."

"I'll get him to reinstate that ten thousand. I'll—I'll promise to sign the papers if he does."

Candra hung up and closed her eyes. She felt sick to her stomach, so ill she thought she might actually throw up. A year ago ten thousand had seemed like pocket change to her, but now it was essential. She hadn't heard from Carson, but then she hadn't expected to so soon. Blackmail wasn't a sure thing, and until Carson came through with the money, she couldn't afford to let a penny slip away. After all, what could she do if he refused to pay blackmail? Making the photos public would ruin his career, perhaps even initiate a criminal investigation because of the drug use, but that wouldn't put any money in her pocket. It would, in fact, totally negate that threat. Her only hope was that he feared exposure enough to pay the money.

God, what had set Richard off? When he had come to the gallery two days before, he had been as cold and stubborn as ever, but though he had tried to convince her to sign the papers then, he hadn't issued any threats. She didn't have any choice about signing, of course, not now. Why hadn't he done this then?

He had to have a reason. Richard always had a reason. He was the least emotional, most logical person she had ever met, something that had made her feel very secure when they were married. No matter what, she had always been able to count on Richard to figure out the best way to handle any situation.

This ultimatum wasn't a bluff; he would do exactly what he said. He wanted the papers signed and the divorce expedited. The question was: Why now? Why not two days ago, or two months ago? He could have done this at any time and the outcome would have been the same.

He had an urgent reason now, one that he hadn't had two days before. It had to be a woman. Just because she hadn't found out about any women he'd had since they separated didn't mean he'd been living like a monk. She knew Richard's sexual appetite, and she also knew women automatically gravitated to him, as if he gave off subliminal signals that said he liked it slow, and often. He also held some ridiculously old-fashioned opinions; if he had accidentally gotten some woman pregnant, he would insist on marrying her. That was another thing she knew about Richard, she thought bitterly: He didn't take a pregnancy lightly.

On the other hand, neither did he tend to repeat his mistakes. Accidents happened, but he would be doubly careful now.

No, more than likely he was interested in another woman. Candra thought of someone taking her place, sleeping in her bed, waking up with Richard, eating breakfast with him, and she wanted to scream. She would have done anything to be able to turn back the clock, undo this past year, but she couldn't and she had to stop wasting time with useless regrets. She had to think.

Sweeney. Of course!

A flash of intuition told her she was right. She hadn't been wrong about that flare of attraction, or the way Richard had stared at Sweeney. Maybe Sweeney was oblivious to Richard—if any woman could be, Sweeney was that woman—but that didn't mean he was oblivious to her. On the contrary, he would enjoy the challenge of enticing her into a relationship.

Candra could work this to her advantage. She knew she could.

"You're plotting something," Kai said, coming into her office without knocking. She frowned; he was becoming entirely too cocky. She would have to trim his wings soon.

On the other hand, at least she could talk to him. "I think I was right about Richard and Sweeney. All of a sudden he's in a hurry to finalize the divorce."

"He's agreed to your terms?" Kai's eyes glittered. The thought of money did that to him.

"No, he's still playing hardball, but now I think I can at least get in the game."

"You're playing with fire," he warned. "Richard won't tolerate threats."

"Then he shouldn't make them," she snapped.

"Oh? What threats has he made?"

"Never mind." Kai didn't know Richard owned the gallery. If he did, he might well quit on the spot and leave her in the lurch. She had no illusions about his loyalty. He was, however, a valuable asset; many of her female clientele were blunt about his attractions and abilities.

"What are you going to do?"

"Talk to him." Rising, Candra picked up her expensive leather tote that doubled as briefcase and purse. Luckily she hadn't gone home to change; she was still wearing the conservative suit she had worn to D.C. that morning. She would take any edge she could get, no matter how tiny.

"Why not just call?" Kai suggested.

"I'd rather talk to him in person." If she called, Kai wasn't above listening in, and he would find out about the gallery.

"What makes you think he'll see you?"

A couple of times Richard had refused to let her in, to Kai's malicious amusement and Candra's fury. "Oh, I think he's expecting me this time."

Richard's gaze flickered immediately over the suit. "Trying out for a part on Broadway?" he asked, letting her know he saw through the little subterfuge. She controlled her irritation. She should have remembered how detail-oriented he was, noticing everything.

"I had a business appointment this morning," she said, which wasn't a lie.

Rather than take her upstairs to the living area, he led her to his bottom-floor office, telling her without words she no longer belonged here, if the notion needed to be reinforced. To him, she was nothing more than unfinished business—unpleasant business, at that.

She was always surprised at how small and spartan his office was, though of course he had been limited in space by the size of the town house. He could have done more with the furnishings or let her do more. Everything in the office was utilitarian, even his big, custom-made leather chair.

"I see your lawyer told you about my new terms," he said coolly, taking a seat and leaning back, hooking his hands behind his head. His dark eyes were unreadable.

She took a seat across the desk from him and cut right to the chase. "Sweeney's been having problems with her painting for quite a while now," she said. "She finally brought some of her new work in yesterday, but she's very uncertain about it. I told her it was wonderful, of course, but the truth is, I may have a difficult time selling any of it."

His expression didn't so much as flicker. "And you're telling me this because . . . ?"

Damn him, could she have been wrong? No, she couldn't have been, and she hated him for making her feel uncertain.

"I know you, darling. I saw how you were looking at her." As if he wanted to fuck her right then, right in front of everyone, Candra thought with sudden viciousness. Jealousy seared her, and she pushed it away.

"With my eyes?" he suggested mildly.

"Don't be witty, please. I can destroy her career. I wouldn't enjoy doing it—I really like Sweeney—but if it's necessary . . ." She shrugged.

"And I can replace you at the gallery tomorrow, if necessary." Eyes narrowed, he leaned forward. His expression wasn't impassive now; it was so grim she found herself drawing back from him. "If you do the slightest thing to harm Sweeney's career, hell will freeze over before you get a dime from me."

"So I was right," she managed to say, but inwardly she was alarmed. Somehow, she hadn't expected him to counter her threats with more of his own.

"Are you?"

"Why else would you care?"

"I can think of several reasons why I wouldn't give in to blackmail," he said.

She wished he hadn't used that word. She paled slightly. "I wouldn't call it *that.*"

"What would you call it? If I pay up, you'll refrain from ruining a career. That sounds remarkably like extortion to me." He got up and seized her by the arm, forcing her up from the chair. "Get out."

"Richard, wait!"

"I said get out." He propelled her toward the door, past the astonished faces of his two assistants. Embarrassment turned her face dark red.

She jerked her arm free and whirled to face him. "I'll make you regret treating me like this," she said in a voice clogged with angry tears.

"Sign the papers," he said, opening the door and ushering her out. "Or *you'll* regret it."

CHAPTER EIGHT

Sweeney moved restlessly around her studio, studying canvases without really seeing them. What did it matter anyway? She seemed to have lost the ability to judge her own work, but Candra was enthusiastic, so all she could do at this point was take the completed pieces to the gallery and go from there.

She had looked up the address for David and Jacob Stokes, attorneys-at-law, and mailed the sketch of their father to them, along with a note of condolence. Then she had spent the rest of the day working, just working, automatically applying paint to canvas and not even thinking about what she was doing.

A lot of disturbing things had happened to her in the past

year, and for the most part, she thought she had handled them with remarkable composure. Though she hadn't been able to find any logical explanation, such as having a near-death experience or being struck by lightning, for why she had suddenly become able to see ghosts, at least she had found references to countless other people who claimed the same ability. She had to believe them, because why would anyone claim to see spirits if they didn't? It wasn't exactly something you wanted on an application for employment.

But in all the books on paranormal subjects she had read, she hadn't found anything to explain that death scene she had painted. She didn't remember painting it, so she had to assume she had been sleepwalking and had done the painting in her sleep. When she had gone out to mail the sketch she had stopped by the library and checked out some books on sleepwalking, but she hadn't had a chance to read them yet. She had flipped through one, though, and found the explanation that people who walked in their sleep were often under stress.

Well, duh. Like seeing ghosts was supposed to be relaxing. But she had been seeing ghosts for a year, and the night the old vendor died was the first time she had ever sleepwalked. The books didn't even have chapters on sleep-*painting*.

But that wasn't even what bothered her most. Guessing the questions to the *Jeopardy!* answers before she knew anything more than the categories was a little annoying, but not alarming. Anyone who had watched the show for years, as she had, was familiar with the categories and possible answers, and could guess right occasionally. Her success rate was a lot higher than that, like one hundred percent, but at least she could rationalize that.

She couldn't rationalize painting in her sleep, especially not the death scene of a man she hadn't known had died. That wasn't just chance, that was . . . weird. Strange. Spooky.

Who was she kidding? She knew the word that applied, having come across it a lot in her research on ghosts.

Clairvoyant.

She kept fighting down a sense of panic. This frightened her more than anything else that had ever happened to her. She had thought her situation was static, but instead it seemed to be intensifying, with new situations being thrown at her just as she thought she had a handle on the old ones. She had even adjusted to seeing ghosts, though that was neither amusing nor enjoyable, like her effect on traffic signals and the growth of plants. The constant cold wasn't enjoyable either, but she had decided that came with the ghosts.

Jeopardy! she realized, had probably just signaled the beginning of clairvoyance. She was terrified that the ugly death-scene painting was just the next step in a progression that would have her foreseeing massacres, plane crashes, famines, and plagues. What did it matter that her plants were beautiful, when mentally she would live with constant death and suffering? The part of painting she loved most was the creation of beauty, and this development threatened to take that away from her.

She had always enjoyed her solitude, but now for the first time she wished she didn't live alone. Even a cat or a dog would be better than this sense of being completely on her own, with no one to turn to for help.

She could always call Richard.

The temptation was almost overpowering. He would hold her as he had before, and she could sleep, warm and safe, in his arms. She had never before felt that way with anyone, certainly not her parents. She had grown up knowing she had to handle things herself, that there was no soft, comforting lap in which she could rest. Not that Richard's lap had been soft; she had a very clear memory of exactly how hard he had been. Nor had his lap been particularly comforting. But she had felt secure, and . . . and cherished. Or at least desired.

She couldn't call him. She had been right to send him away, and her reasons for doing so still existed. She knew her views on morality were much more stringent than was generally held to be normal, but after seeing the harm done by her parents' indiscriminate infidelities, the wonder was she hadn't entered a convent. She was more than a little startled by Richard's desire for her, but she was absolutely astounded by her own desire for him. That had never happened before, and she wasn't certain of her ability to resist it. The urge to lie down with him was so potent she could feel her insides tighten now, just thinking about him. With Richard around, she thought, she would never be cold again. Every time she felt a chill, she could crawl into his lap and let him warm her, maybe from the inside out.

Whoa! She had to stop that line of thinking right now, or she'd be on the phone before she knew it. But she had a very clear vision of herself astride him, his mouth spreading kisses over her breasts and his big hands gripping her hips as he moved her up and down—

Oh, damn. Stop it, she admonished herself. There were serious problems in her life, and she was letting herself get distracted into thinking about Richard. Mother Nature had rigged the game in her favor, making sexual attraction so damn fascinating that once you felt it, you couldn't tune it out. On the other hand, thinking about Richard, picturing him naked, was a lot more pleasant than thinking about death and clairvoyance.

She admitted to herself that she had half-expected him to call or stop by that day. If she read him correctly, and she thought she did, his middle name was persistence. Even though he had agreed to lay off, he had also promised that this thing between them, whatever it was, wasn't over. *I'll be back,* he'd said, and she knew he meant it. The question was, how long would he lay off and when would he be back? To her shame, she had hoped to see him today.

But no one had rung her doorbell all day long, and bedtime was fast approaching. She hadn't slept well the night before—she'd been edgy after the morning's encounter with Richard and the afternoon's encounter with the vendor's ghost—but even though she was tired, she didn't want to go to bed. She was afraid to sleep, she realized, afraid she would sleepwalk or go into a trance, or whatever had happened, and paint another death scene. She had always loved sleeping, and now that pleasure was being stolen from her. That thought made her mad as hell, and it scared her. Most of all, it scared her.

Fear was something she had seldom known in her life, at least as an adult. Once as a child she had spent two days alone, because her father had taken her brother with him on some shoot and her mother had gone to a party and forgotten to come home, and she had been very scared then. She had been only nine years old and afraid they had all left her behind and were never coming home. And once, when she was fourteen, one of her mother's many lovers—his name was Raz, she would never forget that name—had agreed with her mother that Sweeney was old enough to learn about sex.

Fortunately they had both been so drunk that Sweeney was able to pull away and run, her heart pounding so hard in her chest that she had been afraid she would pass out and then they would have her. She had run down to the basement of the apartment building and hidden in the laundry, knowing her mother would never think of looking there, having never set foot in the place. She huddled between a washing machine and the wall for what seemed like hours, afraid to go back go the apartment in case Raz was waiting for her. Finally, growing more disgusted than afraid, she had loosed the handle from a mop and, armed with the handle, returned to the apartment. She didn't like hiding in the laundry; she was going back to her room and the comfort of her books and paints, and if anyone bothered her, she would hit them on the head as hard as she could.

Over the years she had developed the habit of confronting problems rather than hiding from them, but in the current case neither seemed to do any good. How could you confront something so nebulous? Clairvoyance wasn't something you could see, or touch. It was just *there*, like blue eyes; you either had them or you didn't. Same with clairvoyance.

Having blue eyes didn't frighten her, but clairvoyance did. In itself it was scary enough, but now, looking back, she saw everything that had happened in the past year as a progression, from plants to red lights to ghosts to clairvoyance. Looking at it that way, she didn't dare try to guess what would be next. Levitation? Or maybe she would start setting things on fire just by looking at them.

She tried to be amused, but for once her sense of humor wasn't working.

But wandering around the studio afraid to go to bed did remind her of hiding in the laundry when she was fourteen, and she growled aloud at herself. Nothing had happened the night before, and just because the more she thought about the trance painting the more worried she became didn't mean it would happen every night. It might not happen again for a long time, until someone else she knew died—

That was it. A lot of people died every day in New York, but none of their deaths had caused sleepwalking forays. She had known the hot dog vendor, however, so his death had disturbed her on a subconscious level.

For the first time, she wondered how he had died. After she had seen him yesterday, she had been too shocked to think about it, and he had looked as healthy as any ghost she had ever seen. But in the scene she had painted, blood had been coming from his nostrils, and he had clearly suffered a head injury. Had he been hit by a car or maybe fallen down some steps? Just how accurate was that painting?

Sweeney shivered. She didn't want to know the answer to that last question.

She shivered again and realized how cold she was. She was also very tired, very sleepy, and she was not going to stay awake a minute longer worrying about things she couldn't control. She put on her pajamas and crawled into the warm bed, curling into a ball and waiting for the heat from the electric blanket to seep into her flesh.

Just before she slept, she had the drowsy thought that if Richard were in bed with her, she wouldn't need an electric blanket to keep her warm.

Just after midnight she gasped, pulling in a hard, fast breath. She pushed restlessly at the covers, fighting the blankets. She muttered, the sounds indistinct, and rolled her head as if trying to escape something.

In the silence of the night her sudden cessation of breathing was as noticeable as her gasping had been. For a long moment she lay utterly still, then breath returned on a long, slow, gentle inhalation.

She opened her eyes and sat up. Pushing the heavy cover aside, she got out of bed and walked soundlessly through the apartment. When she reached her studio, she put a blank canvas on an easel, stood for a moment with her head cocked to the side as if pondering her next step, then selected a tube of paint and began.

It was the cold that woke her. She huddled under the covers, wondering if her electric blanket was malfunctioning. Even so, the nest she had made for herself should have contained the heat. She fought her way out of the tangle of blankets and rolled over until she could see the blanket control. To her surprise, the little amber light was on, so the blanket should have been warm. She found a coil and pressed her fingers to it. She could feel the heat, but it didn't seem to be transferring to her.

Next she looked at the clock and lifted her eyebrows in surprise. It was almost nine, and she seldom slept past dawn. She didn't have any appointments, though, so it was the cold, not urgency, that drove her from the bed. She paused to turn the thermostat up as high as it would go, then went into the bathroom and turned on the shower, setting the water as hot as she could bear it. By the time she stripped off her pajamas and stepped under the spray, she was shuddering with cold.

She stood with the hot water beating down on her head and back, warming her spine. The shudders stopped, the fading tension unlocking her taut muscles as it drained away. Maybe there *was* something physically wrong with her, she thought, almost sagging as her body relaxed. The chills had started about the same time the other stuff had started happening, but that didn't mean they were related. She wouldn't have to tell a doctor everything, just that she was cold all the time. The realization that she was actually considering seeing a doctor startled her.

As she toweled off, her skin roughened as another chill seized her. Swearing under her breath, she hurriedly got dressed. Getting her head wet hadn't been the brightest idea, she thought, because she didn't own a hair dryer. One disastrous attempt at blow-drying her hair, which resulted in something resembling a hairy explosion, had persuaded her to let her curls dry naturally rather than outrage them with heat. Wrapping a towel around her head, she went into the kitchen for that first cup of coffee.

The light on the coffeemaker wasn't on, but the pot was full. Frowning, she touched the pot and found it cold. "Damn it," she muttered. The coffee had brewed right on time, but she hadn't been up to drink it and the heat pad turned itself off after two hours, one more example of a manufacturer trying to protect itself from lawsuits by careless or forgetful customers who left their coffeemakers turned on and perhaps caused fires.

She poured a cup of coffee and popped it into the microwave, then dumped the rest of the pot down the sink and put some fresh coffee on to brew. By the time she finished that, the buzzer on the microwave had sounded. The warmed-up coffee tasted terrible, sort of like old socks, but it was hot, and at the moment that was more important.

The apartment wasn't getting any warmer. She'd have to call Richard about getting the heating system repaired, she thought desperately. She leaned down and held her hand over the vent, and felt the warm air pouring out. Okay, so the heating system was working. She went to the thermostat to check the temperature; it was already eighty-two degrees, and the thermostat registered only up to eighty-five.

She would just have to tough it out until her hair dried, she thought. That was what was making her so cold this morning. She was loath to unwrap the towel covering her head, but common sense told her that the heat in the apartment would dry her hair much faster if it wasn't wrapped in a towel. Gritting her teeth and bracing for the chill, she ditched the towel. The air on her wet head didn't feel cold, though. Maybe this wouldn't be so bad.

Taking the cup of coffee with her into the bathroom, she sprayed some detangler on her curls and then finger-combed them, noting that most of the moisture had already evaporated. The mirror reflected a face that was white and pinched with cold. Her teeth chattered. "What a lovely sight," she told her reflection.

She poured more coffee and went into the studio. Her hands were shaking so much she wouldn't be able to paint, but the habit was ingrained, so she went.

There was a new canvas on the easel.

Sweeney stood just inside the door, dread congealing in her stomach like cold grease. Her body felt leaden. Not again. Not another one. Who had she killed this time?

No, she thought fiercely. She hadn't killed anyone. Her painting hadn't caused the old vendor to die, rather his death had caused the painting. But if this only happened when someone she knew had died . . . She didn't want to see who was in the painting this time; she didn't want to lose someone else she liked. What if—what if it was Richard?

She was unprepared for the violence of the pain that seized her chest, freezing her lungs, constricting her heart. *Not Richard,* she prayed. Dear God, not Richard.

Somehow she made her feet move, though she wasn't aware of crossing the floor. Somehow she steeled herself to walk around the easel, positioned so the bright morning light fell directly on the canvas. And somehow she made herself look.

The canvas was almost totally blank. She stared at it, the relief so sudden and total she almost couldn't take it in. Not a death scene, then. Not Richard. Maybe . . . maybe this meant her supposition had been totally wrong, that the sleepwalking and painting didn't necessarily have anything to do with death. That one time had been a coincidence, just one more part of the weird stuff that had been happening to her.

She had painted shoes. Two shoes, one a man's and the other a woman's. The man's shoe was the most complete, and it looked as if she had started on the foot inside it. She hadn't finished the woman's shoe, a high-heeled pump from the look of it, stopping before she got to the heel. There was no background, no sense of location, nothing but shoes. Just shoes.

She laughed softly, giddy with relief and happiness. She had let all this funny business get to her, make her imagination go wild. She had almost made herself sick, thinking that Richard was dead when she had no reason to jump to such a hysterical conclusion.

Humming, clutching her coffee cup with both hands in an effort to warm her fingers, she went back into the kitchen to rustle up some breakfast and drink more coffee. Surely she would be warm soon, and then she would get some work done.

But the chill intensified, shaking her so violently she barely managed to eat a slice of toast and it became dangerous to try to drink the hot coffee. She *hurt,* her muscles were so tight. She grabbed a blanket and sat down on one of the vents, making a tent with the blanket to trap the warm air around her.

Why was this happening again? Why now, why not yesterday morning? The only other time the chill had been this intense was the morning after she had done the death painting of the old vendor. No, this was worse. This was the coldest she had ever been in her life.

It had to be linked to the sleepwalking episodes. Once could be coincidence, but not twice. She couldn't imagine what she could be doing to trigger such an extreme reaction, but at the moment all she cared about was getting warm. Afterward she would worry about the why and hows.

A vicious cramp knotted her left thigh. Sweeney moaned, folding double with the agony as she massaged the muscle. She got the muscle unknotted, but moments later another cramp hit. She panted as she rubbed it out, then gingerly stretched out her legs. The constant shivering was causing her muscles to knot. She ached in every joint now, every muscle.

Miserably she began to cry. She felt like a weak crybaby for doing so, but she hurt so much she couldn't help it. She hadn't known being cold was so painful. Why didn't the tears freeze on her cheeks? She felt as if they should, even though she knew the room was warm.

Richard had gotten her warm before. She couldn't bear the pain much longer; with everything in her, she wanted him here with her now.

Keeping the blanket around her, she crawled to the phone and lifted the cordless unit from its stand. She was surprised at how much energy it took to move, how sluggish she was, and she felt the first twinge of fear that her condition was truly serious, rather than being just a major inconvenience.

She didn't know the number. She had never called Candra at home, and she vaguely remembered being told the private line was unlisted. Richard's business line was listed, though, and unless he had an appointment somewhere, he should be in his office now. She wrestled the heavy white pages into her lap and clumsily flipped through to the Ws. "Richard Worth, Richard Worth," she mumbled to herself. In a city the size of New York there were a lot of duplicated names, but she could pinpoint her Richard Worth with his address. Ah, there it was. She punched in the numbers, then huddled deeper into the blanket.

A female voice answered and recited the number. "May I help you?" she pleasantly inquired.

"May I speak to Richard, please?" Maybe she should have called him Mr. Worth instead of Richard.

"Your name?"

"Sweeney."

"S-w-e—?"

"S-w-e-e-n-e-y." Her name wasn't difficult, she thought irritably. Why would anyone have any trouble spelling it? Of course, her teeth were chattering so hard she might be difficult to understand, so she gave the woman the benefit of the doubt.

"Sweeney." Richard's voice sounded in her ear only a few seconds later. "What's wrong?"

"How did you know?" she asked weakly.

"That something was wrong? Why else would you be calling me?"

She tried to laugh but couldn't. "I'm cold," she said, and was appalled to hear a whimper in her voice. "Oh, God, Richard, I'm so cold I think I might die."

"I'll be right there." His tone was quiet and calm. "You'll be okay."

Because he had said it, she clung to the idea while she waited for him. She would be okay. He would arrive soon and get her warm with that miraculous body heat of his. "I'll be okay," she whispered, though her legs began cramping again and she couldn't even crawl back to the vent. Tears wet her face again, and she dried them with the blanket. She didn't want to be crying like a sissy when he got here.

She would have to unlock the door. She tried to get up and fell back with a cry when her thigh seized in a cramp. She knew she should wait until he arrived, that it was dangerous to leave an entry door unlocked, but damn it, what if by then she wasn't able to move at all? She massaged the knotted muscle, digging her fingers deep in a savage effort to buy herself a few relatively comfortable minutes. One minute would be enough, just long enough for her to get to the door and unlock it.

If she couldn't walk, she could crawl. If she couldn't crawl, she would drag herself on her elbows. She *would* get to the door.

She drew her right leg beneath her, pushing herself up, and breathed a sigh of relief when it didn't cramp. Her entire body was trembling violently, both from the cold and in reaction to the incessant shivering. She was unbelievably weak. How could shivering be so debilitating? Wasn't it the body's means of producing heat?

She couldn't stand. Even though her legs weren't cramping at the moment, she simply didn't have the energy to get to her feet. She crawled a few feet, then collapsed on her side, breathing hard from the exertion. After a few moments she rolled, blanket and all, like a large human sausage. If babies could use rolling as a means of locomotion, so could she.

She laughed aloud at the picture she must have made, and then cried because she ached so badly in every muscle. When she reached the door, she stretched to reach the doorknob, then hauled herself up on her knees. In that position she could reach, just barely, the two dead-bolt locks on the door. She fumbled them open, then curled into a ball beside the door to wait for Richard.

CHAPTER NINE

The ringing of the doorbell, when it came, startled her. She had no idea how much time had lapsed. "R-Richard?"

The bell rang again, and she realized her voice had been too weak to penetrate the wood. She took a deep breath, holding it to buy herself a few seconds free from shivering. "Richard," she called, not letting herself think what she would do if someone else was at the door.

"I'm here. Open the door."

"It's u-unlocked."

He opened the door, looked down, and saw her curled on the floor and said, "Shit," in a very quiet, very controlled tone.

He closed and locked the door, then bent down and effortlessly lifted her in his arms.

"How long has this been going on?" he asked as he swiftly carried her to the couch.

"S-since I woke up. A-about n-nine."

"It feels like the Sahara in here," he said grimly. He placed her on the couch and unwrapped the blanket, then with sure, brisk movements unfastened her jeans and stripped them down her legs.

"H-hey!" Sounding indignant and outraged was difficult when your teeth were chattering, she discovered.

"Don't argue," he said, and pulled her sweatshirt off over her head. She wasn't wearing a bra, because she never did when she was at home. Her nipples had pinched into tight little points. She started to cover her breasts with her hands, then abandoned that idea in favor of wrapping her arms around herself to conserve heat. Her eyelids drooped heavily.

"Don't let yourself go to sleep," he ordered.

"I w-won't," she promised, and hoped she wasn't lying.

He left her socks on and went to work on his own clothes. He wasn't wearing a suit today, she noticed, just slacks and a silk shirt. He unbuttoned the shirt, his fingers moving swiftly, and dropped it to the floor. He kicked off his shoes and unbuckled his belt at the same time, stripping himself as efficiently as he had her. His pants hit the floor, he jerked off his socks, and then he was with her, wrapping her in his arms and all but crushing her against the back of the couch. "Easy," he murmured, feeling her convulsive shaking, and pulled the blanket over them.

He pushed his feet under hers and placed one big hand on the back of her head, tucking her face into the hollow between his neck and shoulder, forcing her to breathe air heated by his body.

The shock of his heat was so intense she thought she might faint. At first all she was aware of was warmth, surrounding her, seeping through her skin and penetrating down to her marrow. He held her tightly against him, helping her contain the shivering, adding his strength to hers. "Don't cry," he whispered, making her aware that she still was, and wiped her face with the blanket.

After what seemed like hours but could have been as little as five minutes, the shivering eased for a moment, allowing her to relax. She lay bonelessly in his arms, breathing heavily, then the monster seized her in its jaws again and shook her until her teeth rattled.

The next respite lasted a little longer, long enough that she began to hope it was over. Richard's body heat continued to pour over her, through her, reaching that central core of ice that no amount of coffee, hot water, or heated air had been able to touch. He was sweating; she could feel the moisture on his skin. She tried to stretch, ease her tired and cramped muscles, but the movement triggered more shivering.

He held her through that, too, whispering reassurances in her ear. She didn't need to be reassured, she thought fuzzily. Richard was here, so of course he would get her warm. Funny how she was so positive of that.

She stilled again, lying quietly in his arms. The minutes ticked by, the room silent except for the sound of their breathing and the strong, steady thumping of his heart under her ear.

She was all but naked, wearing only panties and socks. He had on even less, nothing but a pair of tight boxers. The crisp hair on his chest rasped her nipples, keeping them puckered even though she was no longer cold. He was very hard, she thought drowsily, brushing her lips against his shoulder without quite realizing what she was doing. Muscular, too. Her fingers moved over his shoulder, feeling the power beneath his sleek, warm skin as she stroked down to the hard bulge of his triceps. Even his belly was hard, and his legs were heavy with muscle.

His erection prodded her stomach. A different kind of heat gathered in her, pooled between her legs. Instinctively she shifted, pushing her hips against him in an acceptance she knew was dangerous, but the knowledge came a split second after the action. Even then she didn't withdraw. The contact felt too good, too right.

He kissed her forehead, the caress slow and tender. "Warm now?" he asked, and she nodded.

"Good." His breath sighed over her closed eyelids. "Sleepy?"

"*Um hmm.*"

"Go to sleep then, Sweeney." At least she thought he said Sweeney. Something about her name sounded different, but she couldn't quite place what it was. She inhaled with slow, deep precision, drawing his heated scent into her lungs and feeling something deep inside loosen and give way.

His hand covered her breast, his callus-roughened thumb rubbing over her nipple. She had never thought breasts were the great source of pleasure portrayed in books and movies, having never felt more than irritation when some boy grabbed hers and pulled the nipples and expected her to become incoherent with pleasure when what she really felt like doing was punching him in the face. She didn't feel like punching Richard. His circling thumb produced a prickling sort of heat in her nipple, then there was an almost unbearable tightening, and a hot wire of sensation ran from her breast straight to her loins, exploding there and spreading a different kind of heat throughout her body. She moaned, a quiet little whimper of delight.

He repeated the motion over and over, the pleasure building

with every second until it seemed to take over her body. She was glowing with heat now, inside and out. She surged against him, back and forth like the gentle, inexorable wash of the tide. A faint remnant of caution was swamped by the flood of pure physical delight.

He tugged on her hair, pulling her head back. His mouth closed over hers, leisurely intensifying the pressure until her lips parted. He slanted his head then and kissed her, deep and hard, taking her with rhythmic thrusts of his tongue. Sweeney didn't open her eyes, couldn't open them, lost in a combination of fatigue and desire that both demanded and beguiled. Her fingers dug into the deep ridge of his back, slippery with sweat.

He moved a little, adjusting his position so that the hard ridge of his penis nestled against her mound. She felt the soft folds between her legs open, just a little, and he rested between them. She started, a sliver of alarm working through the haze of desire, and that small movement rubbed her against his shaft in a way that sent pleasure rioting along her nerve endings. If the two layers of their underwear hadn't been between them, he would have been inside her then, because she couldn't stop the convulsive thrust of her hips. He groaned, deep in his throat, the sound vibrating in her own mouth.

She felt as if her body were a bow, the hot wire of sensation pulling her tighter and tighter, arching her against him. She made a small, desperate mewling sound, all but clawing at him in her urgency, her thighs opening as she tried to ride the ridge of his erection. She was in pain again, a different kind of pain, hot and empty, almost mindless with need. Richard gripped her bottom and rubbed her against him, and everything inside her tightened, holding her on the verge of shattering for one long, unbearable moment before the tension released and she convulsed on great waves of pleasure. She heard her own cries, thin and wild, muffled by his kiss, and then for a while she didn't know anything.

Her dazed senses gradually regained their function. She was sweating, she realized with astonishment; her body sheened with moisture. As her heartbeat slowed, she realized that his hadn't, but his touch was gentle as he settled her so that her head was pillowed on his arm. "Go to sleep," he whispered.

She didn't have any other choice. Her muscles were like water, unable to function. "I had a climax," she managed to say, and heard her own surprise.

"I know," he said on a low chuckle, his amusement strained but genuine. She nestled her face against him, breathed deeply, and like a child, was asleep.

Richard pushed the sweltering blanket down a little. He didn't want to trigger another of those alarming chills, but neither did he want either one of them to have a heatstroke. The apartment was so hot he could barely breathe. Sweat poured off him, and he hadn't helped the situation by what he had just done. Foreplay with Sweeney was more erotic than any full sex act he had ever experienced; her response was swift and intense, and utterly beguiling. He had never before enjoyed so much something that left him so frustrated; he thought one touch of her hand would take him over the edge.

He could have had her. She wouldn't have accused him afterward of taking advantage of her, because she had the kind of bedrock honesty that made her take responsibility for her own actions. But he would have been taking advantage, and he knew it. She had been alarmingly weak, all her energy sapped by that constant, convulsive shivering. Her defenses had been down, and he could have done anything with her he wanted.

What he had wanted most, it turned out, was to take care of her.

He didn't know how he had managed to control himself. He

closed his eyes as he remembered the sight of her high, round breasts with the delicate blue tracery of veins and her small, tightly puckered nipples. Those soft mounds were flattened against his chest now, her nipples plumped but still firm enough that he could feel both of them.

Her cheek was flushed now with warm color, her skin smooth and supple instead of roughened with chills. Something was very, very wrong, but he couldn't begin to imagine what it was. There was no medical condition he knew of that would let body heat warm her but prevent any other means of heat from doing the same thing. Her condition this time had seemed far more extreme than it had during the other episode; she'd had all the symptoms of hypothermia, including the slurred speech. That was why he had stripped their clothes off, knowing she would get warm faster without the buffer of clothing between them. He had also known the other likely outcome and fought to keep himself under control while he deliberately aroused her.

When she woke, and got some clothes on, he intended to hustle her pretty little ass into the car and get her to a doctor. He knew a couple of very good diagnosticians who would see her without an appointment, as a favor to him. Though he had been acquainted with her for several years, he was only now beginning to *know* her, to plumb the treasure chest of her personality, and he refused to let anything endanger his intoxicating discovery.

She was damp with sweat, her own as well as his. The crisis, whatever it was, was over for now, and he was about to pass out from the heat. He eased away from her and got up, tucking the blanket around her as a safeguard, then went in search of the thermostat. When he found it, he winced at the setting and nudged it down to seventy-five.

The heat had made him thirsty. He opened cabinet doors until he found the drinking glasses, then stood in front of the sink and guzzled two full glasses of water. He wanted a cool shower, but didn't want to leave her alone in case her nap was a short one. She deserved to be held when she woke up after her first orgasm.

He didn't know what made him so certain that had been her first. Her surprise, maybe. He had always thought her totally oblivious to men, so focused on her work that there wasn't room in her life for anything else, and now he knew his supposition had been right. Her experiences were probably few and a long time ago, very likely with boys her age, and had produced damn little pleasure for her. She had probably said to hell with the whole process; she had better things to do. He didn't know why she had suddenly responded to *him*, but he wasn't about to question his good luck.

He went back into the living room, where he could keep an eye on her. The sweat was evaporating on his body, but he still felt too hot to put on his clothes.

When he had been here before, he hadn't paid much attention to his surroundings; he had been almost totally focused on her. Now he looked around, relieved beyond measure that everything wasn't stark white, or black lacquer. Her furniture was traditional, and functional. Her artistry was revealed in her use of color, a deep blue bowl placed where the sunshine would fall on it and make it glow, a light green vase filled with red flowers, a purple afghan thrown across a chair. He noticed the abundance of plants and thought she must have a very green thumb, because all of them had glossy, abundant leaves and several of them were blooming in a riot of color, yellows and pinks and reds.

She had a lot of books, too, most of them on shelves but some stacked on the coffee table. He picked one up, his eyebrows lifting as he read the title, *The Ghost Detectives*. He picked up another book, *Paranormal Phenomena*. Funny, he wouldn't have thought she was the type to be hooked on this paranormal stuff, but he enjoyed *The X-Files* himself and he wasn't normally a science fiction fan, so he couldn't knock her interests.

A third book was *Spirit Sightings.* Another was *Ghosts Among Us.* She was evidently fascinated by ghosts.

He was a little interested himself. When his grandfather died, Richard had gone home for the funeral and stayed for a week with his mother in the tiny run-down house where he had grown up. The entire time he was there, he kept sensing his grandfather's presence, catching a glimpse of movement out of the corner of his eye and then, when he turned, finding no one there. He was a logical man, but logic didn't mean rejecting everything he couldn't touch or see or taste. He couldn't see electricity, but he could see its effects, and maybe in death the body left behind a lingering energy field. He thought it must be at least possible, though he admitted it was equally possible his brain had been playing tricks on him, because he was so accustomed to his grandfather being in that house that he *expected* to see him.

Richard put the books down and checked on Sweeney. She was still sleeping soundly, one hand tucked under her cheek, her lips rosy and her fingertips pink.

Her entire body had been icy when he first arrived. He frowned. He had thought, the first time, that she seemed almost to be in shock, and the impression was stronger now. Had anything happened both times to trigger such an extreme reaction? Or was her blood pressure dropping suddenly because of some physical condition? One way or another, when she woke, he was going to get to the bottom of this.

She slept for over an hour. When she began stirring, he slipped back under the blanket with her, crowding her against the back of the couch. Her legs felt like silk; her breasts flattened gently against him, making his head spin. Gently he rubbed the back of one finger against the underside of a plumped-out breast, reveling in the satiny smoothness. He wanted to taste her, suck her, but his frustration level was so high he knew if he did, there wouldn't be any stopping.

She stirred again, wrinkling her nose and making a disgusted sound, as if she hated waking up. Richard watched her closely, anticipating that moment when her eyes opened and awareness hit her. He couldn't wait to hear what her first words would be.

She stretched, the movement rubbing her body all along his and making him grit his teeth. Her eyelashes fluttered, and sleepy blue eyes looked at him. "Hi," she murmured, an incredibly sweet, drowsy smile curving her lips. She blinked a couple more times, focused, and he saw her eyes widen. She froze in his arms. "Oh my God," she said.

He laughed quietly and kissed her temple. "Don't panic." He didn't think his balls could survive another attack from her knee, even an inadvertent one.

Her face was crimson. "We—I—" she stammered, unable to look at him. She put her hand on his chest and then snatched it away, as if startled by the feel of bare skin.

"It's okay, sweetie. Nothing happened."

"The hell it didn't," she blurted, then blushed even more.

"I made you come." He kept his voice calm. "I did it deliberately, to get you warm."

"I would call that something," she snapped.

"Then call it heavy petting, to use a high-school term. I sure as hell wouldn't call it anything more, or I wouldn't be as damn frustrated as I am." Gently he brushed a curl back from her flushed face. "We need to talk."

She paused, looking truculent, but finally sighed. "Okay.

Let me get up and get dressed, and put on a fresh pot of coffee—"

"I like you right where you are." Once she put some distance between them, she would throw up her defenses again, and he wanted some answers. Until he had them, he intended to keep her mostly naked and half under him. Touch was a powerful force, making babies thrive and gentling the most fractious of women. It had a powerful effect on him, too. Slowly he stroked his hand over her back, feeling the delicate vertebrae of her spine, the smooth warmth of her skin.

She must have sensed his determination, because she was motionless in his arms, waiting. "Unless you have an explanation for what's causing you to go into shock this way, I'm taking you to a doctor," he said. "Today. Even if I have to wrap you in this blanket and carry you the way you are."

She exhaled through her nose, huffing her displeasure. She didn't look at him but stared over his shoulder. Her evasion made him think there was indeed something going on that was causing her to have such drastic reactions. "Richard—"

"Sweetie," he countered, with the exact level of impatience she had used. She darted a suspicious glance at him, not quite certain what he had said. He managed not to smile.

"All right," she said abruptly. "I'm usually cold, but not like—not like today."

"Or day before yesterday?"

"Or then," she agreed. "Both times, I walked in my sleep the night before." She pressed her lips together, looking both mutinous and worried.

She evidently thought that was explanation enough, but Richard didn't. "I've never heard of sleepwalking causing anyone to go into shock."

Mutiny began to override worry in her expression. "Well, that's what happened, whether you believe it or not."

There was more, and she was determined not to tell it. Without another word Richard got up and tucked the blanket around her, wrapping it tight so she couldn't get even her arms free. Then he picked up his pants from the floor and stepped into them.

"Hey!" She began wiggling frantically, trying to fight her way out of the blanket.

"Don't bother." He zipped his fly and buckled his belt. "I'd just have to wrap you up again before I take you to a doctor, and you know I can do it. I'm a helluva lot bigger than you, and a helluva lot stronger."

"Bully!" she threw at him.

"Yep, but a concerned one." He leaned down and kissed her forehead.

Whether it was the concern or the kiss that did it, or maybe her realization that he meant what he said, he saw her expression change. The look she gave him was almost frightened. "It isn't just sleepwalking," she said, her voice so low he could barely hear her. "Both times I've painted something in my sleep, too."

Sleep-painting? Interested, he sat down on the edge of the couch, trapping her between his hip and the couch back. "Why would that be such a shock to your system?"

She bit her lip. "There was an old hot dog vendor who worked a corner about four blocks from the gallery. He had the sweetest expression of anyone I've ever seen. Day before yesterday, when I got up I noticed the canvas I'd been working on had been moved, and another one was on the easel in its place. The p-painting on the easel was of the hot dog vendor, with blood coming out his nose and pooled around his head. In the painting he was dead. That was the first time it happened."

"Painting in your sleep, or being so cold?"

"Both. That afternoon, I found out the vendor really was dead, though I had seen him just the day before."

He didn't know what to say to that. Bad coincidence? That was stretching the boundaries of logic, but unless she had a lot more to tell him, he couldn't think of anything else it could be but coincidence. "And this morning?"

She gave a low, harsh laugh. "This morning, when I saw the canvas had been moved again and another was in its place, all I could think was that someone else I knew had died. I was too scared to look at it, because I was afraid—*terrified*—that I had painted you."

The meaning behind that admission went through him like a bolt of lightning. He clenched his fists to keep himself from reaching for her. He didn't dare touch her now, or they wouldn't get out of bed until sometime tomorrow. The look she gave him was stripped bare of the layers of prickly defenses she usually kept between her and the world.

"Did you?" he asked, and managed to keep his voice calm. He had the feeling she was grateful he hadn't pounced on that telling admission.

She laughed again, this time with real amusement. "No. I painted shoes. Two of them. One man's, and one woman's."

He grinned at the incongruity. "Shoes, huh? This may start a new trend. Some people would be able to read all sorts of deep meaning into two lonely, mismatched shoes."

She snorted. "Yeah, the same people who buy a VanDern and think they've bought anything a monkey couldn't reproduce."

The disdain in her voice made him laugh. Now he felt able to touch her again, so he lifted another curl and watched it wrap around his finger. He examined the curl, rubbed his thumb over it to separate the silky strands, and carefully considered his next question. Maybe it shouldn't be a question at all. "Now tell me why you were convinced that if you had painted me, I would be dead."

He glanced at her in time to see the panic in her eyes. "You'll think I'm crazy," she said.

"Try me. I'm not leaving you alone until I know what's going on."

She wiggled again, frowning impatiently at the blanket. "Let me out of this thing. I feel as if I'm in a straitjacket, and considering what I just said, it's making me very uncomfortable."

Smiling, he tugged hard on the blanket, loosening it. She started to push it aside, then remembered she was almost naked and settled for tucking it under her arms. She sighed. "About a year ago, weird things began happening."

"Weird, how?"

She waved her hand. "Oh, traffic lights turning green whenever I approached, parking spaces at the front of the row emptying just as I got there, that sort of thing."

His eyebrows lifted. "Convenient." He remembered how fast the trip from the gallery to here had been. It had been almost miraculous, the way traffic had cleared out of their way. It had irritated the hell out of him, because he had been looking forward to spending more time with her.

"Yeah, I kind of like that part. And I like the way the plants look. Before, they tended to die on me, but now, no matter what I do, they just keep growing and blooming." She pointed at a plant with delicate pink blossoms. "That's a Christmas cactus. This is the sixth time already it has bloomed this year."

He rubbed his jaw. "I assume it isn't supposed to do that."

"Well, it never has before."

"What else?" There had to be something else. Traffic signals and parking spaces wouldn't make her this uneasy.

She shivered suddenly, alarming him. But her skin remained smooth, and he realized it was her thoughts that had made her shiver. She stared at him, blue eyes stark and haunted. "I began seeing ghosts," she whispered.

CHAPTER TEN

Sweeney couldn't tell if he believed her or not, and for a moment it didn't matter. The relief at having told someone else was enormous, and until now she hadn't realized how much strain she had been under, facing this alone. His dark gaze never wavered from her face, and his hand remained gentle in her hair.

Then she realized that it did matter what he thought. It mattered very much. Three days before she wouldn't have believed she could respond to any man the way she did to him. She was uncertain how he had become so important to her so fast, but she couldn't argue with the truth. And it was because he was important to her that she cared about his opinion. What if he thought she was a crackpot and decided she was more trouble than she was worth?

Suddenly she couldn't look at him, and she felt her face heating again. Oh, God, where had her sense of caution gone? How had she let a threat to *take her to the doctor,* of all things, convince her to spill her guts like that? She had even been thinking of going to a doctor herself, just to see if her constant chill was in any way caused by a physical ailment. As threats went, that one was a real wimp.

"I don't know why I told you all that," she mumbled.

He merely looked at her and continued to play with her hair. "Yes, you do," he finally said in a mild tone. "How do you know they're ghosts?"

"Because they're dead," she said irritably, and scowled at him. "When you go to someone's funeral and then see him in the supermarket parking lot a month later, you pretty well know something strange is going on." She didn't know what to make of that cryptic "Yes, you do," so she ignored it.

"Yeah, I'd say that's a given." His mouth quirked as if he was struggling to hide a grin, and she wondered just what it was about her that he thought was so funny. He frequently looked as if he was trying not to laugh.

"What's so funny?"

"You are. You're so busy trying to rebuild your fences to keep me out you haven't realized I'm already in the pasture with you."

"We agreed not to get involved—"

"That's not exactly how I recall it," he drawled. "We're already 'involved.' We agreed not to have sex. We haven't, though I have to tell you, sweetie, it was mighty tempting."

He was doing something funny to her name, she thought, fluttering the *n* or something like that. Maybe it was caused by that remnant of a Virginia drawl that she had never before noticed, though she didn't know how she could have missed it. And he really should put on his shirt, instead of leaning over her half-naked like that. The guy in the Diet Coke commercial didn't have anything on Richard in the chest department. His chest was broad, and muscled, and wonderfully hairy, and she wanted to lay her hands on his pecs, feel his heart beating against her palm, somehow bank his heat against the cold hours when he wasn't there.

"Tell me more about the ghosts," he coaxed.

Well, she had already let the cat out of the bag, so she might as well tell him everything. He looked as if he had settled in for the duration, determined not to move until he heard the whole story. "The first time was in Clayton, a year ago. A little boy named Sam Beresford died of leukemia, and a month after that I saw him in the supermarket parking lot, trying to get his mom to see him, talk to him, anything."

"Sad," he commented, and she nodded.

"Then I began seeing more and more, and Clayton is such a small town I knew most of them by sight, even if I wasn't actually acquainted with them. They'd wave, and I'd catch myself waving back, or saying hello, and people were beginning to give me really strange looks, so I knew I had to leave. There are a lot of ghosts here, but they're New Yorkers; they rarely speak."

He almost grinned again, but caught that one, too. "I guess seeing ghosts would be a problem in a small town," he murmured.

"You don't believe me, do you?" She sighed, her eyes somber. "I wouldn't believe me either, if it wasn't happening to me."

"I didn't say that." He stopped playing with her hair and cupped her cheek. "I'm open on the subject of ghosts. Tell me more."

She shrugged. "They're sort of translucent, and two-dimensional. When they speak, the sound is tinny. And they always know I can see them. I don't know how, but they do."

"You saw the vendor, the one you painted? That's how you know he's dead?"

"He came up behind me on the street. He asked me to send a sketch I'd made of him to his sons. But how did he know I had made a sketch? I did it the night he died. I never had a chance to show him."

"Did you send the sketch to them?"

She nodded. "Yesterday."

"Do you still have the painting?"

She looked startled. "Sure. Why?"

"I'd like to see it. Just curiosity."

She started to sit up and remembered her state of undress. Considering he had already seen her breasts, and touched them, and considering everything else they had done together, if she had been sophisticated, she would have nonchalantly gotten up and gotten dressed. "I guess this is proof I'm not sophisticated," she said, looking up with a rueful smile to find his dark gaze already locked on her. Her heart fluttered, or maybe it was her stomach. Something fluttered. He really shouldn't look at her that way, there was no telling what sort of damage he was doing to her internal organs.

"What is?"

She gestured to her clothes. "Turn your back."

"Ah." He nodded in understanding, but he didn't get up. That dark gaze was so intense she was afraid to try to read what was in it, though she didn't know if she was afraid he wanted too much from her, or too little.

He rubbed his thumb over her lips, then lightly over one

cheekbone. They looked at each other in silence for a moment, then he said, "I'm expediting the divorce."

So he could be with her. She couldn't play games and pretend she didn't understand the meaning behind that statement. He wanted her, and he was moving legal mountains to get her. It was exhilarating to be the object of such determination, but it was a little—a lot—frightening, too.

She was comfortable alone, comfortable with her life, but in that moment she accepted that things were going to change. He was going to change them. More important, she *wanted* them to change. For the first time in her life, she wanted to be part of a couple. She wanted to give this relationship thing a shot. Life was a lot more predictable when she had only herself to consider, but she wasn't the island she had always thought herself to be. She couldn't always be totally self-sufficient. Twice now she had needed him, and twice he had been there to help. Having someone else on whom she could depend was novel, but intensely comforting. She had never known that kind of security before, not even as a child. Especially not as a child.

"Get dressed," he said softly, standing up and turning his back.

Dressing was only a matter of pulling on her sweatshirt and stepping into her jeans, accomplished in seconds. She pushed her hair back from her face, relaxed and still a little drowsy, wonderfully warm. She didn't feel any chill at all. All she felt was a sense of well-being, of physical contentment.

"This way." She led the way to the studio, though in a four-room apartment it wouldn't have been difficult to find. The studio was actually supposed to be the main bedroom, but her bed fit into the smaller room, so there was never any doubt about where she would sleep and where she would work.

She had put the painting of the vendor in the closet. She couldn't bring herself to throw it away, but neither could she bear to have it out where she could see it. She went to the closet, but instead of following her, Richard walked around the room, pausing before each of the canvases she had already completed. Tension suddenly knotted her shoulders. Candra's opinion of her new work had been important to her career, but Richard's opinion was important to *her*.

"You've changed," he said abruptly, stopping before a particularly vivid landscape she had propped against the wall. He squatted down so he was at eye level with it.

"I didn't know you knew anything about my work," she said, surprised, and still uneasy. She stared at the long line of his tanned back, well-defined muscles delineating the furrow of his spine. Why hadn't he put on his shirt? He should have put it on, for her peace of mind if nothing else.

"Sure. I met a lot of artists through Candra, but I paid attention to the ones I liked."

That could be taken two ways. "Professionally or personally?" she asked, her tone wary.

He glanced over his shoulder at her, a smile in his dark eyes. "In your case, both." He turned his attention back to the landscape, reaching out to run a fingertip over a stream of water swirling around a rock in its path. Running water was difficult to execute, because you had to convey motion and energy as well as capture the play of light on the surface. Water that wasn't muddy took its color from its surroundings; it would look blue under a clear sky, green in the shadow of a mountain, dull on a gray day. She had spent years painting the St. Lawrence and never tired of it because the water was always different.

"How did you do this?" he murmured. "It looks three-dimensional. And the color . . . " He fell silent, moving on to the next painting, a sunset in Manhattan with the dark, faceless buildings silhouetted against a brilliant sky. She had painted the sky a glowing pinkish orange, and what could have been an ordinary skyline was turned into something exuberant. It had taken her two days of experimentation to get that exact shade.

He didn't say anything, and finally she couldn't stand the silence any longer. "Well?" she demanded, the word tart with impatience.

He turned to face her, eyeing her taut stance. "You've always been good, and you know it. Now you're better."

Her shoulders relaxed and she ran a hand through her hair. "I can't paint the way I used to," she confessed. "Like everything else, my style changed a year ago. I look at what I'm doing now and it's almost as if a stranger painted it."

"*You've* changed, and that's what changed your style. Maybe all of this is linked, maybe it isn't, but I'm damn glad it happened."

She gave him a curious look. "Why?"

"Because you never saw me before. Now you do."

He was serious, his gaze intent and unwavering. He could probably hypnotize a cobra with that look, she thought. It was certainly working on her, because she couldn't look away. She started to protest that of course she had seen him before, but then she realized what he meant. She hadn't seen him as a *man* before. In her mind men had been desexed, neutralized, of no importance to her. She hadn't wanted to deal with the messy complications of sex and emotional demands, so she had closed herself off from them. With her parents' example of what *not* to do always before her, and her own desire to concentrate on her painting, she had turned herself into an emotional nun.

Whether the weird changes had something to do with the shift in her attitude or the simple passage of time had healed her fears, that phase of her life was over and she didn't think it would ever be possible for her to return to it. Her eyes were open, and she would never again be oblivious to Richard's sexual nature, to the male hunger in his eyes when he looked at her.

"Did you see me?" she asked. "Before, I mean. We met . . . what? Three times?"

"Four. Yes, I saw you." He smiled. "I've always known you're a woman."

The way he looked at her then made her nipples tingle, and she suspected that if she glanced down, she would see they were nothing more than tight little points poking at her sweatshirt. She didn't look. She didn't want to draw his attention, in case he had missed it.

"Are you turned on, or cold?" he asked softly, and she knew he hadn't missed a thing.

She cleared her throat. "I guess I'm turned on, because I'm sure not cold."

He threw back his head and laughed. She wondered if she should have feigned ignorance, or maybe played it cute and flirted with him. She had a lot to learn about this come-hither stuff, but for the first time she realized the process could be fun.

But not now. Not yet. She cleared her throat again and turned to the closet behind her. "The painting's in here." She had to steel herself to open the door, reluctant to face the ugliness of death. She couldn't avoid looking at it; because the paint hadn't been dry when she put the canvas in the closet, it was turned facing out. The artist in her wouldn't let her do anything to deface even this painting, though ordinarily she would never put anything in the closet to dry.

Hurriedly she reached in and got the canvas, then propped it on the wall next to the closet. Richard walked over and stared down at the painting, his expression hard and shielded. Sweeney went over to the window and stood looking out.

"You did this before you knew he was dead." It was a statement, not a question, but then in any case, she had already said so. "Do you know what happened to him?"

"No, he looked okay to me." She bit her lip. "But they all do, you know?" All the ghosts looked in the pink of health. Talk about ridiculous.

"What was his name?"

"Stokes. I don't know his first name. But his sons are David and Jacob Stokes. They're both attorneys."

"I think I'll check into this, if you don't mind."

"Check into what?" Curiosity made her turn to look at him.

"How he died." He rubbed his thumb against the underside of his jaw. "Maybe it was an accident."

"Because of the blood? I don't know how realistic that painting is; he could have had a stroke, or a heart attack. Maybe the blood's there because—I don't know—I associate blood with death. Or maybe he fell down a flight of stairs."

"I'll check into it," Richard repeated. He turned toward the door. She followed him as he went into the living room and picked up his shirt. She watched him shrug into it, feeling a pang of regret as he covered that broad chest. Without a hint of self-consciousness, he unfastened his pants and began tucking in the shirt. A wave of warmth washed over her. She actually felt flushed.

"I have an appointment I can't put off," he said as he rebuckled his belt. "Get a pen and paper; I'm going to give you my private number."

She didn't have to search for either one; she was an orderly creature, so both were right beside the phone. "Okay, shoot."

He recited the number. "Don't wait until you're so cold you

can't function. Call me immediately. If you're right about it only happening when you've had an episode of sleepwalking, then you'll know as soon as you check the studio whether or not you need to call."

"There's no way to tell how often that will be. You can't take the time to come over here every time I get *cold.*"

"The hell I can't. It isn't just a chill; it's more serious than that and you know it. Look, for my peace of mind, call me every morning when you get up, okay?" He took her chin in his hand and bent down to kiss her. The kiss was light, his lips soft and barely moving on hers. Sweeney kept herself from clinging to him, but it was a struggle; the man was addictive. She wanted more of him, all of him.

He paused at the door. "Does the gallery have exclusive rights to sell your work, except for your portrait commissions?"

"Except for any directly commissioned work, yes."

He nodded. "I want that one with the running water. Take it to the gallery to be framed, and I'll arrange the purchase through another person so Candra won't sell it to someone else just to keep me from getting it."

And so Candra wouldn't know there was anything between them, she thought. She had been right to be reluctant to get involved with him; even though he and Candra had split, the situation was awkward, and finalizing the divorce probably wouldn't help a lot. In that moment she made the decision to dissolve the agreement between herself and Candra and begin the search for another gallery to represent her.

"I'll call you," he said, and hesitated for a moment, looking back at her. She had the impression he wanted to kiss her again. Evidently he thought better of it, though, and he stepped out into the hall. He had probably made the right decision, she thought wistfully, as she shut the door and locked it, but the right decision wasn't always the most pleasurable. They had already become far more involved than was right, but at least he'd had the self-control to keep from taking things any further. Until his divorce was final, she thought, they couldn't risk a repeat of today's situation, because the temptation was too great to resist many times.

Richard frowned as he left the building. Edward saw him come out of the door, and within seconds the car slid to a halt in front of him.

"Just a minute, Edward, let me make a call." He dialed directory assistance, and asked for the number of David Stokes, attorney, then asked to be connected.

A young male voice answered on the second ring. "Mr. Stokes isn't in," he said in answer to Richard's request. "There was a death in the family, and he'll be out of the office for the rest of the week."

"This is about his father's death," Richard replied, taking the chance that Sweeney had been right about the vendor. Her story defied logic, but he wasn't inclined to dismiss it out of hand as nonsense. *Something* was going on, something that was causing her to go into shock, or something resembling shock, and everything she had said could be verified either by investigation or observation.

"Oh, are you a cop?"

"I'm investigating the death," Richard replied easily.

"Everyone is shaken up by this. Have you found out anything?"

"I can't discuss that. Give me Mr. Stokes's home number."

Richard scribbled down the number. He saw Edward watching him in the rearview mirror and their eyes met. Edward was normally the most impassive of men, but he looked interested in this new development.

Richard dialed David Stokes's number. A child answered, and when Richard asked for Mr. Stokes, the little voice said, "Just a minute," then yelled, "Daddy!"

"Hello."

"Mr. Stokes, my name is Richard Worth. I'm sorry to bother you at a time like this, but if you feel up to it, I'd like to ask you some questions about your father's death."

"His murder, you mean," said David Stokes.

CHAPTER
ELEVEN

Elijah Stokes had been murdered, the victim of a violent mugging. He had been attacked, dragged between two buildings, and beaten to death. He had died from severe head injuries, inflicted by a blunt object. A reluctant witness had finally told police she had seen a young man running from the alley on the afternoon in question.

Richard pondered on the details he had learned from the bitter, grief-stricken David Stokes. He didn't like any of them.

His daytime staff had long since gone home, and he was alone in the town house, his favorite time of the day. He usually worked at night, and in fact, he needed to study some reports that he should have read that morning, but he wasn't in the mood for profit margins and stock options.

He snagged a bottle of beer from the refrigerator and sat down in front of the television. His fondness for the occasional beer had always reminded Candra of his peasant origins. Though she seldom said anything about it, he had always been aware of her mingled distress and disdain. When they were first married, when he had cared what she thought, he had restricted himself to her approved list of wines, mixed drinks, and whiskeys. Projecting the right image hadn't been important to him, then or now, but it had been to her. When she started cheating, he stopped caring, and from then on there had always been beer in the refrigerator.

He suspected Sweeney wouldn't know one wine from another, and furthermore wouldn't care to know. It was a refreshing attitude.

He propped his feet on the coffee table and turned to a news channel, but he already knew the Dow Jones, and Standard and Poor's averages. He knew the latest price of gold; he knew what the Asian markets were doing, what the money markets were doing, what the Chicago futures were doing, and he didn't give a shit. Work would wait. He had more important things on his mind.

Sweeney's claim to see ghosts and affect electronics didn't bother him. He didn't necessarily believe it, but it didn't bother him. She was patently sane, so at worst her convictions were eccentric. The electronics effect was easily explained; some people couldn't wear battery-operated watches because their personal energy field made the watches go haywire. If she really did affect traffic signals, that was fine with him.

Several things did bother him, though. Those severe chills she was having, whether caused by shock or something else, were serious enough to incapacitate her. He didn't know if she was in any true physical danger, but judging from what he had seen that morning, he thought it was more than a little possible. Whether triggered by her imagination or some physical condition, the events were real.

He wanted to believe there was some underlying physical cause, something easily adjusted with medication. That would be the simplest, most logical cause and solution.

Unfortunately, there was that painting of Elijah Stokes. He couldn't find any possible explanation for its existence.

As soon as he had seen the painting, he had known it depicted a violent death. Sweeney didn't seem to realize quite what she had painted, but then she hadn't seen a lot of death and violence. He had. In the army, he had been trained to be efficiently violent, to perform his mission and avoid capture, and to kill. He had been good at it, and not just in exercises. The rangers, like all other special-forces groups, were often sent on clandestine missions that were never reported in the news. He knew what death looked like, what blunt-force trauma looked like, so he had been expecting David Stokes to say his father had been murdered.

Sweeney didn't live in Elijah Stokes's neighborhood; she hadn't even known his name until she learned the names of his sons. Nor could she have found out about his death afterward and done the painting, because the paint had been completely dry today. While Sweeney's back was turned, he had touched the paint, especially the thick red of the blood, and it hadn't been sticky. No, she didn't know Elijah Stokes had been murdered, and he didn't intend to tell her. She was already upset about the painting, and he didn't want to do anything that might trigger another episode of hypothermia or shock.

If anyone had told him a month ago, even a week ago, that he would be entertaining the notion such psychic phenomena could be real, he'd have laughed in his face; that was tabloid fodder. But this was Sweeney; she wasn't a good liar, wasn't good at any sort of deception. Watching her reaction to the McMillans had made him want to laugh out loud, because her growing repulsion and desperation to get out of there had been plain on her face. When she didn't want to tell him something, she didn't pretend not to know the answers he wanted; she just got a mutinous, stubborn expression. She didn't play games, didn't know how.

After Candra's deceptiveness, after the social snobbery he had observed for ten years, some of which he had endured, Sweeney was like a drink of fresh water. She was direct and honest, so even if he didn't believe some of the things she had told him, he had to believe that she did. And he had to believe she had painted Elijah Stokes's death scene without having seen it, without having known the old man was dead.

So, with the evidence at hand, he had to discard logic and take a leap of faith. She wasn't crazy and she wasn't deceptive. He had to believe she'd had at least one true psychic experience.

If he loved her, he had to believe her.

Son of a *bitch*. Shocked by the thought, Richard surged to his feet and restlessly paced the room. Wanting her was one thing, a healthy sexual reaction to a desirable woman. He liked her. When he first asked her out, only a few days before, he had known he would like to have a steady, exclusive, and very sexual relationship with her. He hadn't thought about love. He was just getting out of a bad marriage, though the divorce was only the legal epitaph on the tombstone of something that had been dead a long time. Loving Sweeney wasn't convenient. The timing was bad, and he suspected she could be a real pain in the ass. She was difficult and prickly, and probably didn't compromise worth a damn.

But she was honorable, and this morning when she woke in

his arms, the smile she had given him had been as sweet as an angel's. His heart had literally skipped a beat. He had known then he was in real trouble. A man would do a lot for a woman who smiled at him that way, all warm and drowsy and satisfied. He would move mountains for the privilege of making love to her, of watching her face while he brought her to orgasm. Having had a taste of Sweeney's passion, he knew he wouldn't be able to hold out much longer. One way or the other, Candra would sign those papers, and he would call in every favor owed to him to get a hearing before a judge as soon as possible. Sooner. Within a week. Money could work miracles, and he had a lot of money. He couldn't think of a better way to spend it. It was time he did something satisfying with his money, and he couldn't think of anything more satisfying than getting Sweeney in his hands, in his bed, in his life.

He was going to make some drastic changes in his life, and he was going to make them soon. Sweeney was the most drastic change, but the others weren't minor. He was tired of playing the market, tired of the life he led here. It had never been what he wanted on a permanent basis, just the means to an end. He didn't like what he was seeing in the market, and it was time to get out. He thought he'd have at least a year, but liquidating his assets would take time, and he didn't intend to wait until the last minute to do it.

The computer problem looming at the end of 1999 looked like a bitch. From the information that passed through his hands, he knew a lot of companies weren't going to have their computer programs fixed by that time. What that would do to the market was anyone's guess, but if enough companies shut down, the market would crash. If he had been satisfied with what he was doing, with his life here, he might have tried to ride it out. Under the circumstances, though, it was time to get out.

He didn't want to try to predict what would happen, or shift his investments to companies with computer systems that were millennium compliant. He had never intended to spend his whole life playing the market and amassing wealth, anyway. All along he'd had other plans, and now it was time to put them into action.

Sweeney complicated matters, and not just because the timing was inconvenient. He didn't want a long-distance romance. He wanted her with him, and he had no idea how she felt about relocating.

Big plans, he thought in self-mockery. He tilted back his head and killed the rest of the beer. He was planning her future without even asking if she wanted to spend it with him. Hell, why not? She had disrupted his life, so turnabout was fair play. He thought he had a good chance of success, considering what she had given away that morning with her comment about being terrified something had happened to him. He grinned to himself. He wasn't above taking ruthless advantage of her feelings for him; hell, he needed any advantage he could get.

It was almost two A.M. when Sweeney stirred slightly in her sleep, a frown puckering her brow. A barely audible whimper sounded in her throat, a quiet protest from her subconscious. A few moments later she slipped out of bed, her movements so calm the covers were scarcely disturbed; one second she had been lying beneath them, the next she wasn't. She stood beside the bed for some time, her head cocked as if she were listening to something. Then she sighed, and walked silently through the dark apartment to her studio.

She had stood the canvas with two shoes painted on it against the right wall, where it was out of the way but she could still look at it. The shoes had puzzled her. Why had she painted shoes? After her initial relief that she hadn't done another portrait of death, she had gotten more uneasy as the day had gone on. The shoes weren't finished; they needed more work. Knowing that had made her dread the night, for the first time in her life.

Now she went straight to the shoe canvas and placed it on an easel. Her expression was smooth and blank as she selected her tubes of paint and began to work. Her brushstrokes were fast and precise, the narrow, tapered bristles adding detail.

She didn't work for long, no more than an hour. Suddenly she shuddered, her entire body drooping as if overwhelmed with fatigue. She capped the tubes of paint and dropped the brush in a jar of turpentine, and silently returned to bed.

She slept late again, until almost eight, but knew as soon as she woke that she had done it again. She was cold, the heat from the electric blanket somehow not transferring to her flesh, even though she knew it should. When she had gone to bed the night before, the bed had been toasty warm, such a delicious sensation she had almost purred as she crawled between the sheets. It would still be toasty warm, she knew, to anyone else, but she couldn't feel it.

Not being an idiot who couldn't face reality, she hurriedly dressed and went into the living room, where she had left the pad with Richard's number on it. As she picked up the cordless phone and punched numbers, she noticed that her hands were colorless except for her fingernails, which had an interesting bluish tint to them.

Richard answered the phone himself, and something tense inside her relaxed a little at the sound of that deep, calm voice. "This is Sweeney," she said, trying to sound cheerful, but at that moment a violent shiver seized her and her voice shook. "It happened again."

"I'll be right there."

Just like that, she marveled as he hung up. No questions, no "I'm tied up right now, but I'll be there as soon as I can." She needed him, and he was dropping everything else to be there with her. The sheer wonder of it made her chest feel tight, as if she were catching a cold. Tears stung her eyes and she blinked them back, determined not to be such a sissy again.

She went into the kitchen. The coffee was made and already cold. She poured a cup and put it in the microwave to heat, waiting impatiently for the ding. Chills raced down her spine, roughened her skin. She felt her muscles tensing with another shudder.

She gulped down the first cup of coffee and heated another one. She had to hold it with both hands to keep the coffee from sloshing out, but still she was shaking so hard she risked scalding herself.

The attacks were getting worse, she realized; she was getting colder, faster. Maybe she should move the coffeemaker into the bedroom, put it right there on the nightstand so she wouldn't even have to get out of bed. Not that the coffee seemed to be helping much; nothing helped, except for Richard.

Just the thought of him caused a small spurt of warmth deep inside. That's the ticket, she thought. Just think of Richard. She had thought about him incessantly the day before, constantly replaying those remarkably carnal moments in his arms. The fact that they hadn't had sex was a tribute to his self-control, not hers, and she was still astounded at herself, astounded at the heat that had poured through her, the blind physical drive for fulfillment. She had never experienced that before, and now that she had, she was no longer so certain of her ability to keep their relationship platonic.

She snorted into the cup of coffee. Who was she kidding? They hadn't consummated their relationship, but it was far from platonic. All these years she had felt so smug about her imperviousness to sexual temptation, but with one look Richard could get inside her defenses and have her insides jumping around. Face it, she thought. With Richard, she was a pushover.

Shivering, she looked at the clock. How much longer would he be? He should be here any time.

Her shoulders were hunched against the cold, but abruptly she straightened, her eyes going wide. She shot out of the kitchen chair and raced for the bathroom. Hastily she rinsed her mouth with mouthwash, then grabbed a comb and attacked her hair, which stood out from her head like a bush. Her efforts only made it wilder. She threw down the comb, squirted a dab of something that was supposed to control the frizzies into her hand, and rubbed it over the worst spots. Makeup? Should she put on lipstick? She stared at herself in the mirror, wondering what shade looked best on blue lips. Perfume, maybe. Damn it, she didn't have any.

"Oh, I've got it bad," she whispered. Here she stood, shivering so hard she was beginning to hurt, worrying about makeup and perfume. In horror, she realized she was *prettying up.*

The doorbell rang. Hurriedly she wiped her hands and ran to the door. Her teeth were chattering as she jerked it open. "I've lost my mind," she told him grimly, walking into his arms. "I'm freezing to death, and I was worrying about lipstick. Then I opened the door without checking first. This is all your fault."

"I know," he murmured, lifting her off her feet and stepping inside. He hugged her tight, helping her brace against the shudders that wracked her. She buried her face against his neck, seeking to breathe in his warmth, and her nose was so cold he jumped. An exuberant curl tickled his lips as he turned and locked the door.

"It isn't as bad today. I c-c-called you as soon as I got up."

Since she'd lost control of her teeth in the middle of the sentence and they'd done their castanet imitation again, her statement wasn't as believable as it could have been.

"Good." He carried her to the couch. "Where's the blanket?"

"On the ch-chair in my bedroom."

He set her down. "I'll get it."

He was back in seconds, guiding her to lie down on the couch and lying down beside her, then gathering her full length against him and covering them both with the blanket. Then he sat up again and shucked his lightweight crewneck off over his head, carelessly dropping it to the floor; then he lay down beside her and tucked her hands between them, warming them on his torso.

His skin felt hot against her cold fingers. He put his hands on her back and pressed them against her spine, and she shuddered with relief as his heat began sinking into her. "It's already easing," she said against his throat, feeling her tight muscles slowly relax as a sense of profound well-being spread through her. She breathed in slowly, deeply, filling her lungs with the scent of him. He smelled warm and musky, undeniably male. The aroma of testosterone, she thought, and smiled to herself.

"Better?" he asked. His voice was low, deeper than usual. The bass notes reverberated under her ear.

"*Mmm.* This wasn't bad at all."

"Because you didn't wait." His lips brushed her ear, moved over her temple. His hand slowly stroked down her back, urging her even closer. Their legs tangled, and one hard-muscled thigh slid between hers.

Her breath caught as she felt his erection. "I can't keep calling you over to get me warm," she murmured. "This is too tempting."

"You're telling me," he said ruefully. She felt his lips curve against her temple as he smiled, then he pressed another kiss there. He smoothed her curls back, gently traced a fingertip around the sworl of her ear. "I couldn't take a repeat of yesterday. If I'd had to take your clothes off today, I'd be fucking you right now."

His voice was low and intimate, impossibly tender. The graphic promise invoked a breathtaking image, making her loins clench with almost unbearable anticipation. She couldn't protest, not when she wanted nothing more than for him to do exactly what he had said. She slipped her hand around his bare back, feeling the strength of the muscles there and the way they tightened under her touch. "I want you to," she whispered, unable to pretend, as if he didn't know exactly how she reacted to him. He had known from the first, before she was willing to admit it to herself.

His entire body flexed and surged, pressing her hard into the couch. His thigh wedged higher between her legs. A ragged breath shuddered out of him. "I feel like a teenager making out on the living room couch. I'd forgotten how damn frustrating it is."

Sweeney brushed her lips over the underside of his jaw. She was inexperienced, but not naive or ignorant. There were several ways they could satisfy each other, without actually having sex, and the temptation was strong to suggest one or more, or all. She didn't. Not only did she doubt her willpower would stand the test, but to do so seemed like cheating—getting off on a technicality, so to speak. It would be delicious, and wonderfully satisfying, and wrong. Until his divorce was final, it was wrong. Maybe most women wouldn't feel that way, but then they hadn't grown up with her parents as examples.

She didn't dare even kiss him, though she hungered for his

taste. She could feel the tension humming through his big body, feel her own flesh throbbing in response. It would take so little to push them both over the edge that she was afraid to move.

But there was pleasure in just lying there with him, his arms around her, feeling his chest expand with each breath, hearing his heart beating. There was animal comfort in sharing his heat. Above all, there was a sense of belonging that she had never before known, the startling realization that she was *not* alone in the world, that somehow she had become part of a couple.

It was a heady sensation, to know that he cared for her, that she was important to him. Sweeney couldn't remember ever being important to anyone before. She didn't know how this sense of connection had formed so fast, or how she had so quickly come to trust and rely on him, but it had and she did.

"What did you paint this time?" he asked, after ten minutes had passed without a return of the chill. She was warm and drowsy, almost in a daze.

"I don't know," she said, a little surprised. "I didn't even go in the studio. I have an electric blanket on my bed, and when I woke up cold anyway, I just assumed I had been sleepwalking again. What if I called you for nothing?"

"I would rather you call me whenever you have the least chill, than let things get as bad as they were yesterday morning. You worried the hell out of me."

"I worried the hell out of myself," she said wryly, and listened to his laughter rumble in his chest. It was nice, the way his voice was so deep. The hair on his chest was rough under her cheek, and that was nice, too. Everything about him was so damn masculine she could barely control herself.

"Are you warm?"

"Toasty."

"Then we need to get up."

"Why? I'm so comfortable."

"Because I'm not a saint. Come on, let's see what you painted."

She wanted to groan and moan at the loss of his body heat, but for his sake she decided to be gracious about it. "Oh, all right."

He grabbed his sweater from the floor and tugged her to her feet, then headed toward the studio. Sweeney detoured into the kitchen and nuked another cup of coffee. Richard declined her offer of coffee and leaned against the cabinets with his ankles crossed while he pulled the sweater on over his head. She didn't think she'd ever had a man in her kitchen before, and she sneaked a couple of admiring glances at him. As the sweater settled in place, she stifled a sigh of regret. It was a damn shame to cover a chest that looked like his.

"Come on, quit stalling," he said, and until then she hadn't realized she was. Yesterday she had painted shoes; who knew what she had painted last night, if indeed she had done anything.

With his hand resting comfortably on the small of her back, they went into the studio. Sweeney looked around and saw that the shoe canvas wasn't leaning against the wall where she had left it. "Looks like I worked on shoes again last night," she said, relaxing inside. She didn't like walking in her sleep and doing paintings that she didn't remember doing, but she could have picked subjects a lot more upsetting than shoes.

An easel had been moved, positioned so the canvas was facing the north wall of windows.

Together they went over to study the canvas. Sweeney studied the details she had added during the night, clinically examining the brushstrokes. The details were so fine, the lines so soft, that the painting looked like a portion of a photograph. It wasn't her usual technique, but the work was still undoubtedly hers.

She had added another shoe to the painting, a high heel that matched the other one. Last night's shoe was still being worn; she had completed a woman's foot to the ankle. And she had painted a woman's bare foot and part of that leg, up to the knee, lying close to the empty shoe. All in all there was nothing horrible about the painting, not in what she had done so far, but still she felt her stomach knot in dread, and she shivered.

"Great," she muttered. "I added some body parts." Despite her flippancy, her voice was tight.

Richard felt her shiver and gathered her close, hugging her to him. His expression was grim as he stared at the painting.

"It's going to be like the hot dog vendor, isn't it? She's dead. She's lying down; she's lost one shoe. Or if she isn't dead now, she will be soon, and it feels as if it's my fault." Sweeney tried to pull away, but Richard turned her to him and held her tighter, cradling the back of her head in one big hand and pressing her face into his chest.

"It isn't your fault and you know it."

Her voice muffled, she said, "Logically I do, but emotionally—" She waved a hand. "You know how emotions are."

"Yeah, they're unruly as hell." He kissed the top of her head.

"I wonder what would happen if I destroyed the canvas."

"Nothing. Whether or not you paint the scene will have no effect on this person. Get that straight, sweetie. Whatever . . . vibes, or whatever the hell they are, that you're picking up, *you're* the one being affected, not the other way around."

"I wish I could be sure of that."

"You can, because you painted Elijah Stokes after he was dead, not before."

Startled, she jerked her head back to stare at him. "How do you know?"

"I talked to his son David. Mr. Stokes died late in the afternoon. You didn't do the painting until that night."

She mulled that over, feeling relieved but as if there were some questions she should ask, if only she could think what they were. Sighing, she slid her arms around his waist and was comforted by the feel of his body. He was so solid and strong. Had she held him before? She had touched him and stroked her hand up his back, but she didn't know if she had actually put her arms around him before now. her conscience twinged. She had been taking and taking, while he had been doing all the giving, but even strong people needed to be held. She had always considered herself strong, and look how much she had needed him.

He leaned back a little so he could peer down at her face. "Feel better about it?"

"Relieved. Still worried." She managed a smile, pushing away her uneasy feelings. "And hungry. Have you had breakfast?"

"A long time ago, but I could eat again. Would you like to go out for breakfast? It'll be our first date."

"Wow, a date. I don't know if we should do that." She grinned at him, thinking of all the things they *had* done—and the things they had yet to do.

His answering grin was both amused and rueful. "My day will come, sweetie. When I finally get you flat on your back, just remember that I have a lot of built-up frustration that will have to be worked off."

"You say the sweetest things," she purred, and laughed because she had never done this kind of love play before, never teased a man and felt his desire for her like a tidal wave about to break over her head. It was heady, and exciting, and . . . and wonderful.

He turned her to the door and urged her on with a small

push. "Put on some shoes—and a bra, while you're at it. That little jiggle is hell on my self-control."

She did more than put on shoes and a bra. She exchanged her gray sweatshirt for a blue sweater and did the mascara-and-lipstick thing. She frowned at her hair, blew a curl out of her eyes, and decided to leave it alone. Grabbing her purse, she went out into the living room, where Richard sat reading one of the books on ghosts.

"I've been researching ghosts since all this started," she said. "I keep hoping I'll find some explanation of what caused me to start seeing them, but so far all the books are just about the ghosts themselves. Some spirits leave immediately; some hang around for a little while; some never leave at all."

"So why would any of them hang around?" He stood up and walked with her to the door.

"There are all sorts of theories. Maybe there are loose ends to be tied up, maybe they're just confused and don't cooperate—who knows? One book said that only unhappy spirits become ghosts, so technically the ones who stay just a little longer aren't really ghosts, they're just on a layover."

"That's one way of looking at it," he murmured.

Sweeney locked the door behind them, and they walked to the elevator. She noticed Richard looking around him, studying the building for signs of decay. The apartments weren't luxurious, or even upscale, but everything was usually in good repair. If the elevator malfunctioned, the tenants didn't have to wait weeks for it to be repaired. Lightbulbs were replaced and the plumbing was maintained. The building was old, but the tenants, herself included, generally considered themselves lucky.

They stood waiting for the elevator, watching the old-fashioned dial at the top with the needle that indicated at which floor the car was stopped. The needle was coming up. Richard put his hand on her waist, his fingers flexing slightly as if he savored the feel of her. Sweeney tilted her head to smile at him just as the elevator chimed and the doors slid open, and Candra stepped out.

She froze when she saw them, her face blanching of color. She took in Richard's hand on Sweeney's waist, the way they were standing close together, and angry color flooded back into her face. "Fancy meeting you here," she said to Richard, her hands clenched into bloodless fists.

The elevator closed behind her. Richard leaned forward and punched the button again, and the doors obediently reopened. "Where would you like to go for breakfast?" he calmly asked Sweeney, ushering her into the car and hitting the button for the lobby. Sweeney blinked at him, admiring his cool unconcern; she felt almost paralyzed by the awkwardness of the situation.

Infuriated, Candra stepped back into the elevator as the doors began to close. "Don't you dare try to ignore me!"

"What Sweeney and I do is none of your business." His voice was still calm, his demeanor completely unruffled. His hand was firmer on Sweeney's waist, however, keeping her anchored at his side.

Sweeney noted the linking of her name with him, and so did Candra. "The hell it isn't!" She was so furious her voice was shaking. "You're still my husband—"

Standing so closely to him, Sweeney felt the sudden tension in his body, and his eyes narrowed into dangerous slits. For the first time in his presence she felt a frisson of fear, and that look wasn't even directed at her. "You don't want to go there," he told Candra, very softly.

"Don't tell me where I want to go or what I want to do." Trembling, Candra reached out to steady herself as the car descended. Her chocolate gaze switched to Sweeney. "You! I asked you if anything was going on between you and Richard, and you lied to me, you little bitch—"

"That's enough," Richard snapped, wrapping his arm around Sweeney and bodily moving her out of Candra's reach. He moved so his own body completely blocked hers.

"Oh, don't worry," Candra sneered. "I'm too adult to brawl over a man, though that's probably what you were used to before you met me. Isn't that what your beer-swilling, country-fried little southern girls do?"

Sweeney cleared her throat. "Actually," she said to Richard's back, "I was born in Italy."

"Who gives a fuck where you were born!" Candra screamed. Sweeney peeked around Richard's back and saw tears running down Candra's face, ruining her perfect makeup. "You're an unsophisticated hayseed, so he should feel very comfortable with you! But I promise you, you'll never sell another piece of work at *my* gallery, and no one else in town will touch you either after I—"

Sweeney felt Richard's temper snap. He took a single step toward Candra as the elevator lurched to a stop and the doors slid open. Her face blanching, Candra backed away from him.

"You're damn right I feel comfortable with her," he said in a tone so low Sweeney could barely hear him. "You don't know how great it feels to be with a woman who doesn't crawl into bed with every swinging dick she meets, the way you did. Yeah, I knew about all your men, every one of them, but you know what? I didn't give a damn, because I didn't give a damn about you. I do give a damn that you aborted my baby, though. Do you know what *hate* means, Candra? That's the best I feel about you. I warned you what I would do if you did anything to harm Sweeney's career, and I meant it, so you'd better think long and hard about any step you take."

He towed Sweeney out of the elevator and clamped his arm around her waist again. He had taken two steps when he halted and swung back to Candra. "By the way, I've just added another condition to the settlement. Sweeney is released from any agreement with the gallery, without penalty, effective immediately."

"Damn you, you can't keep adding conditions—"

"I can, and I have. Your only hope of getting the gallery is if you meet those conditions. If not, within three days you won't have to worry about Sweeney's career, because I'll replace you at the gallery and bar you from the premises."

"I'll kill you if you do," Candra shrieked, sobbing. The only other people in the small lobby were the super and a guy who lived on the second floor, but they were staring, not wanting to miss a second of the excitement. "The gallery is *mine*—"

"No," Richard interrupted. "The gallery is mine. Until you sign those papers the gallery is mine, and if you wait much longer, it will always be mine."

CHAPTER TWELVE

Richard ushered Sweeney out onto the sidewalk, leaving Candra weeping in the lobby. He had driven himself, she saw as he led her down the street to where he had parked the Mercedes. The neighborhood wasn't the best, sort of residential going-to-seed, but neither was it the sort where such a car left parked on the street would be stripped bare within ten minutes.

They were both silent as he unlocked the car and opened the passenger door for her. She got in, trying to think what she could say. She had just learned more about Candra, and the reasons for their divorce, than she had ever wanted to know. She was a little shaken, but more for Richard's sake than her own.

He pulled the car out into traffic. "I'm sorry," he said gruffly, after another minute of silence. "I know one of the reasons you didn't want to get involved with me was because you wanted to avoid scenes like that."

"It wasn't your fault; it was hers." The traffic light ahead of them turned green. She looked down at her hands. "I'm sorry, too. About—about the abortion. I didn't know."

"She did it over two years ago." His mouth was a grim line. "I didn't find out about it until right after you moved to the city. I put her out of the town house right then, and filed for divorce the next day."

"You wanted children?" Stupid, she berated herself. Of course he had wanted the child, even after the fact, or he wouldn't have been so upset on learning about the abortion.

"Not by then. Not with her. Her pregnancy was an accident. But once she was pregnant—that was different. It existed. It was my child."

Sweeney couldn't imagine being Richard's wife and aborting his child. She had never thought of children in relation to herself, period. She especially couldn't imagine her father caring what happened to any of his offspring, unborn or born. "How did you find out?"

"She told me. We were arguing, she was drinking—she told me."

The second traffic light turned green as they approached. He glanced at her. "I think I need you in the car with me from now on."

Understanding that he needed to change the subject, she relaxed back against the seat. "Where are we going?"

"To a little diner I know, nothing fancy."

"Good. I don't do fancy very well."

The little diner was across the river in New Jersey. They made it to and through the Holland tunnel in record time, which made Sweeney feel a little smug. If he had doubted her about the traffic lights, he couldn't now.

They managed to snag a booth in the diner, which couldn't have changed much since the 1950s. Over eggs and coffee she said, "I thought the gallery was Candra's."

"She ran it. I own it."

"You were going to buy one of my paintings from your own gallery? And pay commission?"

He shrugged. "If Candra doesn't sign the papers by the deadline and I keep the gallery, commission doesn't come into it. She'll sign, though. It's in her best interest."

"What if she doesn't? She was furious to find you with me, and she might make the divorce as difficult as possible."

"I'd break her," he said softly. "She wouldn't have a dime left, and she knows it."

Something else occurred to her. "I wonder why she was going to my apartment."

"She isn't stupid, and she knows me too well. She could tell I was interested in you, that day in the gallery, and she figured it out almost immediately. A few days ago she came to the town house and made an offer: if I upped the settlement amount, she wouldn't prevent any future sales of your work. She didn't like my counteroffer."

"I can imagine." And she could; Richard would make a dangerous enemy. "But still, why come to me?"

"To ask you to convince me to raise the settlement."

"Then why act so shocked to see us together, if she already thought we were involved?"

"Until then, she was just guessing. And thinking I was interested in you isn't the same as seeing us together so early in the morning, at your apartment."

Not to mention Candra had immediately realized Richard's presence thwarted her plan to ask Sweeney for assistance. Sweeney said, "I've made things more difficult for you, haven't I?"

"By existing? Yeah, you have." He eyed her over the table. "You keep me awake nights, you worry me, you drive me crazy."

She nudged his leg with her toe. "I'm serious."

"So am I, sweetie."

She frowned at him, diverted. "You're saying my name funny. What're you doing to it?"

"Nothing," he said, but he smiled.

Deciding she wasn't going to get anything out of him right now, Sweeney looked out the window of the diner, indulging herself for a moment by watching faces. A stooped old man, with tufts of hair on his ears and in his nostrils, walked by holding the hand of a chattering preschooler, a little girl wearing a dainty yellow sundress and a perky ponytail. The indulgent smile on his face shouted "grandfather." Or maybe "great-grandfather." Next was a young woman carrying her toddler in a backpack. She strode along as if she had a world to conquer, but she had tied a red balloon to the frame of the backpack and the baby's chubby little hand had managed to grab the string; he was staring in wonder at the balloon, which bobbed every time he moved. His eyes were round, his lips a perfect pink bow, and his cornsilk hair stood straight out like a dandelion. Sweeney watched until they were out of sight.

She applied herself to her eggs for a moment, then snorted as she remembered something.

"What?" Richard said, and she marveled at how fast they had settled into the shorthand communication of longtime couples.

" 'Beer-swilling, country-fried little southern girls,' " she said, and they both began laughing.

Candra couldn't stop crying, even though she knew it was stupid. She caught a taxi to the gallery, blubbering all the while. The cabdriver kept eyeing her in the mirror, but he didn't speak much English and she made it a point not to encourage chatty cabdrivers anyway.

She had one tissue in her purse, and it was inadequate for the repair job needed. She blotted her eyes instead of wiping them, to keep from destroying the remnants of her makeup, but more damn tears kept falling.

Damn him. Damn Sweeney. Damn both of them, for looking so . . . so together. She couldn't believe *Sweeney,* of all people, could be so sly and sneaky, or could lie so effectively. When Candra remembered her phone call to Sweeney the morning after the McMillan fiasco, she burned with humiliation. Richard had probably been with her then; they might have just gotten out of bed, and afterward they had laughed probably about the phone call.

Candra hurt, in a way she had never imagined she could hurt. Until now, though she had known she had lost him, in a way he had still been hers, because no one else had taken her place. Now someone had, and she knew, finally, irrevocably, deep in her bones, that Richard was gone. She had lost him, thrown him away, and she would never love anyone else the way she loved him. Still loved him, even now. He was the strongest person she had ever known and she couldn't stop admiring him even when that strength was turned against her. Was Sweeney capable of understanding, of appreciating what she had, or was she so damn inexperienced she had no idea?

That inexperience was what had drawn Richard to her, of

course, because God knows she had no style, and her conversation often bordered on the absurd. He had even admitted as much. Candra couldn't understand what men saw in her, but even Kai said Sweeney was "cool." She was pretty enough, Candra supposed, if you could overlook the fact that she often had paint in her hair and didn't know what day of the week it was.

She couldn't imagine Richard finding that attractive. He was so organized, so logical and work-oriented, she would have thought Sweeney would drive him mad within two days.

Her nails dug into her palms. Today Sweeney had . . . glowed. Candra closed her eyes against the remembered shock of stepping out of the elevator and seeing Richard and Sweeney together. Sweeney wore the look of a woman who had been well and truly loved the night before, and perhaps that morning, too—and, knowing Richard, several times during the night.

Candra couldn't believe she had made such a fool of herself. Screaming like a fishwife, *crying,* for God's sake. Richard had known why she was there, of course. Now she wouldn't have any chance of getting to Sweeney, not that Sweeney was likely to listen to her after that little scene. She had blown her last chance to get the settlement reinstated. Now her only hope was Carson, and it looked as if he needed nudging.

Kai had just opened the gallery when she got there; no customers had come in yet, thank God. She paid the cab and hurried through the door before anyone she knew saw her.

Kai stared at her, eyebrows lifted. "Rough morning?" he silkily inquired.

"Go to hell." She sailed past him into her office and got her cosmetic bag from the desk, then went into the bathroom. She winced when she looked in the mirror. Her face was blotched, her nose red, and her eyes looked like raccoon eyes. She needed to completely remove her makeup and start over, but she didn't have any cream with her. She did the best she could with wet paper napkins, and applied cool compresses to her eyes and face to take down the swelling and even out her color.

Kai sauntered in as she was reapplying her foundation. "Do you mind?" she snapped.

He ignored her protest and propped his rear end beside her on the vanity, crossing his arms over his chest. "There, there. What's Richard done now?"

"What makes you think this is about Richard?" She blew her nose and threw the tissue in the trash, then repaired the smudges.

He watched her take out her compact and dab powder over her face. "Because he's been making you dance to his tune for a year now, and you have a temper tantrum every time things don't go your way."

"I do not 'dance to his tune,' or anyone else's," she said furiously.

"Of course not, darling."

"I'm not your darling, and don't forget it. You're just an occasional lay."

"My, we are in a snit, aren't we? He must have refused to reinstate the settlement."

She whirled on him, mouth working with rage. "How do you know anything about the settlement?"

"There was a message from your lawyer on the answering machine. She strongly advises you to sign the papers posthaste, before you lose your ass and can't pay her. She didn't say so in so many words, of course, but that's what she means."

"How dare you listen to my messages!" She sounded like a Victorian maiden, she thought in disgust.

"It was on your business machine, darling, not your home machine. Perhaps you should instruct your attorney not to leave personal messages at work—assuming you'll be here much longer, that is."

"If I am, you can bet you won't be, pretty boy," she snarled. She jerked open the door. "Get out."

He went, with a sulky look on his pretty face. Candra took a deep breath, fighting the urge to sit down on the toilet lid and bawl. She had to get control of herself. She had totally ruined things this morning by being emotional, and now she would have to pacify Kai. She didn't feel like having sex, but it would probably take that to get him over his pout.

She took several deep breaths, and when she felt steady again, she finished her makeup. When she was finished, she critically studied herself in the mirror and dabbed more powder on a blotch. There. Her makeup wasn't perfect, but she knew she still looked better than most women would after a day at a salon.

She had to call Olivia, she realized; she had been a fool to put off signing the papers these few days, thinking she could somehow recoup what Richard had already deducted. She couldn't. She accepted that now. Richard had known, of course, that she would rage and protest against his conditions, but in the end accept them; he had left her no other choice. He didn't bluff and she knew it. Richard was one of those say-what-you-mean and mean-what-you-say people, the bastard.

She almost started crying again, but took a deep breath and controlled the urge. Walking briskly, she went into her office, closed the door, and called her attorney.

"Set up an appointment," she said calmly. "I'll sign. I assume the punitive action stops as soon as you call Gavin Welles?"

"I'll make certain it does, if I can't get an appointment for today. The papers will have to be redone and that will take some time, so it might be put off until tomorrow."

"Tomorrow is fine," Candra said. Of course a new agreement would have to be drawn up, to reflect the deduction in the settlement amount. She had no doubt Richard had already called his attorney instructing him to draw up papers concerning his new condition about Sweeney. That wouldn't go in the divorce agreement, but some sort of legal agreement would be reached allowing Sweeney a clean break from the gallery.

After hanging up with Olivia, Candra flipped through her Rolodex and found the McMillans' number. A maid answered, of course. "Has the senator returned from Washington yet?"

"Yes, ma'am, he has. May I say who is calling?"

"Candra Worth." There was no point in hiding her identity, she thought. Carson was more likely to take the call if he knew who she was; he wouldn't like it, but he would do it.

She was on hold for several minutes, long enough that she was beginning to get angry when Carson's richly modulated voice finally came on, except today it wasn't so modulated. It sounded rather tight, she thought with satisfaction. Good. That meant he was worried.

"What do you want?" he said abruptly.

Candra managed a light laugh. Actually, it felt good to be the one in control for a change. "Really, Carson, that's a silly question."

"Raising that kind of money in cash isn't easy."

"How difficult can it be? Sell a few stocks, cash in a few bonds, dip into a few accounts. You can't put me off with that excuse. If you don't have the money by tomorrow afternoon, a photograph will be at *The Washington Post* first thing the next morning. Let's see, which picture should I choose? The one of you snorting coke, I think."

"I want you to know this conversation is being taped," he said, his voice full of satisfaction. "You are now on record attempting blackmail. Is that a felony? You know, I rather think it is. I believe, my dear, we now have each other by the short hairs."

"Do we?" Carson would have benefited from having encountered Richard's style of negotiating, Candra thought grimly. Make the stakes too high for the other person to tolerate, and don't back down. It was a brutally effective tactic. "You don't quite understand my position. If I don't get that money, I lose everything, so I don't give a damn what you've taped. You have heard the old saw about desperate people and desperate measures, haven't you?"

"You fucking—"

"Now, now, let's be civilized." She'd had enough scenes for one day.

"Civilized, my ass." He was breathing heavily, the sound echoing in her ear.

"Face it, Carson; the only way you can use that tape is if those photographs have been made public, which is too late for you. Your career would be in the toilet. We would both lose, but if you don't come through with the money, I've lost anyway, so I might as well take you down with me." Her voice was cool, controlled. She meant every word.

He knew it, too. There was more heavy breathing before he accepted the inevitable. "All right, goddamn you. But tomorrow is too soon. It'll take at least two days to get that kind of cash."

"Day after tomorrow, then, but not a day longer."

At his desk, Kai smiled, and carefully timed his disconnect to coincide with Candra's so she wouldn't see the telltale light above her line stay on a second too long. He had perfected the art of eavesdropping over the years he had worked for her, just to keep the upper hand. She thought she had control, of course, but only because he had allowed her to think it.

So the little bitch was trying her hand at blackmail. He shouldn't be surprised, because he knew Richard had her over a barrel and Candra wasn't a woman who could do without money.

When she signed the divorce agreement, the gallery would become hers. She would probably fire him as she had threatened, he thought. Things were fine with her as long as he kept his mouth shut and performed on cue in bed, but he was tired of being her whore.

She sailed out of her office, all smiles now. "Darling," she said, coming over to his desk and lightly placing her hand on the back of his neck. "I'm so sorry I snapped at you. You were right; I had a fight with Richard and I took it out on you."

Now she would offer sex to pacify him, he thought cynically.

She lightly stroked her fingers through his hair. "Is there anything I can do to make it up to you?" Her tone was light, teasing, seductive.

He stood, moving away from her touch. "That isn't necessary," he said, at his most polite. He would have taken her up on the offer if he hadn't had an appointment at lunchtime and needed to be fresh for that. Too bad, he thought. He would have enjoyed being rough with her, maybe even rougher than she liked.

"Don't pout, darling; it isn't attractive."

He shrugged his disinterest. "I'm not in the mood."

"Nonsense, you're always in the mood."

"Maybe I'm getting picky," he said, and watched her temper flare. Candra didn't deal well with rejection. She was truly a beautiful woman, he thought, so beautiful she had always been able to get any man she wanted. Richard's rejection of her had startled her, shaken her out of her complacency, and now her lowly assistant was refusing her offer. Her world must be wobbling off its axis.

"Then enjoy your sulk," she said, her lips tight. "Oh, by the way. Get Sweeney's new pieces back from the framer. We won't be displaying her work anymore."

"Really." Interested in this latest development, he raised his eyebrows. "That's a shame, since her new stuff is better than anything she's ever done before. What's the problem?"

Her perfect fingernails tapped a tattoo on his desk. "Just a small complication. I found her and Richard together this morning."

Oho! Kai threw back his head and laughed. It wasn't the most politic thing to do, but the image was just so delicious. "So that's what ruffled your feathers! Did you catch them doing the nasty?"

She was annoyed that he'd laughed, he could tell. If her lips got any tighter, they would disappear. "I caught him coming out of her apartment. He must have spent the night."

Kai whistled. "He's a fast worker. I wouldn't tag Sweeney as an easy lay, so he must have put some effort into getting her." He put admiration into his tone, knowing Candra would be infuriated. "I wouldn't mind taking her for a ride myself."

"I don't see the attraction." The words were so stiff, they would barely come out of her mouth.

"You mean other than those big blue eyes and all that hair? Well, her tits are nice. They aren't very big, but they don't sag at all, and her ass is fine—"

"I don't need a rundown," Candra snapped, whirling away from the desk and going back into her office. Kai laughed softly. He was turned on, he realized. He liked baiting Candra, and envisioning Sweeney's body, imaging her naked, was exciting.

He kept that pleasant heat all during the morning, even while he was assisting some tourists from Omaha who wanted some "real art," in their words, to take back to Nebraska with them. Knowing instinctively what they wouldn't like, he steered them away from the abstract and modern, and smiled to himself as he showed them the last piece Sweeney had in the gallery. Candra would be furious if they bought it.

They did, to his delight.

At twelve-thirty he left the gallery and walked the eleven blocks to his apartment. A hotel would have been more convenient, but the woman he was meeting was afraid she would be recognized at a hotel. He had given her his key and knew she would be waiting for him. He would probably be late getting back to work, he thought.

She was cautious; she had relocked the door. He knocked once, and watched the peephole darken as she put her eye to it. She opened the door.

"Kai, darling, you're late."

Kai smiled. She had already taken off her clothes and was wearing his robe, the one he himself never wore but kept because women seemed to think they looked sexy in it. The belt was loosely tied, of course, and the robe open just enough to show most of one breast. She was in good shape, for a woman old enough to be his mother. There was no telling how many lifts and tucks a cosmetic surgeon had done on her.

"You look beautiful," he said as he took her in his arms and undid the robe, pushing it off her shoulders. Margo McMillan arched her fashionably thin body, offering him her breasts, and Kai performed as expected.

CHAPTER

THIRTEEN

The damn painting was calling her. It wasn't anything as overt as "Here, Sweeney Sweeney Sweeney," but nevertheless, she couldn't get it out of her mind.

She'd had a wonderful afternoon. Breakfast with Richard had been so relaxing she was able to push the ugly scene with Candra out of her mind. Not being a dummy, she realized Richard had intended exactly that. It was almost eerie, the way he seemed to read her every mood and anticipate exactly what she needed, but at the same time she couldn't stop reveling in his care. Having someone take care of her was such a novelty she wanted to enjoy every minute.

After Richard had brought her home from the diner and left her at the building entrance with a quick, domestic peck on the lips, having made a date for breakfast again tomorrow, Sweeney had gone humming up to her apartment. The scene with Candra, despite its awkwardness and nasty drama, had been a relief. Breaking her ties with Candra and the gallery would be so much easier now, with no regrets. She made a mental note to call the gallery and make arrangements to pick up the new pieces she had left there a few days before, as well as whatever old paintings were left.

Then she began to paint.

For the first time in a long while, it was joyous. She didn't worry about the colors being too lavish for reality; she simply let her instincts carry her. After doing a quick charcoal sketch on a canvas and brushing it off so that only the outline was left behind, she lost herself in the creation of a chubby toddler with dandelion hair, staring in awe up at a brilliant red balloon. She played with technique, completely smoothing and blending the colors she used for the baby, softening the outlines, so that he took on the realism of a snapshot. Everything around him, though, was an explosion of color and movement, intensified, slightly exaggerated, so that his surrounding world was a fantastical place begging for exploration.

It was the technique she used for the baby that jarred a memory of the shoes. She had used the same realistic technique on the shoe painting. Her concentration broken, she stepped back and wiped her hands on a cloth, frowning as she glanced over at the other canvas. She didn't want to think about it, but now all her former feelings about it came roaring back, like water that had been seeking a crack in the dam so it could burst through.

The woman the legs and shoes belonged to was dead, or would soon be dead. Sweeney knew that with every cell in her body. Her theory that these paintings were triggered only when someone she knew died was a bit thin, since she had only one instance on which to base it, but instinctively she knew she was on the right track. She would know this woman. But perhaps she wasn't dead yet, perhaps that was why Sweeney hadn't finished the painting, hadn't put a face to the woman. If she could hurry and finish the painting, anticipate the future, maybe she could do something to prevent the woman's death. Warn her against crossing the street, maybe. There weren't enough details in the painting yet to give any hint of location, not even whether it was indoors or out, but if she could *consciously* finish the painting instead of waiting for the night muse to move her—

The responsibilities of this new gift hit her like a runaway bus. Yes, *gift*. Not inconvenience, though it was damned inconvenient. Not a nuisance, though it could be annoying. For whatever reason, she had changed or been changed, and been given gifts. The traffic lights, the lush plants, the ability to know lines of dialogue on a television show before they were spoken, even seeing the ghosts—all that had been a prelude, a sort of building up, to this. It was as if the door to another world had opened slowly, perhaps because she wouldn't have been able to handle everything rushing at her at once.

The door probably still wasn't open all the way. The painting of Elijah Stokes had been done after the fact. This new painting, she was sure, was anticipating the future. As the door opened wider, her gifts would expand as her view of that new world widened. She would be able to warn people, prevent their deaths. She had no idea what the limits would be, because they seemed to be expanding all the time. Perhaps this gift wouldn't be limited to people she knew; perhaps there were other gifts waiting to manifest themselves.

She hadn't wanted this. She had been perfectly content in

her self-contained world, isolating herself from people and not letting anyone really touch her. She knew analysts would say that in her childhood she had learned to protect herself by mentally distancing herself from the people in her world, and she knew they would be right. But the change had opened her up, made her really see people, made her feel, and she didn't know if she would return to the old way even if she could. There was Richard now; she didn't know what she felt for him; she was afraid to even try to put a name to it, but she knew her life would be poorer without him in it. There was passion growing in her, passion he was carefully feeding, and she could never be content now if she didn't discover the full reach of it.

There was no going back. Instead of fighting the changes, or at best trying to ignore them, she should be opening herself up to the experience. For the first time in her life, she should *live*.

As much as she loved the painting of the baby and the balloon, she could no longer focus on it. She could see, from the corner of her eye, the other canvas. Waiting. Waiting for the night, when sleep lowered all her mental barriers, or perhaps just waiting. Perhaps she could do it now.

She approached the easel as one would a snake, cautiously, ready to run. Her heart hammered, and her breathing was quick and shallow. What was wrong with her? This was just a painting, even if it was a weird one. Okay, maybe not *just* a painting, but neither was it a snake. She knew art, knew the techniques, knew how to scale and shadow and foreshorten, how to manipulate light with the thickness of the paint, how to highlight or downplay with her choice of colors. Since art was the medium in which this particular gift was expressing herself, perhaps she could look at the painting strictly on that level: assess it on its artistic merits, and go from there.

Yes. She could do that. Calm descended on her. She took several deep breaths, just as insurance, and forced herself to study the composition objectively.

The composition and scale were good. The position of the woman's feet looked as if she had just fallen. The shoe lying on its side would have come off when she fell. They were nice black pumps, three-inch heels, and light gleamed on the rich leather. But they weren't right, she thought, frowning at them. The shoes weren't right. Something was missing.

She had no idea what it could be. All the basic parts of a pump were there: heel, sole, upper. There were endless designs and decorations one could put on shoes, however. This might be something she would have to do in her sleep, when she was open to suggestions.

The man's shoe disturbed her, not because there was just one, but because of the way it was positioned. He would be looking directly down at the woman. He was too close. A bystander wouldn't be so close. Anyone running up to give aid would be crouched beside her. A cop . . . Where would a cop be? An investigator would be crouched, she thought. Medics would be crouched. The way this shoe was positioned, the man was just . . . looking at her.

He had killed her.

The thought was a flash, electrifying in its surety. She was painting a murder scene.

She hurried to the phone, called Richard. When he answered she said, without preamble, "Was Elijah Stokes murdered?"

He hesitated. "Why do you ask?"

Sweeney gripped the phone tighter. "Because I think this shoe thing is the beginning of a murder scene. Don't try to protect me or humor me; just tell me the truth: was he murdered? Did you see something in the painting I missed? Is that why you contacted his son?"

"Yes," he said. "Look—I'm scheduled for a business dinner tonight, but I'll cancel it and be right over."

"No, don't do that. I'm okay, I've just been doing a lot of thinking. Besides, I'm working."

Another pause, then he gave a low laugh. "And don't bother you, right?"

"Right." She stopped, frowning. Having to consider some- one else's feelings when she wanted to work was a new concern for her. "Did that hurt your feelings?"

"Of course not." There was a hint of tenderness now.

"Good." She took a deep breath. "What made you think Mr. Stokes had been murdered? What did you see?"

"The head injury. You didn't paint any stairs, and he was obviously lying between two buildings. It looked like blunt-force trauma to me."

" 'Blunt-force trauma,' " she repeated. That wasn't laymen's lingo. She had the exciting sense of discovering a facet of Richard she hadn't suspected existed. "Do you have medical training?"

"Only in the rough first-aid stuff we needed in the field. I can set a simple fracture, rotate a dislocated joint back into place, stop bleeding. Things like that."

"But you know what blunt-force trauma looks like."

"I've seen it."

Somehow she had absorbed enough information about the military to know that, in general, only medics were given that kind of training. Of course, her information came from books and movies, so her impression might be wrong. But a medic would have had much more extensive training than what Richard had described. "Just what kind of army were you in?" she asked curiously.

"The United States Army," he said, amused again. She could almost see his lips curving. "But I was in a special unit. I was a Ranger."

She knew about forest rangers. She knew about the Lone Ranger. Other than that, her memory bank was empty of information on rangers. "My military experience is kind of limited. What do Rangers do?"

"They wear really snazzy black berets."

"Other than that."

"Rough stuff. It's a specialized infantry organization."

"Specialized in what?"

He sighed. "Raids."

"Raids."

"You sound like a parrot."

"You were a *commando,* weren't you?" Her voice rang with astonishment. She had known nothing but gentleness from him. No, not gentleness. That was the wrong word. Tender was more accurate. But determined, too. And she had seen firsthand how he could affect people with just a look, seen how easily he dominated Senator McMillan.

"That's one term for it, yes. Honey, I'm thirty-nine years old. I've been out of the army for fifteen years. What I did back then doesn't matter."

"In a way it does. You knew what blunt-force trauma to the head looked like, knew to ask questions. Knowing Mr. Stokes was murdered gives me a different view of what I'm doing now. I think the murderer is standing looking down at her."

He followed her thoughts with ease. "Because of the way the man's shoe is positioned?"

"If he were there to help her, or investigate, wouldn't he be crouched down? A bystander wouldn't stand so close. I'm going to try working on the painting while I'm awake, see what happens. I don't think she's dead yet; I think I'm picking up on something in the future and that's why I'm doing just a little at a time. If I can finish it, see who she is, then maybe I can stop it from happening."

He said, very gently, "I don't think you'll be able to finish the painting until it's too late."

His concern furled around her like tender arms. "But I have to try," she whispered, her throat suddenly tight. She swallowed. She refused to cry in front of him again. When she cried, she wanted it to be about something real important, like being cold.

"I know. Got a pen?"

She reached for the pen and pad beside the phone. "Got it."

"Here's my cell phone number." He rattled it off. "I'll have the phone with me tonight. Call me if anything happens and you go into shock again."

"How many numbers do you have?" she muttered. "That's three."

"Well, there's the fax number, too, if you want it."

"I don't think I'll be sending you any faxes."

He chuckled, then said, "Take care of yourself. The last few days have been rough on you. Don't let this get the upper hand."

"I'll be careful," she promised, and went back to the studio warmed by the ease with which they communicated, the sense of being linked. No matter how upsetting this situation got, she wasn't alone.

She stared at the painting for a long time. Assuming she was looking at a murder scene changed her perspective. Picking up a stick of charcoal, she lightly sketched in the logical position of the woman's body, given the position of her legs. And if the man's right foot was *here,* then his left foot would be *here.* No, that was wrong. The angle was too severe. She needed a more direct angle, not exactly head-on but close to it.

She knew instinctively when she got it right. Her fingers moved rapidly over the canvas, sketching a rough outline of two people around the details she had already painted.

When she finished, she was trembling, as exhausted as if she had worked for days instead of—of however long she had worked. Glancing out the window, she saw night had fallen. She had no idea what time it was, but her stomach growled a warning that it was a long time past supper. She was a little chilly, but nothing unusual. Her efforts hadn't triggered that scary, bone-deep cold, at least not immediately. She had no idea how she would feel in a few hours.

She rubbed her eyes, then remembered her hands were black with charcoal. Muttering under her breath, she went into the bathroom and peered in the mirror. The black smudges all over her face weren't a surprise. She washed her face and hands, then went into the kitchen.

Soup was always good. It was fast and hot. She opened a can of chicken noodle soup and nuked it. What did Richard eat at business dinners? she wondered. More to the point, would he ever expect her to eat *with* him at those business dinners? The prospect wasn't a pleasant one. She would manage, she decided. If necessary, she would even buy some high heels.

Good God, this was serious. She should be running as far and fast as she could. Instead she sipped her chicken noodle soup and smiled a little at the lengths to which she was willing to go for Richard, should he ask.

She showered and went to bed, and woke a little after dawn

feeling warm and relaxed. She was almost disappointed; lying in Richard's arms wasn't exactly a hardship, no matter how cold she was.

She lay there for a while, enjoying the warmth. An electric blanket wasn't as good as Richard, but she would have to make do. She daydreamed for a while, smiling, before noticing that the sunlight wasn't getting any brighter.

She sat up and looked out the window. Fog pressed against the panes, white and a little luminous, as if it were just thin enough to allow a little sunshine through. The light was strangely reflective, filling all the shadows in the room the way sunshine on snow did.

Afterward, she didn't remember getting out of bed. She got dressed, in her usual thick socks, sweatshirt, and jeans. The coffee hadn't started brewing yet—she had got up too early—so she turned off the timer and turned on the maker herself. Then she went into the studio, because this white light was too unusual to miss.

She knew exactly what was missing from the high-heeled pumps.

Twenty minutes later she stepped back, blinking. The heels weren't solid. A small gold ball formed the middle of each heel. The shoes were very distinctive, impossibly stylish. If she had ever seen a pair like them before, she would have remembered.

And the skirt . . . the skirt was fuller than she had sketched it last night. Flirty. *Black.* The woman was wearing a black dress.

In some corner of her mind, she laughed. This was New York City; what else would the woman be wearing but black?

Hours later, the ringing of the phone jerked her out of her trance. She shuddered and stepped back, for a moment unsure of where she was or what that noise meant. Then she realized it was the phone and raced to answer it.

"Are you all right?" Richard demanded, and she realized she should have called him.

"I was," she said, still more in a daze than out of it. "Nothing happened last night. But this morning—I was painting. I just *knew* how it should look. What time is it?"

"Nine-thirty."

She had been working for almost four hours. She remembered very little of it.

CHAPTER FOURTEEN

She was wrapped in a blanket when Richard arrived, a freshly nuked cup of coffee in her hand. She was cold, but the cold wasn't unbearable, at least not yet. He bent down for a quick kiss, then started to take her in his arms to battle the chill.

"Wait," she said. "I want you to see the painting first."

He went with her into the studio and in silence studied the canvas. The scene was graphic in its violence. The woman's body was sprawled in a pool of blood, which had soaked into a pale carpet. Her chic black dress had been slashed to pieces, and one arm, the only one Sweeney had completed, was covered with wounds.

The man standing over her was relaxed, the knife he had used in his right hand, which was hanging at his side. Working from his shoes up, she had completed him to just above the waist. He wore black pants, perhaps jeans, though jeans were a bit incongruous with the wing tips. She had also painted the beginnings of a black shirt.

"A burglar, maybe," Richard said with the cool distance in his voice that said he had switched into his analytical mode. "They're both in black, but she looks as if she's been to a party. The shoes are wrong, though; a burglar would wear track shoes, or something else with a soft sole."

"I thought there was something strange about the shoes, too. They look awkward." She didn't like the way she had done the feet; they were vaguely out of proportion. But when she had begun studying how she could correct them, the mental image refused to form. Perhaps she was just exhausted and she would be able to think better after she had rested.

"I need to get this finished," she said, and even though she heard the fretful tone, she couldn't do anything about it. She was just about an inch short of whining. "I have to know who she is."

"Honey—" He clasped her shoulders and turned her toward him. "You have to assume you won't know until after the fact. That's the way it was with Elijah Stokes—"

"But this thing, whatever it is, is getting stronger all the time. Or maybe I'm just getting better at it. What I'm painting now is in the future, so why shouldn't the scope broaden and let me see her identity before it's too late?"

"This might not be a burglary that went sour. This might be a planned murder."

She didn't follow him. "What difference would that make?"

"The plan could already be formed. If I were going to commit murder, I'd have it planned down to the ground. So what you're picking up on could be a plan that exists *now,* not in the future."

She gave him a sour look, or at least as sour as she could make it when she was shaking like a leaf. "Don't be so analytical," she said, even though she knew he was right.

"Being analytical is how I got rich. Come on; there's nothing you can do about this right now. At least when the painting is complete, you'll also have the murderer's face. You probably can't save her, but you can help in other ways." With her firmly clamped against his side, he began easing her toward the door.

"You're handling me, right? I hate being handled. I'm not one of those temperamental *artistes* who get hysterical if the least thing goes wrong."

"I know," he said soothingly, and smiled at the ferocious look she threw him.

He got her settled on the couch, in his lap, with the blanket wrapped around them. He wasn't going to take his shirt off today, she thought, disappointed. Nor was he going to lie down with her. She understood; the temptation was just too great. The transfer of body heat wasn't as efficient with their clothes on, but neither was the need as great.

He held her locked tight against him, absorbing the force of her shivering. "I didn't think it would happen this time," she said, with her face buried against his chest. "I was awake. I worked on the painting last night and felt fine, so why am I cold this morning?"

"Depth of involvement, maybe, or the length of time you worked."

Trust Richard, she thought, to come up with a reasonable, logical explanation for what was innately illogical. At least he took her seriously and didn't assume she was having panic attacks or was hysterical. He believed her, about something she herself had a difficult time believing.

She lay quietly for a time, letting his heat soak through her skin, and felt herself begin to grow drowsy as she warmed. With this to look forward to, she was beginning to think getting severe chills wasn't such a bad thing. Remembering the time he had stripped them both down to their underwear made her breasts tighten and caused an ache deep inside. Maybe, she thought mischievously, if she put off calling him until she was really, really cold, he would do that again. Her entire body flushed as she remembered the explosion of pleasure she had experienced just rocking against him. She wanted to do that again. Often.

Sitting in his lap, she discovered, wasn't much better than lying down with him, in terms of temptation. She ached with a physical need that shook her with its intensity. His erection was rock hard against her hip, and only sheer determination kept her from squirming around until she was astride him. "Sheer" described her determination very well. It was gossamer thin, and getting thinner every day.

He stroked her hair back from her temple and pressed his lips to the fragile skin. "Good news," he murmured. "Candra has an appointment to sign the papers tomorrow. She would have done it today, but there had to be some additions and corrections made. I've already arranged to have the petition come before a judge next week."

She tilted her head back a little, staring at him. Considering the well-known backlog in New York City's civil court, she was astounded. He had "arranged" a small miracle. "How did you manage that?"

"Money." His tone was careless. "I have it, so people come to me for favors. I collected on a lot of debts." His hand on the back of her head, he settled her against him once more. His mouth lightly brushed her temple, and over to her eyelid. "After next week, when you get cold, I'll be able to warm you from the inside out."

Oh, God, he managed it now. Her heart leaped, and her pulse rate jumped to double time. "You're doing just fine as it is," she gasped.

"The way you shake and shudder, I won't even have to do any work. All I'll have to do is set you in place, then lie back and enjoy the ride."

Laughter burst out of her. Her arms were confined by the blanket he had wrapped around her, but she punched him with as much force as she could muster. Grinning, he subdued her by the simple method of kissing her.

She had never before had so much fun, she thought as she relaxed in his arms, her head cradled on his shoulder. Even under the circumstances, she enjoyed every moment with him. She managed to work one hand free and curled it around the back of his neck, nestling her fingers in his hair. The sensation was delicious; his hair, silky soft, was warm close to his scalp and cool on the outside. Evidently he detected some remnant of rebellion, because he kept on kissing her.

She wanted him to deepen the kisses. She waited for him to do so. But he pulled back with a sigh, his face taut, and she knew his determination was in the same shape as hers. His dark eyes were heavy-lidded, and a faint flush rode his high cheekbones. "If this keeps up, I won't be able to even kiss you," he said gruffly.

"Keeps up, or *stays* up?" She meant to tease, but her voice came out too husky for that.

The sound he made was more growl than laugh. "Either. Both." He breathed hard through his nostrils. "Talk. Distract me."

"What do you want to talk about?" Her mind felt mushy.

She didn't know if she could muster a conversation, at least not a detailed one.

"Anything. *Were you really born in Italy?*"

"Really. Florence, to be exact. My mother felt the need to make some sort of pilgrimage—for her art, you understand. I was two weeks early, which evidently really fouled up her itinerary. I couldn't keep the formula down and was losing weight, so I stayed in the hospital while she salvaged as much of her trip as she could. Hardy woman, my mother. She was back on the road two days after having me. When she was ready to come home, she swung by the hospital to pick me up, but when she tried to leave the country, there was a problem with the paperwork—she hadn't done any of it—so I ended up staying another week until everything was straightened out."

She said it humorously, because she had long since become accustomed to her mother's lack of concern for her offspring—not just for Sweeney, but for her brother, too. Richard didn't laugh, though. He didn't even smile. His gaze turned flinty. "Do you mean," he said in an almost toneless voice, "that your mother left her sick baby in the hospital while she resumed her *vacation?*"

"Yeah, well, that's Mom." Sweeney tried to lighten the mood with an awkward laugh. It didn't work.

"Where was your father?"

"Working on a movie somewhere, I guess. I don't think I've ever heard."

Fascinated, she watched his jaw set. If it got any harder, it would probably shatter under the pressure. His reaction startled her. She had long since stopped worrying about her parents' behavior; she neither justified or analyzed. "Hey," she said mildly, "they didn't beat me. They didn't pay any attention to us, period, but there are worse things."

"Us?"

"I have one full brother, and several half-brothers and -sisters from my father's various marriages. It's possible he's added to the total since I last heard from him."

"Are you close to your brother?"

"No. He went by the 'if you can't beat them' philosophy. His goal in life is to be stoned and trendy. I haven't heard from him in . . . oh, I guess it's been three years or longer."

"Jesus," he muttered.

"I sent everyone a postcard when I moved, so they would have my current address and telephone number, but I haven't heard from anyone. I don't know if their addresses were current. What about your family?"

"I don't have any immediate family. My father died when I was three, and my mother and I lived with my grandfather. He died eight years ago, and Mom's been dead five years. I have two uncles and an aunt on my father's side, and a lot of cousins, most of them in Virginia. I get home for family reunions and the odd Christmas every now and then, but Candra hated being around my relatives, so I always went alone."

Just from the way he talked, she could tell he enjoyed being with his relatives. She tried to imagine a big, noisy family reunion where everyone was glad to see each other. "Excuse me while my mind boggles," she said. "I can't imagine a family reunion in *my* family."

"What do you do for Thanksgiving and Christmas?"

"Nothing." She shrugged. "Work. We aren't big on holidays, either."

"We'll spend the holidays in Virginia, then," he said.

She sat up, surprised. "You mean you want to take me with you?"

"Well, I sure as hell don't mean to leave you here alone."

Now she was more than surprised; she was downright astonished. She hadn't thought about their relationship in terms of the future. She was so new to this relationship business that she had no idea what the normal expectations would be; she certainly hadn't thought about where she would spend the holidays.

"Do you think we'll still be . . . you know?" she said hesitantly.

"Oh, yeah." His tone was as confident as hers was hesitant.

"Well." She rubbed her nose. "Okay."

He grinned. "Don't overwhelm me with your enthusiasm." He glanced at his watch. "I have an appointment I need to cancel if—"

"No, go ahead," she said swiftly, sitting up. "I'm toasty warm; I was just enjoying sitting here."

He eyed her, judging her color for himself. He took her hand to feel if her fingers were cold. They weren't, and he dropped a quick kiss on them. "Okay. You know how to reach me if you need me. I have business dinners tonight and tomorrow night, but after that my week is clear." He winked at her. "I think it's time for a second date."

At eleven-thirty that night, Candra let herself into her apartment. She usually loved parties, but she hadn't been able to enjoy the one tonight, even though it had been attended by a lot of her favorite people. She couldn't stop thinking about the coming day. Tomorrow, she would sign the papers on the divorce settlement, and she couldn't help thinking that the best part of her life was over. She would likely never see Richard again. Perhaps someday she would meet another man who could compare with him, but she didn't really think so.

He had won. If there was a winner, there had to be a loser, and she was it. She had played him all wrong, because her mistake was in trying to play him at all. If she had simply given him his freedom with the least fuss possible, and tried to salvage some dignity for herself, he would likely have been more generous. Richard couldn't be coerced; it was that simple.

She felt ineffably weary. Even though she had no doubt Carson would come through with the money, at the moment she couldn't summon up much enthusiasm for the future.

She had left lamps on in the living room and foyer because she didn't like walking into a dark apartment. Once she hadn't worried about anything like that, because Richard had been with her. Sometimes, when she couldn't bear the thought of being alone, she would have Kai spend the night, but tonight she would rather be alone than be with him. He seemed to enjoy seeing Richard get the best of her. She *would* fire him, she thought. His looks were undoubtedly an asset to the gallery, but there were a lot of good-looking young men in New York who were looking for an in to the art world, and a side door was as good as a front one.

She dropped her tiny antique beaded purse on the hall table and set the locks. Her heels tapped on the faux marble tiles as she crossed the foyer and stepped onto the plush oatmeal-colored Berber pile of the living room carpet. She caught movement out of the corner of her eye and whirled, panic momentarily robbing her of her voice. Pressing her hand to her chest as if she could calm her racing heart, she said, "How in hell did you get into the building?"

"I have a key. Convenient, isn't it?"

"A key! I don't believe you. How would you get a key to my apartment?"

"You know the old saying, it isn't what you know, it's who you know."

"I don't care who you know; no one has a key to this apartment but me."

"Obviously, my dear, you're wrong."

The smugness rasped on Candra's nerves. She let her gaze drift downward, and put a hint of contempt in her tone. "Are you going to a costume party, or have you mistaken the date for Halloween?"

"I'm not the one who's made a mistake. You are."

There didn't seem to be any point in pretending ignorance. Candra was too tired and too angry to try, anyway. "This is because of the money. Look, it isn't personal. I need money, a lot of it, and this is the only way I can think of to get it. It's a one-time thing."

Her assurance seemed to pass unheard. "Did you really think I'd let you wreck what I've worked so hard for?"

"You knew what you were getting into, so don't play the victim."

"What I know is that if there's a victim, I won't be it." The words were soft, almost serene. The approach was not.

Suddenly alarmed, Candra backed up. "Get away from me! Get out of my apartment."

"You aren't giving the orders now, darling." A gloved hand lifted, and in it was a long-bladed kitchen knife.

Candra made an instant decision, feinting to her left as if she would make a break for the door. Immediately she cut back right and dived for the telephone. It wasn't a cordless; she had gone for style over convenience and chosen an ornate European desk model. She had time to punch in the 9 before the blade slashed downward, catching her on the arm. She screamed and threw herself backward, catching her right heel on the leg of the telephone table and sprawling on her back. She rolled, still screaming, and managed to gain her feet before the knife plunged into her back. An agony that was both icy and burning-hot speared through her, almost making her faint.

Desperately, her vision dimming, Candra threw herself forward, away from that searing blade. "No no no," she heard herself babbling. She lurched to the side, trying to throw herself over the back of the sofa to gain some time, but she was clumsy from shock. Her elegant high heel caught on the carpet and her ankle turned with a sickening wrench that almost overrode the pain in her back. The shoe twisted off, and she fell on her hands and knees. Another tongue of cold fire pierced her, below her right shoulder blade. And again, farther down in her side.

The pain convulsed her, drew her body tight with agony. She couldn't even scream. Her mouth gaped open in a silent battle for air, but her lungs refused to cooperate. Somehow she rolled again, gained her hands and knees, and crawled. The effort was superhuman, and yet she knew it wasn't enough. She knew.

She toppled over onto the thick carpet and feebly kicked out. Through a dark haze she saw the blade flashing down again, and she managed to raise her left arm. She felt the shock of the blow, but no pain. Then there was another thud, this time in her chest; her ribs gave under the force of the impact. Another blow, into the soft flesh of her belly.

She gasped, flopping on the carpet like a landed fish. Time slowed to a feeble crawl, or perhaps it only seemed as if a long time passed. The terrible pain ebbed, to be replaced by a growing lassitude. Something must have happened to all the lamps; all she could see was a faint glimmer of light coming through the darkness. She needed to move . . . The knife . . . but the knife wasn't there anymore. She could just lie there, in the dark, feeling an odd coldness spread through her body, feeling her heartbeat slow . . . slow . . . slow . . . stop.

Her assailant watched the moment of death. The disgusting release of bladder and bowels was somehow pleasing; the bitch deserved to be found in her own embarrassing waste.

The scene had already been set. The apartment had been thoroughly searched, but no interesting packet had turned up, damn it. That was a problem, a big one. It was a good thing they had been smart enough to take precautions.

Thank God for the phone call warning that Candra had left the party early and was on her way home, otherwise the outcome could have been very different. What money Candra kept in the apartment, as well as her jewelry, had been gathered. The refrigerator door was open, which would suggest a burglar had been in the kitchen when Candra surprised him. That would also explain the use of one of the knives from the expensive set Candra kept next to the cutting board: a weapon of opportunity.

The gloved fingers opened, let the knife drop to the floor beside the body. The knife belonged here; it couldn't be tied to anyone but the victim.

A screwdriver was taken from a hip pocket. A few minutes at the door with the tool made the lock look as if it had been carefully jimmied. No real damage done, not enough for a woman coming home to a dimly lit hallway to notice, but the police certainly would. An unforced entry would mean she either opened the door herself, which would imply she knew the person, or that a key had been used. A forced entry would indicate a stranger.

The money and the jewelry—mostly jewelry, very little cash—were in a small black bag. That bag would be put in a very, very safe place—just in case it were ever needed.

CHAPTER FIFTEEN

Sweeney left her bed a little after three A.M. She made the trip through the dark apartment without stumbling or hesitating. Her expression was calmly distant; she scarcely blinked. Her heartbeat was slow and regular.

When she reached the unfinished painting, still propped on the easel, she stood before it for a long time with her head slightly tilted, as if listening to some unseen voice.

Her movements were slow, dreamy, as she mixed a rich brown pigment and then darkened it with black. When the shade was that of dark, lustrous mink, she began to paint, her precise brushstrokes re-creating a fan of dark hair, spread in disarray across an oatmeal carpet.

The face was much more difficult, the expression not one she had ever seen. The late summer dawn crept closer as she painstakingly filled in a lovely face that had turned ashen, dark eyes open and glazed in death, lipsticked mouth slack. The studio was already filling with light when she methodically put her brushes into a can of turpentine, capped the tubes of paint, and returned to bed as quietly as she had left it.

The sun was streaming brightly in the window when Sweeney woke. She was huddled in a tight ball, her arms wrapped around herself in an unconscious effort to conserve heat. The chill was incredible, colder and deeper than it had ever been before. She was shaking so violently the bed trembled.

Richard. She needed Richard.

Whimpering, she managed to crawl to the side of the bed. The red numerals on the digital clock were dimmed by the bright light, but they were undoubtedly a one, a zero, a three, and a four. Ten-thirty-four.

Why hadn't Richard called?

He should have called. If she didn't call him, then he called her. How fast their routine had been established! She had come to rely on him even faster. His absence shook her, rattled a newborn security that she was just beginning to believe.

"Richard," she whispered, as if she could call him to her. Her voice was thin and weak.

Don't panic, don't panic, she thought. She could do this. She wasn't likely to die, she reassured herself; she just thought that she would. Whatever weird rules governed this psychic stuff, she had never heard that practicing it killed off the practitioner. Not that she'd had time to research clairvoyance or anything like that; she had concentrated on ghosts. Maybe a psychic only got one shot, like a male praying mantis.

Call Richard. Maybe he overslept. He had probably been out late on that business dinner.

She reached for the bedside phone, but as she did a sickening certainty shot through her. The painting. She was beginning to notice a trend: the more work she did, the colder she was when the reaction hit her. This was the coldest she had been.

During the night, she had put a face on the victim.

Urgency drove her to her feet. She stumbled to the studio, her coordination slow and clumsy. She had to know, she had to know *now*. Every second could count. Richard thought she did the work after the fact, but deep inside she wasn't certain, and that uncertainty kept her feet moving, even though they felt as if they didn't belong to her and didn't go quite where she wanted to place them. She wobbled across the room, wincing at the effort it took to move, at the deep internal aches that were beginning to make themselves felt.

Then she reached the painting, and wished she hadn't. She hung in front of it, blood roaring in her ears, shaking so hard she clenched her teeth to keep from breaking them.

Candra.

She stared at the canvas until her eyes hurt, hoping the features would suddenly rearrange themselves into someone else's. She was mistaken. She was seeing only a superficial likeness, and because Candra was so prominent in her life these days, naturally she jumped to that conclusion.

But the face was eerily accurate, with the photographic quality of a Gerhard Richter painting. And Sweeney knew she was very, very good at portraits.

Candra.

Oh God, oh God.

She didn't know Candra's number. It would be unlisted, because Candra had once said she never allowed her number to be published. The gallery. She should be at the gallery, and Sweeney knew that number.

She made it to the living room and the cordless phone. But the phone rang and rang, and finally an answering machine picked up. Frustrated, Sweeney disconnected. Her hands shook so violently she dropped the phone, and when she bent to pick it up, her strength seemed to give out and she just kept going, down to the floor.

She landed on the phone, a hard plastic corner digging into her ribs. Groaning, she managed to sit up and cradled the phone in her lap while she punched in Richard's number.

One of his assistants answered, her voice strangely muted.

"This is S-Sweeney. Is Richard in?"

"I'm sorry, Ms. Sweeney, but he won't be in today." She hesitated, then said, "Mrs. Worth—Candra—has been killed."

"No," Sweeney moaned, almost weeping.

"The housekeeper found the . . . the body when she arrived this morning. Mr. Worth is with the police right now."

She *was* crying after all, Sweeney discovered. She gulped, and in a thick voice said, "Tell Richard I c-called."

"I will, Ms. Sweeney, as soon as possible."

So Richard had been right; she couldn't help, couldn't stop anything. Sobbing, Sweeney rested her head on her drawn-up knees. What good was any of this, then, if she couldn't do anything about the horrors she painted? Why suffer this savage chill, when there was no opportunity to keep bad things from happening? There should be a payback, something to make this pain worthwhile.

Her leg muscles suddenly protested their prolonged tension

and knotted into cramps so vicious she cried out. Panting, crying, she dug the heels of her hands into her thighs and stroked toward her knees, trying to knead the muscles into relaxing. Over and over she did it, but her muscles seem to knot again just behind the stroking motion.

Once she had seen a trainer rub a cramp out of the calf of a football player. He had used both hands in a back-and-forth motion. She held her breath to steady herself and placed both hands on one thigh. She could feel the knotted muscle between her palms. A half-cry of pain burst from her throat as she began that brisk washing motion, but within seconds the pain began to ebb, at least in that thigh.

With that leg finally relaxed, she did the same thing to her right thigh. That cramp was more stubborn, returning as soon as she stopped the massage. She kept at it for five minutes and finally her thigh relaxed. Her entire body felt like a balloon with a leak; she toppled over, going boneless, without the strength to sit up any longer.

Heat. She had to have heat. Richard wouldn't be coming. He was still legally Candra's husband; he would be giving information to the police, filling out reports, probably identifying Candra's body, making arrangements. Sweeney had his cell phone number, but calling him was out of the question. She had to take care of this herself.

The electric blanket wouldn't help. Hot coffee would help a little, but not enough. Body heat was moist heat, because the body was mostly water. That was what she needed: moist heat. The shower wouldn't be enough. She needed to immerse herself in hot water.

She crawled into the bathroom, dragging herself like a wounded animal. Her arms and legs barely functioned, and she could feel her thoughts slowing.

She never took a tub bath; she always showered. She stared at the lever that closed the drain for several long moments before she figured out how to work it, though of course she knew. The cold was making her stupid.

She turned the hot water on full blast and watched steam begin to fill the air. A remnant of common sense kicked in, and she turned on the cold water, too. If she got the water too hot, she would scald herself, and even if it wasn't hot enough to scald, it could still kill; a lot of people had died in hot tubs when prolonged immersion caused heart failure. She had to be careful.

She put her hand under the faucet, and blessed heat poured over her fingers. It felt so good she put the other hand under the faucet, too, lying with her body draped over the edge of the tub because she didn't have the strength to sit up.

When the water was deep enough to reach the overflow drain, she turned off the faucet and crawled into the tub without bothering to take off her pajamas. She almost howled as she sank into the hot water, the heat was so intense. Her toes throbbed. She stared at her bare feet through the clear water; they looked white with cold, almost shrunken.

She sank down until her chin touched the surface of the water. Tendrils of hair floated around her shoulders. Her trembling sent little wavelets sloshing to-and-fro. "Please please please," she heard herself saying, over and over. Please let this work. If it didn't, she would have to call 911. Probably she should already have done it, but a part of her just couldn't believe a chill was serious.

She began to warm. It was a gradual process, the heat of the water transferring to her flesh. The shivering began to dwindle, so that it wasn't ceaseless, letting her relax between the episodes. Exhausted, she laid her head against the sloping back of the tub. Always before, when she was warm, she got sleepy, and the colder she had been the sleepier she got. She would have to be careful not to fall asleep in the tub.

The water began to cool. Her fingers and toes grew pink and wrinkled. She let out some of the water, then turned on the hot water to refill the tub, but she forced herself to sit up. The danger of falling asleep was a real one, and so was staying in the water too long. Just a few more minutes, she promised herself.

Sometime during those few minutes she began crying again. Like most people, Candra had been neither wholly good nor wholly bad. Until she had seen Sweeney and Richard together, she had always been warm and friendly. Candra's support had meant a lot to Sweeney's career.

Sweeney regretted the way they had parted. She didn't, couldn't, regret her involvement with Richard, but the timing could have been better. If the divorce had been final, if Candra hadn't been bitter about the settlement— There were so many things to which she could tack an "if," and not one of them could be changed.

She didn't dare stay in the water any longer. She opened the drain and hauled herself, trembling, to a standing position. Her muscles felt like boiled noodles. She removed her dripping pajamas, peeling them off and hanging them over the shower curtain rod to drip. Toweling off required immense effort. She finally had to sit down on the toilet lid to finish drying her legs and feet.

She blotted the dripping ends of her hair. She had to go back to bed, at least for a while, but she didn't want to do it with wet hair. That seemed to be asking for another chill. Her eyelids drooped, and she sagged sideways, catching herself at the last moment. She couldn't wait for her hair to dry, either. She could always cut it off, she thought, and then shook her head as a measure of common sense kicked in again. She plucked a dry towel from the stack and wrapped it around her head, tucking all the wet ends up under the cloth. That was the best she could do.

She wobbled her way to bed. The electric blanket was still on. Naked, she crawled between the blissfully warm sheets and was asleep as soon as her muscles relaxed.

Detective Joseph Aquino was a burly guy with shrewd eyes and a homely, lived-in face that invited confidences. Detective H. E. Ritenour was lean and more pugnacious, his sandy hair cut military short, and he had a habit of fixing his pale gaze on suspects and not blinking until they began to squirm.

Richard didn't play games. He didn't fidget, and he would bet the discipline trained into him would outlast the detective's technique. He wondered if Ritenour would stare until his eyes dried out.

When they had come to his house early that morning to tell him of Candra's death, he had known immediately he was at the top of their list of most-likely suspects. He kept his behavior low-key and cooperated with everything they asked of him, functioning despite the shock that tried to numb his brain.

He hadn't loved Candra in a long time, and for the past year had actively hated her, but he had never wanted her dead. He just wanted her out of his life. Now she was, in the most final way. The death of someone you knew well was always a shock, like a wound in your concept of reality. The world had changed, and for a while you had to struggle with the abrupt alteration.

Because their divorce wasn't final, he was still legally responsible for the arrangements. He identified her body, and though he had seen bodies before, that had been in military action, undeclared war, where they had gone in knowing there could be casualties and accepted the risk, doing it anyway. This was different. This was the woman with whom he had shared his life, even if only superficially, for ten years. He had slept with her, made love to her, and, in the beginning at least, loved her. All he could feel now was regret, but it was genuine.

He called her parents, who had moved from Manhattan when her father lost almost every penny he had in some bad stock decisions. Now Charles and Helene Maxson lived just outside Ithaca, their circumstances so reduced Candra had always invited them to the city rather than spend a night in what she called "little more than a shack," though Richard thought the brick ranch house was upper-middle-class and a lot better than what most people had. But Candra had grown up in wealth, while Richard had a different perspective.

Because of the circumstances, Richard quietly told Charles he would defer to him and Helene in the necessary decisions. Candra was their daughter; their grief was sharp. The location and means of interment would be their choice, as would the service.

Every step he took, Richard was aware of the pair of detectives. One or both of them was always within earshot when he was on the phone. Any resentment he felt was immediately controlled, because they had a job to do and murder statistics showed that any time a woman was murdered, either her husband or boyfriend was the one most likely to have done the deed. Because he and Candra had been embroiled in a divorce, that tipped the percentages heavily against him. So he remained calm, even when the detectives finally took the step of taking him into precinct headquarters and sat down with him in an interrogation room, a small, dingy square space occupied by three chairs and a beat-up table that wobbled.

He was read his rights and asked if he wanted to call his attorney. "No," he said, surprising both of them.

"You want a cup of coffee, some water?" Ritenour asked.

"No, thank you," Richard said, and managed to hide a small spurt of amusement. That was a basic trick; offer the suspect anything he wanted to drink, keep the coffee coming, and pretty soon he would be squirming with the need to piss. Only they wouldn't let him go; they would keep him there, asking the same questions over and over, maybe phrased a little differently, while the sap's bladder got more and more uncomfortable.

He made himself as comfortable as possible in the chair to which they had steered him, which made him wonder if the front legs had been shortened a little so he would slide forward every time he tried to relax. He put both feet solidly on the floor and kept them there.

Detective Ritenour started. "The housekeeper says you and Mrs. Worth were divorcing."

"That's right." Richard kept his tone neutral. "We've been separated a year."

"Divorces are messy things. I've been through two of them myself."

"They aren't pleasant, no."

"People get all upset. It's understandable. You'd have a lot to lose, wouldn't you, Mr. Worth?"

"In what way?"

"C'mon, you're worth a lot of money, no pun intended. A woman can take a man to the cleaners, get everything he's worked for, unless he's smart enough to protect himself from the beginning. You didn't have much money when you and Mrs. Worth married, though, did you?"

"No."

"So there wouldn't have been any need for a prenup then."

"Gentlemen." Richard said it quietly, because he sympathized with them. He wanted them to succeed. "If you're asking if I stood to lose half of everything I own, the answer is no. When we married, my wife's family was wealthy. Her father insisted on a prenuptial agreement. His intent was to protect his money from me in case of divorce, but the agreement went both ways. She kept what was hers; I kept what was mine. Candra couldn't touch anything."

He saw the quick glance that went between the two detectives. One of their motives had just gone down the drain.

"You'll have a copy of that agreement, of course."

"My lawyer has it. Gavin Welles. Candra's attorney, Olivia Yu, also has a copy."

They made a note of the names.

"The housekeeper said you and Mrs. Worth had been having some trouble coming to an agreement about the settlement."

The housekeeper had said a lot, Richard thought. "Candra wasn't happy with the settlement. She wanted more. We had several arguments about it, but she had agreed to sign the papers. We had an appointment with the attorneys today, at one o'clock, to sign the papers." Automatically Richard glanced at his watch and saw that it was after two already. He hadn't called Gavin to cancel the appointment, but Gavin would know. Someone would have called him. Olivia, probably. One of Candra's friends would have called Olivia immediately, in the guise of passing along the news but really trying to find out some of the details.

The news that Candra had agreed to a settlement took away another of their motives. The two detectives looked thoughtful.

"Did you have a key to her new apartment?" Detective Aquino asked, the first words he had spoken since they entered the interrogation room.

Richard shook his head. "No, not likely. I've never been in her apartment."

"Never?"

"Never." Never was an absolute term, difficult to support. Knowing they were now thinking along the lines of fiber samples, he said, "She came to my town house a couple of times to talk, and to collect her belongings, but I never went to her place."

They hid their disappointment well. Any cross-contamination of fiber samples between the two dwellings now had an explanation. Everything Richard had said was something that could be easily verified, and they knew it.

"Mrs. Worth was a popular woman. Were you jealous of her male friends?"

Richard couldn't help it. He laughed. The sound wasn't particularly humorous. "No."

"When she filed for divorce—"

"She didn't file. I did."

"You did?" Another quick look between them. "Why was that?"

Richard had never told another soul why his break with Candra had been so abrupt and final. Sweeney knew, but only because she had been present during that last argument. He didn't want to say anything against Candra now, especially not anything that would get back to her parents.

"I don't want her family to know," he finally said. "It would hurt them."

"Know what, Mr. Worth?"

"I found out she had an abortion two years ago. She hadn't told me she was pregnant."

Both men sat back, frowning.

"I guess you were upset," Detective Aquino said.

Richard flashed him a disbelieving look. "A little." He couldn't hold back the sarcastic edge. "Our marriage was over right then. I never wanted to see her again. I threw her out, changed the locks on the town house, and filed for divorce the next day."

"Were you still angry with her?"

"Bitter. Regretful."

"Where were you last night, Mr. Worth?"

"I had a business dinner at the Four Seasons." That too would be easily verified.

"What time did you leave?"

"Ten-thirty."

"Where did you go then?"

"Home."

"Were you alone?"

"Yes."

"Did you make any calls, talk to anyone?"

"No. I did some stock analysis on my computer, cleared up E-mail messages, that kind of thing. The time will be on the computer log."

"What time did you stop work?"

"After midnight. Closer to one, I guess." He had no idea what time they thought Candra had been killed, though he had heard someone remark she had still been wearing the dress she wore to a party. Logically, that would put the time of death close to when she arrived home. Candra had been known to stay until a party died, whether that was midnight or dawn.

"What did you do then?"

"Went to bed."

"Alone?"

"Yes."

Detective Aquino sighed. Detective Ritenour looked tired. Richard knew he was their best bet, and he had taken away all the usual motives. What had probably looked like a fairly simple case had become more complicated.

"We'd like you to stay while we verify a few things," Detective Ritenour said.

"I understand." Richard flashed a level look at them, one that said he was well aware of everything that had been going on. "And I'll take you up on that coffee now, if I'll be allowed near a bathroom."

Rueful smiles flashed across their faces, quickly erased. "Sure thing. How do you want it?"

"Black."

"Not a good choice," Aquino said on his way out. "This stuff needs diluting with something, even if it's paint thinner."

"I'll take my chances." He thought of Sweeney, wondering, fearing, how she had weathered the night. The painting she had been doing was, he was certain now, of Candra. Had she completed it last night? Was she in shock? Did she need him?

He wanted to call her. The urge was so powerful he could barely contain it, but he fought it down. Bringing her to the detectives' notice would only involve her in this. He hadn't been to the death scene, but if Sweeney's painting was in any way accurate in the details, he could see that any detective would find that suspicious. And he wondered if the other face, the killer's, was still blank.

"May I call my office?" he asked. Sweeney would have called there if she needed him.

"Sure. Use the telephone on my desk," Ritenour offered. He would be able to listen to every word Richard said. Their suspicion had eased, but not completely disappeared. It wouldn't until everything Richard told them had been verified.

Richard stood beside the desk and dialed the office number. Tabitha Hamrick, budding financial genius, answered the phone. "Tab, it's Richard. Any messages?"

"Thousands of them." She sighed. "Richard, I'm so sorry. Is there anything I can do?"

"No, I've notified her family, and I'm giving them their

choice in everything. They should be here soon. Ah, hell, I forgot to make their hotel reservations. Would you do that for me? The Plaza. I'll pick up the tab."

"Sure thing. Oh, Ms. Sweeney called this morning. I told her I'd tell you."

"Thanks." He wanted to ask how Sweeney had sounded, but couldn't. "What time was that?"

"I think it was close to eleven. I made a note. . . . Here it is. Ten-fifty-seven."

Fairly late in the morning. She should have been okay by then. He breathed a sigh of relief. "Okay. Thanks."

"Will you be in this afternoon?"

Richard glanced over at Ritenour. "This will take another couple of hours, right?"

"Right." Ritenour gave a faintly apologetic shrug. He wasn't nearly as pugnacious as he had been before the interview.

"No, I won't make it in. I'll see you in the morning."

He hung up and worked his shoulders, shrugging the kinks out of them. Aquino appeared with three cups of coffee sand-wiched in his hands. Richard took the one that was black. Aquino and Ritenour both drank theirs with so much cream the liquid was barely brown. After the first sip, Richard knew why. But in the military he had gotten accustomed to drinking coffee this strong, for the caffeine kick.

The coffee made him think of Sweeney again, and her need for it. He needed her as he had never needed anyone, and right now he didn't dare go anywhere near her.

CHAPTER

SIXTEEN

Richard kept tight control of himself as the afternoon dragged on. He didn't fidget; he didn't protest; he didn't threaten. The detectives were doing their job, and it wasn't their fault the things he had told them took longer to verify than he had expected. He wasn't officially under arrest; judging from the detectives' attitude, they no longer suspected him, or at least not much. He could have left. But they kept coming back to him with questions that would help them put together a picture, questions about Candra's habits and friends. Though he and Candra had been separated for a year, they had lived together for ten, and he knew her better than even her parents did.

Tabitha had canceled all his appointments. Candra's parents had arrived and were installed in the Plaza; he had spoken to them on the phone—with Detective Ritenour listening—and apologized for not being able to see them that evening. The Maxson's weren't alone; in the background he could hear the rise and fall of several voices, and knew they had called some of their old friends as soon as they checked into the hotel.

The urge to call Sweeney was almost overwhelming, and that was the one urge he had to resist. In his shock at Candra's murder, he had left his cell phone at home; he had no way of knowing if Sweeney had tried to contact him by that number. The sense of being out of touch with her gnawed at him, as if part of him were missing. He needed her, needed to feel the freshness of her personality, see the clear honesty of her gaze. It was unfair of him, now that Candra was dead, but he couldn't help comparing the two women. Candra had come from a privileged background; she had been pampered and adored, her every whim satisfied, always certain she was loved—and she had grown up to be innately selfish, unable to handle situations in which she didn't get what she wanted. She had been undeniably charming and friendly—God, it was jarring to think of her in the past tense!—so those situations hadn't come about very often, but when they did, she erupted.

On the other hand, from what little Sweeney had told him, she had been mostly ignored by her parents. Her mother's lack of feeling for her own children was appalling. He knew Sweeney's mother, though he had never met her. He had met her type. Because she was artistic, she thought that excused her from responsible behavior. She probably indulged in indiscriminate sex and drugs, and had exposed her children to God knows what.

Sweeney had grown up without love and had closed herself off from the pain by simply not letting herself form attachments.

Richard strongly suspected he wouldn't have been able to get to her so fast if he hadn't caught her at this particular time, when the shock of those psychic episodes was sending *her* into a form of shock. Otherwise, she would have kept him at a distance for months. But despite her parents' example, or maybe because of it, she shunned their dangerous, juvenile lifestyle and had made herself into a woman of strong moral fiber.

He didn't want her touched by this, not any more than she already was. The painting involved her; if she eventually painted the face of the man standing over Candra's body—and he had no reason to doubt she would—then that knowledge would have to be shared with the detectives. It wasn't proof; the painting would in no way be admissible in court. But, if the detectives gave the information any credence, it would point them in the right direction. If they knew where to look, they would probably find the proof they needed. Perhaps he could steer them in that direction without mentioning the painting or involving Sweeney at all.

"Did Mrs. Worth have a will?" Detective Aquino asked abruptly.

"I don't know," Richard replied, dragging his thoughts away from Sweeney. "We had one when we were together, but as soon as we separated, I made a new one. She didn't have a lot of assets, though. I own the gallery, and from what I gather, she ran up a lot of debt in the past year. I had agreed to give her the gallery as part of the settlement, but that wouldn't have been included in any new will she made, if she made one at all."

"Why?" Aquino asked curiously. "Why give her the gallery? With your prenup, you didn't have to give her anything."

Richard shrugged and said simply, "So she would have the means to live."

"Mr. Worth . . ." Ritenour tapped his pen on the desk, his brow furrowed as he framed his question. "I know you've been

separated a long time, but would you know any of the men she's
been with lately? The housekeeper didn't know any names. She
said when Mrs. Worth had company, she tried to stay out of the
way and do her job as quietly as possible."

Richard didn't make any comment on Candra's sexual
habits. "How far back do you want to go?"

They looked at each other. Aquino shrugged. "Since you
separated."

"My attorney has a list." Seeing their surprise, he said, "I
made it a point to know, in case I needed the information."

They both perked up. "Did you have her watched?" An
investigator's report could be an invaluable aid, telling them
where she went and when, whom she saw.

"Yes, but I don't think it will help. There wasn't anyone she
saw more than any of the others. Candra didn't have long-term
affairs. Her attractions were of the moment, and more concerned
with satisfying her own appetite than with her partner. Kai, her
assistant at the gallery, was probably her most frequent partner,
but only because he was convenient."

There was another perking of investigative ears. "How do
you spell that name?" Ritenour asked.

"K-a-i. Last name Stengel, as in Casey."

"Was he in love with her, do you think?"

"Kai doesn't love anyone but himself. I can't see him killing
her, because it wouldn't be in his best interest. I gave Candra a
free hand with the gallery and she hired whom she pleased, but
her death before the divorce was final means the gallery remains
mine, and Kai would know he was out of a job in that event."

"Because of his involvement with your wife?"

Richard shook his head. "Because he's an alley cat."

"Mr. Worth, pardon me for asking," Detective Aquino said,

"but a man like you—How did you stand it, knowing your wife had all these affairs?"

Richard's eyes were cold. "After the first time, I didn't give a damn what she did."

"But you stayed married to her."

"I took vows." And he had taken them seriously. He would have remained married to her, making the best of a bad situation, if she hadn't had the abortion. He had taken her for better or for worse, but "worse" didn't include aborting his child.

He called Gavin and had the entire investigator's report faxed to the precinct station. Gavin offered to come down in case Richard needed his legal protection, but Richard told him there was no need. He had put in an electronic buy order with his broker just before he disconnected last night, his entry coded with his password, and his Internet provider could also verify the time he was on-line, so he was covered in case the detectives had any lingering doubt. He had no motive or opportunity, and he had cooperated with them to the fullest extent.

The next time he checked the clock, the hands had ticked past seven-thirty. He was tired and hungry, having refused their offer of stale cookies or peanut-butter crackers from a vending machine. The detectives looked more tired than he felt, but they doggedly kept at it. He appreciated their persistence, but the need to reassure himself Sweeney was all right was growing more urgent with every passing minute.

He had been containing his emotions all day, until he felt like a pressure cooker with the release valve stuck in the closed position. Candra's murder had stirred a cauldron of emotions; first he had been shocked by the violent death. Next came a cold fury, one so strong he could feel it surging inside him, demanding action. He had been intimate with violence, but his military missions had been against other militaries or terrorist groups, people who signed on knowing what the risks were and were armed and ready to kill him if they had the chance. Candra had been a non-combatant, unarmed, untrained, unaware. She hadn't had a prayer, and the unfairness of the attack revolted him.

He didn't resent being questioned. He did resent, bitterly, not being able to see Sweeney, or at least contact her. The choice was his own, an effort to protect her from this same sort of suspicion and questioning, but that didn't make him resent any less the necessity of making that choice. If the detectives saw that painting, they might even arrest her, and he would do whatever he could to prevent that.

Because he was growing desperate to see her, he locked himself down even tighter. If he revealed any hint of what he was feeling, the detectives' suspicions would be refueled and this would drag on longer.

At last, a little after eight, Detective Aquino stretched tiredly and said, "You've been a lot of help, Mr. Worth. Thanks for your patience. Most people would have gotten upset, but we had to ask the questions."

"I know the statistics," Richard said. "I understood. I assume I'm no longer a suspect?"

"Everything you told us checked out. Your Internet server verified the times you were on-line last night at the crucial time—and thank you for giving them permission to give us that information without having to get papers on it. That saved us a lot of time."

"She didn't deserve what happened," Richard said. "No matter what our differences were, she didn't deserve that." He stood and stretched his tired back muscles. "I'll be at home if you have any more questions."

"I'll get a patrolman to take you home," Detective Ritenour offered.

"Thanks, that isn't necessary. I'll catch a cab." Calling Edward to pick him up would be a waste of time; by the time Edward got here, he could be home.

Leaving the precinct, he walked down to the corner to catch a cab, but traffic seemed to be light on that street. Two blocks over was a busier street, so he kept walking. The tension in him was building. Home. In less than thirty minutes now he would be home. He would talk to Sweeney. He thought about taking the cab directly to her place, but caution kept him from it. Any direct contact with her now could bring unwanted attention down on her. The detectives would probably find out about her anyway, eventually—depending on whom Candra had told about seeing Richard and Sweeney together—but every minute he could hold off the inevitable was important. She might paint the killer's face tonight, and then he would have a direction in which to steer the detectives.

He needed to shower and shave and go to the Plaza, to see Helene and Charles. Respect and common courtesy demanded that he do so, but he didn't know if he had any common courtesy left in him. He was tired, and relations between them would be awkward because of the divorce. When people were grieving, they could lash out, trying to ease their pain by placing the blame on someone or something, and he could easily see Helene making a tearful charge that if only Candra had still been living with him, this wouldn't have happened, because she wouldn't have been coming home alone. He didn't have the patience to deal with that right now. He would call them, after he talked to Sweeney, and tell them he would be over first thing in the morning.

But Sweeney came first. Until he knew she was all right, he couldn't think of anything else.

"Son of a bitch," Detective Joseph Aquino said, tiredly closing a folder and leaning back in his chair. He was actually the more impatient, rougher-edged of the two detectives, but his looks inclined people to trust him, so Ritenour usually played the hard-ass. "Nine times outta ten, it's gonna be the estranged husband kills his wife. This looked like a perfect setup, but what have we got?"

"We've got jack shit, is what we've got." Ritenour ticked the points off on his fingers. They both knew the points, but saying them out loud always helped. "Worth is the one who wanted the divorce. He has a prenup agreement protecting all his assets, so he doesn't have to worry about that. She had been giving him a hard time about the settlement, but she had an appointment today to sign the papers, so that wasn't an issue. He was on his computer last night at the time we estimate she got home from the party, and the M.E.'s preliminary time of death puts the murder roughly at that same time. You know the first thing a woman does when she walks in the door? She kicks off the spike heels. Mrs. Worth still had on her shoes."

"You ever run across a customer that cool, though?" Aquino rubbed his eyes. He had taken the call for the Worth murder a little before seven that morning, and had been working nonstop since. "Nothing got to him. He showed us only what he wanted us to see."

"Joey," Ritenour said. "He didn't do it."

"The scene looked fishy, though. It looks like she surprised a burglar, but—"

"But it looks like someone wanted it to look that way."

"Yeah. The place wasn't messed up much. And those

scratches on the lock. Looks like they were deliberately made. They sure as hell didn't have anything to do with popping the lock."

"Another point in Mr. Worth's favor," Ritenour said. "Don't get me wrong; I'm not suggestin' this as something he could have done. But he struck me as the kinda guy, if he wanted to make a scene look like a burglary, then it would look like a fucking burglary."

"Yeah, I know. But whoever it was knew her, and was pissed as hell. A burglar wouldn't have hacked her up like that." Aquino drew a preliminary report to him. "He got her three times in the back, so she was running from him. Defense wounds on her arm; she was trying to fight him off. Then when she was down, he kept stabbing her."

"No signs of sexual assault. Underwear was in place; prelim shows no semen present. Her friends say she left the party last night unusually early, so the timing couldn't have been planned. She left alone." Ritenour yawned, bleary eyes focused on his notes. "The knife was from a set in her kitchen and was left at the scene. No prints. We have a lot of smears on the doorknob, a partial of Mrs. Worth's right thumb, and a good set of the housekeeper's prints."

"Doesn't look like a disgruntled boyfriend, either. She spread her joy around. There were a lot of men, but no one in particular."

"But maybe one of them wanted to be particular. You know, the sour grapes thing. If I can't have you, blah blah blah. Anybody on that list she was seeing regularly, then *stopped* seeing?" Ritenour doodled on his pad. Like all detectives, he and Joe kicked things back and forth between them. The give-and-take sometimes triggered a new insight.

"Nobody that recent." Aquino paused. "Senator McMil-

Ian's name on that list was interesting, but while he might not want his wife to know about it, I don't think he'd kill to keep it secret."

"Not to mention he doesn't know this list exists."

"Not to mention. Has the insurance company come through with a list of the jewelry she had insured, so we can tell what's missing?"

"Not yet. They're supposed to fax it over in the morning."

"Let's walk through this."

"We've walked through it twice already, Joe."

"Humor me." Aquino leaned back and laced his fingers behind his head. "Guy breaks in. He's already got the jewelry. Maybe he plans on taking the television and stereo, too, but it's just one guy, so I doubt it. He's in the kitchen, looking in the refrigerator. Lot of people hide stuff in their refrigerators and freezers; they think it's an original hiding place, so of course a good thief always checks the fridge."

Ritenour picked up the narrative. "When she comes in, catches him, he panics. He grabs one of the knives. But he already has the jewelry, and he's stronger than she is; he can get away any time he wants. There wasn't any reason to kill her, unless she knew him."

"Like an acquaintance trying to feed a drug habit? That might fly, except for the overkill. The punk enjoyed it. That brings me back to the setup. I think the murder was deliberate, and the rest of it is just stage setting. I don't think there was a burglar."

"Then the guys on this list are our best possibilities." Sourly, Ritenour surveyed the names. "Jesus, the lady saw a lot of action. The problem is, I don't think any of these names are on the security log."

"What, you think a guy planning to commit murder is going to sign his real name for the guard?"

"Then how did he get in? *Somebody* would have to okay him, or the guard wouldn't let him go up. So he would have had to use his real name."

"Or somebody in the building was in on it with him."

Glumly they stared at each other. They were getting into wild territory with a conspiracy theory, and they knew it. The murder had been too personal. So they were left with the puzzle of how the killer got into an upscale apartment building with round-the-clock security. They kept staring at each other. Ritenour arched his eyebrows. "We need a list of recent tenants."

"Yeah, we sure as hell do."

"The name won't be right, but we'll be looking for a single man, and odds are if we get photos of all the guys on this list, the guards will be able to match one of them to the new tenant."

Suddenly energized, they hit the phones. The late hour was working against them, though. There was no one in the office of the apartment building to give them a list of recent applicants. Getting photos of the men on the list would also take time; the photos of the ones who had driver's licenses could be got from the DMV, but a lot of people who lived in the city didn't drive because owning a car was such a bitch of a hassle. There was also the possibility that the guy could live across the river in New Jersey, or in Connecticut. Both were easy commutes.

"Jesus," Aquino muttered, looking at the list of Mrs. Worth's lovers. "This could take the rest of the year. Have you counted how many guys are here? The woman must have had the brains of a flea, what with AIDS and everything. Look at this. I count twenty-three *new* guys in the past year; then there were all the repeaters. She was in the sack with somebody at least twice a week, on average."

"My love life should be so active," Ritenour said mournfully.

"The strain would kill you. Ah, hell, we aren't going to get anything accomplished tonight." Aquino stood and stretched. "I'm going home. See ya in the morning."

"Going home's the best idea you've had all day." Following suit, Ritenour grabbed his coat. "You wanna stop off for a couple of beers?"

"Nah, you go on. I'm whacked." They were both divorced, and all either of them had waiting for them at home was laundry. The beers sounded tempting. But something was nibbling at Aquino, and he couldn't quite figure out what it was. Something about Richard Worth. It wasn't that he thought Worth was the killer; the man had no motive, and no opportunity. But he was too controlled; there hadn't been any shakes, any fidgeting, any show of temper, no visible emotion when he identified his wife's body—okay, soon-to-be ex-wife, and considering the abortion thing and all the other men, he could understand why Worth wouldn't give a damn—*nothing*. No sign he had a single nerve in his body. He had been patient and helpful, giving them access to his records so they could get the information a lot faster than if they had to go through legal channels. Aquino knew he had no reason to be suspicious of Worth, and he wasn't, not really. It was just a gut feeling that the guy was hiding something, that there was some loose end that needed to be secured.

He waved a careless good-bye to Ritenour, then slid his bulk behind the wheel of the nondescript tan sedan the city provided for his use. On impulse, he decided to drive by Richard Worth's town house, just to see what he could see. Hell, he might even park and keep an eye on the place for a while. In a detective, a little healthy curiosity was a good thing.

Richard gave the cabdriver a twenty and didn't wait for the change, just bounded up the steps to the town house. When he renovated the bottom floor for his offices, he had added a separate entrance for them tucked under the steps that went up to the main part of the house. The office floor was half underground, with the windows at street level protected by steel bars. He entered into a foyer, a ten-by-ten square laid with imported slate tiles. The rug centered on the tiles was a two-hundred-year-old Turkish rug so tightly woven it didn't depress under his weight as he strode across it.

He checked the answering machine in the den for messages. There were eleven of them, and he listened impatiently, fast-forwarding to the next one as soon as he identified each voice. Sweeney's wasn't one of them. He dialed her number and listened to the rings, counting them in his head. On the sixth ring, her machine picked up. Her voice recited the number; then she ended with a terse, "Leave a message." Normally he would have been amused. Now he was worried sick. Goddamn it, where was she?

Sweeney hadn't meant to walk so far. The severe episode that morning had left her feeling dazed and dopey, even after she woke from the deathlike, three-hour nap. She had wandered around the apartment for hours, not expecting Richard to call but hanging around anyway, just in case he did. He would be so busy with the arrangements that she didn't expect to hear from him for a couple of days, at least.

Around sundown, though, she began to feel as if she couldn't stay inside another moment. Her thought processes felt slow and clumsy, as if she had been drugged, and she thought some fresh air might help clear her mind. Not trusting the chirpy weather lady who said the temperature was a pleasant sixty-four degrees, she pulled on a denim jacket and hit the street.

She didn't have any destination in mind. She just walked. She lived on the fringes of the Lower East Side, and the area was full of color, especially the human variety. The relatively low rents attracted artists and students by the thousands. Actors and musicians mostly gravitated to Greenwich Village, but some of the overflow ended up in the Lower East Side. The faces were fascinating, young and old. A young couple were out for a stroll, pushing their infant in a stroller, pride and contentment shining on their faces. She caught a glimpse of the baby's tiny, flowerlike face and its minuscule hands curled on the edge of the blanket, and her hands ached to touch the fuzz that covered its head.

A teenager was walking a tangle of dogs, ranging in size from an English sheepdog, peeping through its mop of hair, down to a dachshund, trotting along in double time. A big grin lit the boy's face as he was literally towed along the sidewalk: he was on roller skates. The dogs looked happy to be of use.

Gradually the neighborhood changed. Sweeney looked at window displays, stopped in a tiny bakery for a cinnamon roll with thick icing on top, then had to have a cup of coffee to wash it down. She strolled along, hands in the pockets of her jacket, a light breeze flirting with her curls.

She tried not to think about Candra. She deliberately did not allow the image of the painting to form in her mind. She didn't think about much of anything, just kept walking.

Still, it wasn't a surprise when she looked around her and recognized the luxurious town houses and high-rise apartment buildings of the Upper East Side. She had walked at least a couple of miles, maybe more; she didn't know how many blocks constituted a mile. Richard lived here, in a town house off of Park Avenue. Candra had lived somewhere near here; Sweeney remembered Kai telling her that Candra's new apartment was in the upper somethings; she didn't remember which block.

Sweeney hadn't watched the news, just the weather. The local news would probably be full of the murder; such things

didn't happen every day in one of the swank apartment buildings, and Candra was socially prominent, which made her murder even more newsworthy. Sweeney hadn't wanted to see
anything about it, or hear any of the speculation.

All she wanted was to see Richard.

She walked up the street and stood looking up at the town
house for several moments. She had been here once, three or four
years ago, when she had briefly been in town and had stopped by
at Candra's invitation while a party was in progress. Sweeney
had stayed just long enough to pretend to sip some champagne,
tell Candra hello, then she escaped.

Light shone through the fantail window above the door. She
stared at the window, wondering if he was at home or if the light
was on to make people think someone was there.

This was a bad idea. If he *was* home, surely there were other
people with him. Friends would be offering their condolences—
or perhaps not, considering the circumstances. But they would
definitely be trying to get all the gory details, hot gossip they
could share over coffee with other friends the next day.

She wouldn't have to go in. Just ring the doorbell, tell
him . . . tell him something inane, such as she was thinking about
him, or offer her sympathy, something like that. Maybe he had
staff and didn't answer the door himself. In that case, she would
leave a message. He would know she had been there, and that
was the important thing.

She climbed the steps and punched the doorbell, then
stuffed her hands back in her pockets, standing with her head
down and the night breeze ruffling her hair while she waited for
the door to open.

It was jerked open so abruptly she jumped, startled.

Richard loomed over her, glaring. "Where in hell have you
been?" he barked.

She blinked. "Walking."

"Walking," he repeated in disbelief. "From your apartment?"

"Yeah. I just took a walk and . . . ended up here."

He stared down at her, his face expressionless but his dark eyes glittering with some unreadable emotion. "Come in," he said, stepping back so she could pass by him, and after a slight hesitation, she did.

Sitting in his car thirty yards down the block, Detective Aquino raised his eyebrows, and made note of the woman's time of arrival. No particular reason why, he thought, just a cop's general nosiness.

They hadn't touched, but there had been that indefinable air of connection between them. So Worth had himself a honey; there was no law against it. In fact, after being separated for a year, the man would have had to be a damn saint not to have a lady friend.

What puzzled Aquino was why, in answering all the questions they had asked that day, not once had another woman's name been mentioned. Worth was a private man—Aquino had gathered that much—but when the issue came up, he had, reluctantly, told them about his wife's abortion. Having a lady friend was a lot less sensitive than that information. In fact, being involved with another woman would have been another point in his favor, making him even less likely to care what his estranged wife did.

But Worth hadn't mentioned his friend, and Aquino found that interesting.

CHAPTER
SEVENTEEN

The foyer floor was some kind of dark gray tile, covered by a thick rug in the richest colors Sweeney had ever seen. She would have paused there, but Richard held out his hand, indicating she should precede him, and uncomfortably she did so. His expression was at its most stony, as if he didn't want her there but was too polite to say so. She jammed her hands deeper into her jacket pockets, feeling like an interloper.

She had felt like an interloper the other time she had been here, too. Of course, then she had been under the strain of trying to socialize—briefly—but she wasn't any more comfortable this time. Luxury made her nervous. As a child, she had always been the one who spilled the Kool-Aid on the irreplaceable lace table-cloth, or inadvertently smeared paint on a silk blouse, or stepped on a dropped ink pen and cracked it so the ink ran all over a gazillion-dollar rug. Her mother had always put on that dramatic tone of voice and said the world would be safer if she could only keep Paris in a cage, and then she always profusely apologized for the child's clumsiness. For a while Sweeney had been terrified her mother really would put her in a cage.

She had gotten over that fear, but the fact was she actually had been that accident prone. There was something about expensive stuff that brought out the klutz in her. She walked in the middle of the foyer, staying well away from that beautiful lamp.

The spacious living room was on the right. She went there, with Richard walking silently behind her. She had a vague sense of being herded. She shouldn't be here; not only was she out of place, but now certainly wasn't the time. She had presumed too much on their relationship, which was far too new and unformed for her to presume anything.

Despite her unease, Sweeney was, as always, aware of colors, and she immediately noticed that the room was different. Candra had liked a lot of neutral, light tones; everything now was more colorful, more substantial. Nothing looked any cheaper than what it had replaced.

She stood in the middle of the room, shifting nervously from one foot to the other. "Sit down," Richard said.

"I can't stay." Damn, she hadn't gotten any better at social lies. She could hear the bright falseness of her own tone. "I know I shouldn't be here. This is a private time and I'm intruding—"

"Sit down," he said again, only this time the words sounded as if he growled them.

She chose a big leather wing chair and perched on the edge of the cushion. There was some sort of statuette on the table next to the chair. She put both hands between her knees so she wouldn't accidently knock the thing over.

She didn't like feeling uncomfortable with Richard. She was totally at ease with him in her own apartment, or on neutral territory. Here, for the first time, she was painfully aware of the huge financial gap between them. She had never seen anything snobbish about him, so the distinction had to be within herself, and reverse snobbery was as irrational as the other.

"I don't know what you're thinking, but I don't like the expression on your face." At least this time his tone was wry, instead of a growl. He was still standing, looking down at her with an unreadable expression.

"I'm thinking I don't belong here." That was the unvarnished truth, whether he liked it or not. She pinned her gaze on a flower arrangement, comforting herself by studying the colors.

He shrugged. "I don't either."

Startled, she looked up. "But you own it."

"I'm an old country boy at heart. This isn't where I want to be; it's just a place to live."

She couldn't seem to look away from him. His dark eyes were black in the low, soothing light of the lamps, and he wasn't looking away from her, either. Physical awareness, never far from the surface when she was with him, shimmered through her. Instantly she tried to tamp it down; now wasn't the time.

"I've been with the police all day long," he said in a low, controlled tone. "I've been worried sick about you, but I couldn't call."

She said quickly, "I understand. I didn't expect you to call. And I'm all right. I finally figured out I can crawl into a tub of hot water and soak until the chill is gone."

"I'd rather you crawl into a hot bed with me whenever you need warming up."

The words lay between them like a live wire. She felt her insides jolt as if she had actually been shocked, and realization clicked into place. He wasn't looking at her and thinking she shouldn't be here; he was watching her with the intense focus of a man who intends to have sex. Here. Now.

She found herself on her feet, pulled there by a tension so acute it was almost painful. Nerves and need warred inside her. With just that blunt statement from him she was aroused, her body readying itself for him. Her breasts ached, and without looking down, she knew her nipples had hardened. Liquid heat, sweetly painful, pooled between her legs. She clenched her inner muscles against the pain and found she had only intensified the hurt.

She had accepted, and enjoyed, the force of her attraction to him. She loved those wildly frustrating kisses, the tempting touch of bare skin, the intoxicating blend of feeling on the edge of danger and at the same time utterly safe in his arms. As much as she wanted the completion of actually making love with him, she had also felt comforted by his restraint. Commitment wasn't easy for her, and what he wanted from her right now was the most basic commitment of all. What she had enjoyed so much in theory was a little scary in reality.

"I think I should go," she blurted, turning to do exactly that.

His hands closed around her waist, catching her before she could take a step. "I think you should stay." He pulled her solidly against him, hips to hips, thighs to thighs, nestling the hard ridge of his erection against the softness of her belly. "Don't you want me?" he murmured, bending his head to nuzzle her temple, and lower to the sensitive hollow just below her ear.

Her breath caught. Want him? She wanted him more than she had ever wanted anything or anyone in her life. She was only beginning to realize just how much she did want him, and not only in a physical sense. That was the scariest part about this, acknowledging how emotionally important he was to her. As a child she had loved her family and desperately needed for them to love her in return, but that love hadn't been forthcoming, and since then she hadn't allowed herself to be so vulnerable.

But it was too late for caution, she thought wildly. She already loved him. Her body was already melting against his, seeking the heady pleasure he had given her once before.

She couldn't give him the permission he had asked for, at least not in words. Panic and excitement mingled in a wild rush that closed her throat. So she slid her hands up his chest and locked them around his neck, going on tiptoe to cradle his erection at the junction of her thighs, and that was all the permission he needed.

His arms closed around her and his mouth covered hers, hard and voracious. His tongue moved deep into her mouth, taking her, shaking her with the sudden awareness that until now he had always held himself back. He wasn't holding anything back now. Sweeney had the sensation of being crushed and devoured, except he wasn't hurting her at all, the only pain she felt was the pain of emptiness.

He stripped her jacket down her arms and let it drop to the floor. He delved his hands under her shirt and closed them over her breasts, his palms hot and rough against her tightened nipples. Her whole body arched into his touch, and she heard herself making soft, panting sounds. Everything was spinning out of control, going too fast. "Richard," she gasped, a weak cry, or a plea, she never knew which.

He jerked her shirt off over her head, and the next second she was lying sprawled on her back on the oversized couch. Ten seconds later she was naked, her shoes and socks gone, her jeans and panties tugged down and off. His hands were on her thighs, pulling them open.

Dazedly she stared at him as he knelt between her legs, one knee on the couch and his other foot planted on the floor, tearing at the fastening of his pants. She felt as if her entire body was throbbing with anticipation, the blood running hot and thick through her veins, gathering in her loins. He leaned over her and she braced her hands on his chest, his heartbeat pounding under her right palm. Their eyes met, hers wide, his fiercely narrowed, and their gazes locked and held as he entered her, thrusting hard and deep.

The pain ambushed her. It was sharp and burning, just as if she were virgin again. She caught her breath on a cry, stiffening beneath him. He muttered an indistinct curse as he withdrew a little and more slowly worked himself back in to the hilt. The pain was only momentary, her body's reaction to the unaccustomed invasion; his second thrust wrung another cry from her, this time sharp with pleasure.

"God," he said, his voice stifled, his body held still and tight, as if one more thrust would shatter his control and he wouldn't stop until he climaxed.

Sweeney hooked her legs around his waist, tilting her pelvis up to take him deeper inside. Her breath came in short, choppy pants. He felt so thick and hard inside her she thought she couldn't bear it if he moved, and yet she thought she would explode if he didn't. She felt hot, glowing, the heat boiling through her veins. She tightened her inner muscles around him, trying to pull him deeper. His entire body flexed, and with a guttural sound he surged forward, plunging so deep she almost screamed; then he held himself motionless once more. She arched upward, her nails digging into his chest muscles. "Damn you," she choked. "Do it!"

He caught her wrists in his hands and peeled them off his chest, slamming them down to the cushion and anchoring them over her head. He leaned over her, sweat gleaming on his face, and in the fierce dark depths of his eyes she saw his control shatter.

He took her then with powerful thrusts that made her entire body shudder under the impact. His grip on her hands arched her into him, lifted her for him. With each inward thrust the heat and tension inside her increased, her loins throbbing, her hips rocking back and forth and taking everything he had to give her. She climaxed hard and fast, sobbing and crying out, and without mercy he rode her through it, so that the tension began rebuilding as soon as the spasms ended. His big body stiffened over her, then he shuddered and bucked from the force of his own orgasm.

In the silence afterward, she heard her own breathing, rapid and jerky. Her heart was pounding so hard she could feel it thudding against her rib cage. Every muscle in her felt like butter, mushy and helpless. He lay heavily on her, crushing her into the couch, and she could happily have lain there forever. The pleasure she'd had with him before didn't compare to actually making love. She felt exhilarated, and exhausted, as if she could move mountains if only she could manage to move herself, but at the moment, she wanted nothing more than to just lie there with Richard's weight on her, feeling the tremor in those powerful muscles, and know that she had been enough for him, that he was satisfied.

This was, she realized, what women had always felt at these times, with the men they loved. It was sweeter than she had imagined, in those brief, rare moments when she had allowed herself to think of what she might be missing in her solitary state.

Richard lifted his head. His dark hair was black with sweat, his face stark with triumph and possessiveness and a very male satisfaction. "Are you okay?" His voice was low and rough.

She swallowed. "You tell me," she managed to say. "I haven't had much practice."

A quick grin lit the hard places of his face. "I'd say you're damn wonderful." He released her wrists to balance his weight on his elbows, framing her face with his hands and kissing her with slow, deep deliberation, mimicking with his tongue the small strokes between her legs that kept him semierect and inside her. She quivered beneath him, her swollen inner tissues almost too sensitive to bear even that gentle stimulation.

He knew, and withdrew from her so gently she wanted to weep. He drew back on his knees and restored his pants to rough order, then stood and scooped her up. She lay draped in his arms like a naked offering, clinging to his shoulders as he carried her out of the living room and up the stairs. "I hope you can stay the night," he murmured, "because I'm not even close to being through with you."

"No . . . Candra's bed—"

"She never slept in this bed," he reassured her, gentle but implacable. "Or in this room. I had the house renovated and redecorated." He shouldered open a set of double doors and carried her across a large expanse of gleaming hardwood floors, strewn with rugs the colors of jewels, to a bed that looked large enough to sleep six. He let her legs drop, so that she was standing, but kept her clamped to his side as he bent and stripped back the covers.

Her knees wobbled. "I need to wash," she said. She needed to find a robe, or a towel, or even a couple of washcloths she could hold over strategic places. She had never felt more naked than she did right now, or more aware of her body.

He stiffened. "I'll be damned," he said softly. "I didn't wear a rubber."

They stared at each other, and Sweeney became acutely aware of the wetness between her legs. She did some fast counting. "I think we're safe. It's been almost three weeks since my last period." She had a brief moment of insanity, a flash of regret that the timing hadn't been better—or worse. At the moment she couldn't decide which it would be.

He opened a drawer in the bedside table and took out a box of condoms, placing it on the tabletop. He extracted one from the box. "We both need a shower. The bathroom's through there." He turned her and pointed her in the direction of two white louvered doors.

He intended to shower with her. He intended to do more than that, considering the condom in his hand. Sweeney's heartbeat speeded up as she walked to the bathroom with as much poise as she could muster, though she could feel her cheeks heating. By the time they reached the bathroom, he had shed all his clothes except for his pants and shorts, leaving them strewn in a trail from bed to bath.

She stopped in the doorway. His bathroom was bigger than her bedroom. A square whirlpool tub sat directly in front of her, with thick white towels stacked on the ceramic tile ledge beside it, next to a crystal container filled with small, round, multicolored soaps. To the right a glass door opened into a large shower. The floor was laid with glossy tiles in a soft, rosy brown color that seemed to glow under the bright lights. To the left was a small private enclosure for the toilet, and at her left hand stretched a long, long double vanity in some sort of shiny, rich brown. Gold faucets arched over the bowls. Thick, soft rugs were spread in front of the shower and bathtub.

"This is decadent," she pronounced.

A large warm hand moved over the bare curves of her bottom. "Glad you like it."

She didn't just like it; she loved it. The colors were wonderful. A dull brown would have been awful, but this brown was so deep and rich she felt as if she could sink into it. The gold of the faucets seemed to pick up gold flecks in the vanity top, making it glow.

She opened the shower door and peered in. "Wow." The shower stall was at least eight by five feet, fashioned in marble streaked with brown and rose. There was a showerhead at each end of the enclosure, positioned so one would be rinsed front and back simultaneously.

The hand on her bottom became more insistent, urging her into the shower. She turned, and faced a very naked man. Her breath caught. She had already seen him mostly naked and had imagined him completely so, but the reality was so much better than her imagination. He was in marvelous shape, but it was more than that; he looked exactly the way a man should look, in her opinion, mature and muscular and interested. Impulsively she reached out and closed her hand around his stiffened penis, only half-hearing his involuntary hum of pleasure, and concentrating instead on how the thick shaft jumped in her hand.

He said, "If you aren't careful, you won't get that shower just yet."

"Is that important?" she murmured.

"I'm trying to be considerate and romantic."

She tilted her head back, lifting her brows in interest. "Romantic?"

"I've been thinking about this for a solid week, planning what I would do."

One hand remained at his crotch. The other stroked over his hairy chest. Her breath panted softly between her parted lips. "What romantic plans have you made?"

"Well, there's really only one."

"One? What is it?"

"Fucking your brains out," he said matter-of-factly, and when she fell back shrieking with laughter, he prudently removed her hand from his sex. While she was helpless, he herded her completely into the shower and turned on the water.

He had showered with a woman before, she realized; he adjusted the showerheads so the streams of water hit close to her waist, leaving her hair mostly dry. A few minutes later, with his soap-slick hands roaming all over her body, she conceded that he also knew a good bit about bathing a woman. A few minutes after that, condom in place, he demonstrated what he knew about having sex in the shower. It was fast and hard and carnal, with her pinned against the marble wall while he hammered into her. She came fast, writhing and bucking in his arms. Afterward she could barely stand, and he supported her as he dried both of them. He was still hard, not having climaxed, and the realization dawned on her that he would be much, much slower to climax the second time, and that she could look forward to a long session of lovemaking. She didn't know whether to rejoice or plead for mercy.

Then he carried her to the bed, and all thoughts of pleading for mercy went right out of her head. He spent a long time kissing her, from head to foot. He sucked her nipples until she was almost sobbing with pleasure and frustration; his finger probed and stroked between her legs, and then he replaced his fingers with his tongue and she climaxed again, screaming from the intensity of the sensations. He let her rest for a little while, then rolled her over on her stomach and took her from behind. She was so swollen that he felt impossibly huge, barely able to fit inside her; she was acutely aware of every inch of him, probing deep into her. His slow thrusts rubbed her body against the sheets, and against the hand he had tucked under her so that every movement moved her on his wickedly knowledgeable fingers.

The fourth time she climaxed, he was with her, and afterward they lay close together, her head cradled on his shoulder and his hands leisurely stroking her buttocks, her breasts, her hips and belly and thighs, as if he couldn't get enough of the feel of her. Closing her eyes, she listened to his heartbeat, and her own, as they gradually slowed and adjusted until they were beating in time, two hearts, one rhythm.

"Tell me if you need to sleep," he murmured after a while, rolling on top of her.

She felt him probing, but not yet entering, and knew he wouldn't if she told him she was tired. "No," she whispered, clutching his back and tilting her hips so that he slipped inside her a tantalizing couple of inches. "Don't let me sleep tonight." She had had enough of murders and paintings and feeling as if her life was subject to the whim of an unseen, unknown power. She wanted to drown her senses with Richard, lose herself in the purely physical.

He did just as she asked. A couple of times she thought she dozed, but perhaps not, perhaps she was in a daze of completion. He made love to her endlessly, and even when they rested, he was inside her. When she became too dry to take him, he used lubricant to ease his way into her. He pushed her hard, and a couple of times she cried because she didn't think she could take any more, but she always found that she could, and for that night he kept the cold away.

They were lying quietly together when the sky began to lighten. He stroked her hair back from her face, his touch infinitely tender. "Tell me about the painting."

She tensed, momentarily resisting the ugly intrusion into the happiness of the moment. Then she sighed, accepting the return of reality. "I finished her face." She found she had to swallow. "When I woke up and saw it, I tried to call the gallery, but there wasn't any answer. I didn't have her number, so I called you and—and I found out I was too late."

"Don't blame yourself," he said fiercely, cupping her chin in his hand and turning her face up to his. "The detectives think she was killed around midnight. By the time you finished her face, it was already too late."

"I—" Her throat closed. She knew he was right. Given the time she had gone to bed and the length of time it would have taken her to finish the face, Candra had already been dead. The artist in her knew that. The woman, the human being, felt as if there should have been something, anything, that she could have done.

She could feel the tension in him, thrumming through his muscles and communicating itself to her through his hands. "God, I was so worried about you," he said in a tone of stifled violence, crushing her against him.

"I'm okay." She kissed his collarbone and thought how wonderful it was to be safe and warm, and so thoroughly satisfied. Love for him filled her, making her heart swell. She wrenched her thoughts back to the subject. "I won't lie to you; it was pretty rough, but I managed. You don't have to worry; this proves I can handle it on my own."

His dark eyes glittered. "You shouldn't have to do it on your own. I should have been there."

"You couldn't. You had to—You had to take care of Candra."
Her throat tightened again. "She was your wife for ten years. I
know you must be upset—"

He made a harsh sound in his throat and released her,
rolling over onto his back. He stared up at the ceiling. "I don't
mourn her, if that's what you're asking. I can't be a hypocrite and
fake grief. Maybe people think I should, but I'm not going to put
on a show for them."

Sweeney felt the power and frustrated rage in him and gave
him the same comfort he had given her, putting her arms around
him and gently stroking his face, his chest. "Of course not. It
wouldn't be honest."

He glanced down at her. "You didn't do any work on the
man's face?"

She shook her head. She tried to be nonchalant, but her
eyes filled with dread for what was coming, and he knew that yesterday morning's episode had been the roughest yet.

It was his turn to stroke. "I wanted to call you," he whispered. "I spent all day with the police."

"I know. I knew you had to make arrangements—"

"Not to mention being the prime suspect."

Her pupils flared. *"What?"* She would have bolted up in
bed, but he controlled the surge of her body, keeping her clamped
to him.

"I was the most logical person. When a woman is murdered,
it's usually the husband or boyfriend who did it. We were getting
divorced. They had to eliminate me as a suspect."

"Are you? Eliminated, I mean."

"Yeah, I'm eliminated." His smile was crooked. "I didn't
have a motive, and I could prove I was here."

"How?"

"The computer. I was on-line, and my server had a record of the time."

Sweeney closed her eyes in relief. She tilted her head a little, rubbing her cheek against his chest. "I need to go," she murmured. "I know you have a million things to do today. And . . . shouldn't I take the painting to the police?"

"No," he said forcefully. "Promise me you won't do that."

"Why?" she asked, bewildered.

"Do you really think they'll believe you painted it in your sleep? Honey, *you'll* become their prime suspect, at least for a while. I don't want you to have to go through that; plus if they're concentrating on you, they're wasting time when they could be looking for the real killer. When you finish the painting, and we see who you paint, then I'll think of some way to point the cops in the right direction." He rubbed his thumbs under her chin. "Promise me."

"Okay." Her smile was wobbly. "I guess the whole thing is a little out there, isn't it?"

"No more so than your average *Twilight Zone* episode."

Her smile widened, became more genuine. "That bad, huh?"

"That bad. When you paint the killer's face, then I'll think of some way to point the cops in the right direction, but other than that, I don't want you involved at all."

Outside in his car, Detective Aquino yawned and stretched, battling the need for sleep. He really, really needed to take a leak, and he really, really needed some coffee. Staying awake today was gonna be hell. He should have gone home, and he knew it. It didn't mean a damn thing that Worth had a girlfriend.

But curiosity was his besetting sin, and he wanted to know

more about the woman. He wanted to know who she was and where she lived, and why she had arrived on foot, apparently unexpected, then stayed all night.

Maybe it was nothing, but then again, his hunches had worked out before. He intended to see what happened with this one.

CHAPTER EIGHTEEN

Richard sent her home in a taxi. Sweeney had been prepared to walk home, since she hadn't carried her purse with her the evening before when she set out for a stroll. All she had in her jeans pocket was a couple of crumpled ones and some change, but that was enough for a bus if she got tired of walking. He glared at her as he called a cab, and that was that. He paid the driver, kissed her, and handed her into the cab as if she were royalty.

It was nice not to have to walk home, she admitted as she let herself into her apartment. Her knees felt dangerously wobbly and all her muscles were weak. She thought about taking a nap, but dread kept her awake. She couldn't face another episode of sleep-painting and the awful cold that came afterward, not now. Both physically and emotionally, she wasn't up to the strain. She thought about the painting, with the big blank space where the killer's head would be, and her head began to hurt, sharp pains stabbing through her temples. She didn't even want to go into the studio to work on other paintings, where she would see the murder scene. She didn't want to think about Candra being dead or imagine the terror she must have felt in those last horrible minutes of her life. She wanted to be at peace for a little while, to gather strength for the finish. She wanted to think about Richard, remember his lovemaking and the incredible night she had just spent with him.

She wanted to revel in, and marvel at, the miracle of loving him. She *loved*, fully and wholeheartedly, when she hadn't thought she ever would. She had felt so smug about her ability to concentrate wholly on her work, confident she was immune to the emotional uproar called love. Hah! She was not only not immune, where Richard was concerned she was downright *easy*.

Even more, she was eager for an opportunity to demonstrate to him again just how easy she was.

But for now, she faced a day of doing nothing, or at least nothing much. She didn't dare nap and couldn't work. She was too tired to go out for a day of sketching. That left watching television, reading, or doing the laundry. She leaned toward reading, but the need to do laundry nagged at her conscience. Promising herself she would do the laundry after an hour of reading, she put on a pot of coffee and settled down with an oversized book about the use of acrylic paints.

The doorbell jerked her out of a study of brilliant colors. Muttering to herself, because she knew it couldn't possibly be Richard and therefore had to be a nuisance, she went to the door and looked through the peephole. Two men in suits stood in the hallway. "Who is it?" she asked, keeping her eye to the lens.

"Detectives Aquino and Ritenour, New York Police Department." The beefy man closest to the lens was the one who answered, and he used the entire phrase rather than the initials. Both men held out badges to the lens, as if she could read them through a fish-eye.

There was no way they could know about the painting, as only she and Richard knew she was doing it, but evidently someone had told them she was involved with Richard. She sighed as she opened the door. They were only doing their job, checking out all possibilities, but still she felt uneasy.

"Ms. Paris Sweeney?" the burly cop asked.

Her brows snapped together in a ferocious scowl. "Just Sweeney," she growled.

He looked a little startled, then his expression smoothed into impassivity. "May we come in?"

He looked more tired than she felt, with dark circles under his eyes and his complexion gray. He looked freshly shaved and his hair was still the teeniest bit damp, indicating he had showered and probably changed clothes, but that couldn't hide his exhaustion. The other detective, lean and sandy-haired, looked much more rested but not nearly as friendly.

"Would you like a pot of coffee?" she asked as they both sat down, because the burly guy really looked as if he could use a caffeine kick. "I mean, a cup of coffee."

The sandy-haired detective got that stony, wild-eyed look of someone trying not to laugh. Detective Aquino shot him a dirty look. "That would be appreciated. Sugar and cream. A lot of both."

"Same here," Detective Ritenour said.

She freshened her own cup, and prepared two more, loading

them down with enough sugar to send the average kid bouncing off the walls for ten hours, and enough cream to raise their cholesterol levels several points. They must drink a lot of bad coffee, she thought, for both of them to disguise the taste this way.

She put the cups on a small tray and carried it through to the living room, setting it down on the coffee table. Telling herself there was no reason to be nervous, she sat down and lifted her own cup. What was the procedure for interrogation? Should she invite them to begin?

The burly cop, after an appreciative sip of the coffee, began without her help. "Ms. Sweeney, are you acquainted with Richard Worth?"

She gave him a disbelieving look. "Well, of course I am, otherwise you wouldn't be here."

He coughed. "You're aware that his estranged wife was murdered night before last." That was a statement, not a question.

"Yes."

"Were you also acquainted with Mrs. Worth?"

Sweeney's eyes darkened. "Yes," she repeated, softly. "I've known her for years. I exhibited at the gallery."

"Oh, so you're an artist."

"Yes."

"No kidding." He looked at a large landscape on the wall. "Did you do that?"

"No." She didn't hang her own work. When she relaxed, she liked to look at something someone else had done.

That conversational gambit exhausted, he returned to the subject at hand. "Mrs. Worth wasn't happy about your involvement with Mr. Worth, was she?"

The super, Sweeney thought. That scene in the entrance lobby. "She told me she didn't care, but then when she came here one morning to see me and Richard was here, she was upset." She was pleased with that masterful understatement.

"When was this?"

They already knew, she thought. They had already talked to the super. They were asking questions to which they already knew the answers, to see if she would tell the truth. "A few days ago."

"How long have you been involved with Mr. Worth?"

She blinked at him, more taken aback by the question than most people would have been. "I don't know. What day of the week is it?"

They shared a quick glance. "Thursday," Detective Ritenour said.

"Then it's been a week. I think. I lose track of days."

"A week," Detective Aquino echoed. He made a note in his little book. "You stayed at Mr. Worth's town house last night."

Sweeney blushed. Great. Now they knew how easy she was. "Yes."

"Where were you night before last, Ms. Sweeney?"

Ah, now they were getting down to the meat of their questions. Sweeney felt a flicker of alarm. She had been alone here, with no calls, no witnesses—no alibis. "Here."

"Alone?"

"Yes."

"All night?"

"Yes."

"Did you maybe step out for some fresh air, a walk before bedtime, anything like that?"

"No. I didn't leave the apartment."

Ritenour rubbed his nose. "Did you make any calls, talk to anyone?"

"No."

"Have you ever been to Mrs. Worth's apartment?"

"No. I don't know exactly where she lived."

"Did you have any contact with Mrs. Worth after the scene a few days ago? Since she was so upset, did she call you afterwards and maybe make a couple of threats, you know, the way people do when affairs of the heart are concerned?"

His phraseology was charming. She lost herself in a moment of bemusement at hearing a cop actually say "affairs of the heart." Then she shook herself. "No. That was the last time I either saw her or heard from her."

"Do you have any knowledge of someone, say, holding a grudge against Mrs. Worth?"

Only Richard, she started to say. Thank God he had cleared himself. "No. Candra and I were business associates, not friends. But I liked her," she said softly, looking down. "Until that scene the other day, I had never seen her be anything but polite and friendly to everyone."

They both smiled at her. "That's all the questions I have," Detective Aquino said, closing his little notebook. "Thank you for your time, Ms. Sweeney."

"You're welcome." She went with them to the door.

As they started to leave, Aquino stopped and turned back. "Are you planning on going out of town, Ms. Sweeney? In case we have more questions."

"No," she said. "I'm not going anywhere."

As soon as they were gone, Sweeney picked up the phone to call Richard, then put it down without dialing. There was no point in worrying him with this. The detectives had asked a few questions; that was all. Granted, she had no way of proving she hadn't left the apartment all night, but neither had she ever been in Candra's apartment, so there couldn't be any evidence tying her in any way to the murder. She had nothing to worry about.

Despite her best intentions to stay out of the studio, after lunch and laundry she began to think about the painting. She hadn't really examined it yesterday, looking at it only long enough to recognize Candra. She didn't want to look at it again, and yet she knew she must. She had to finish it. The cops didn't seem to have any solid leads, or they wouldn't have been questioning her, so unless she finished the painting, the killer would probably get away with the murder.

The other day—two days ago? three?—she had worked on the painting while awake. If she could do that again, the shock to her system wouldn't be as severe and the chill wouldn't be as bad. She didn't want to go through a repeat of yesterday morning, even though she now knew she could get through it on her own.

When she went into the studio, though, she couldn't bring herself to walk right up to the painting. She wandered around looking at other works in progress, other things she had done, recalling what had been difficult or fascinating about each subject. For her, looking at her work was what looking at a photo album was to other people, calling up memories of times past.

But eventually she came to the unfinished painting, and she stopped cold, struck by the stark power of the work. The terror of Candra's last minutes seemed to leap off the canvas, as well as the nothingness of death. And there was menace as well, in the stance of the man standing over her, a sort of gloating satisfaction that was sickening.

She stared at the blank space where the man's face would be, and she felt a sort of floating sensation, faint but detectable. Her vision seemed to narrow, her focus tightening on the canvas.

The ringing of the doorbell was a jarring intrusion, making her jump. She lost the focus, the growing sense of seeing something that wasn't yet there. Muttering to herself, she went to the door.

Her unexpected visitor was Kai, his arms loaded with wrapped canvases. "Hi," he said when Sweeney opened the door. "I brought these by. The framer tried to deliver them to the gallery, but of course it isn't open, so he called me. Candra told me to send them back to you, but I thought, what the hell, why not bring them to you myself? Who knows if or when the gallery will open again."

He looked at her as if expecting her to tell him Richard's plans for the gallery, but since she had no idea, she merely shrugged.

"In here," she said, leading the way to the studio.

"By the way, the last of your old work sold."

"That's good." She cleared some space where she could stand the canvases against the wall. "Put them here."

He did as she directed, looking around at the other things she had completed. "Hey, these are really great. You're gonna make a fortune; wait and see."

"I hope," she said, smiling at him.

"The light is great in here." He walked over to the huge windows and looked out at the street below. Then he turned, and saw the painting.

All color leached out of his face. He stared at it, mouth agape, eyes blank with shock. "My God," he blurted.

"Don't tell anyone." Uncomfortable, she shifted her feet, unable to look him in the eye.

"When did you—You did all this in a day and a half?"

She cringed inside, but she had to come up with some reasonable explanation for the painting, and she couldn't think of one. "No, I've been working on it several days."

"What? How?"

"I—" Her mind went blank. Furious with herself for not being able to lie, she said, "I swear to God, Kai, if you spill the beans on this, I'll pull every hair out of your head."

"Spill the beans?" He was looking back and forth from the painting to her, as if he couldn't believe what he was seeing.

"I'm sort of psychic," she snapped.

"Sort of—?"

"I do paintings of things that haven't happened yet. When I finish this, it will show who killed her." She glared at him. "And I don't want you to ever mention any of this to anyone."

He was all but backing away from her, inching toward the door. "I won't," he said.

"I mean it, Kai. I don't want the cops to know; not yet."

He drew a deep breath. "I understand," he said. "I won't tell the cops, I promise." Then he laughed, the sound shaky. "Son of a bitch," he said. "No one would ever expect this, would he?"

CHAPTER NINETEEN

"I'm telling you, I saw it."

"That's impossible. You must be mistaken."

"That isn't something I'd be mistaken about," Kai said, annoyed.

"There's no such thing as a psychic; that's all just parlor games. She must have already done the painting, and when she heard about Candra, she just painted in her face."

"Then explain how Sweeney knew what Candra was wearing. I saw Candra at the party, remember? I know how she was dressed. Sweeney had the dress, the shoes, the jewelry, everything, down right."

"This is unbelievable. She had to have found out some other way."

"There *is* no other way," Kai insisted. "I don't care if you believe real psychics exist or not; the painting exists—because I've seen it. And you have to decide what in hell you're going to do about it."

"Do? What is there to do? *I* don't know anything about what's going on. *You,* on the other hand, are going to do your civic duty and tell the police about this very interesting painting Sweeney has, which couldn't possibly exist unless she saw the killing or did the killing. At the very least they'll take the painting, and she won't be able to finish it."

"You don't think the cops would be interested in letting her finish the face?"

"Why should they?"

Kai felt as if he were beating his head against a rock. He began ticking off points on his fingers. "A: Initially, the cops will think she did it, but unfortunately there isn't any evidence except the painting to tie her to the murder. B: She'll demonstrate how she did the painting, and once they're believers, they'll be watching every brushstroke she makes."

"That would never hold up in court."

"No, but once they know where to look, do you honestly think they won't find some little shred of evidence to tie you up like a Christmas turkey?"

"No, I don't. Anything they find will point to someone else and you know it."

"But what about your fucking *face?*" he said from between gritted teeth. "Once they have it, don't you think it will occur to the cops to show your picture to the guard? What's going to happen then?"

Finally, the danger of the situation began to sink in. They stared at each other in silence for a moment. "Okay, we have to contain the damage. I still think you should go to the police; it will take suspicion off you. And they won't allow her to work on the painting because if they do, then it's inadmissible as evidence against her, if they can make the case, and they wouldn't take that chance."

"What if they do?"

"Then we'll fall back on our safety net. With hard physical evidence, and the tape as motive, do you think the cops are really going to believe a kooky painting? He'd have to die, of course, and leave a suicide note telling why. Such a shame."

Kai relaxed. The logic of the plan was comforting. For the first time since seeing the painting in Sweeney's apartment, he felt as if he might slip out of this trap after all.

"And there's always the most obvious step."

"What?" he asked.

"Why, killing Sweeney, of course. *Before* she finishes the painting."

Late that afternoon, Sweeney opened the door once again to Detectives Aquino and Ritenour. As soon as she saw their cold eyes and impassive faces, the bottom dropped out of her stomach. She knew exactly what Kai had done. "That rotten tattletale," she muttered.

"Ms. Sweeney," said Detective Aquino, "with your permission, we'd like to search your apartment. If you insist, we can get a search warrant within the hour, but things will go much smoother if you cooperate." Smoother for them, he meant. Right now smooth was probably very important to him; he didn't look as if he had gotten any sleep that day, either.

She sighed. "The painting's in the studio. I'll get it."

"If you don't mind, we'll go with you," Ritenour said immediately, and they both fell in step just behind her.

She was so tired she didn't care, or almost didn't care. She had been fighting the need for sleep all day, hoping she would get to spend the night with Richard again and he would somehow protect her from whatever happened when she slept. If she was at his town house, then she couldn't work on the painting, could she? But her conscience hurt her whenever she thought of avoiding the completion of the painting, as if she were planning to let a murderer go free. She had to do the painting. But she would very much prefer that Richard be with her when she did, to help her through the aftermath. That meant he needed to be here.

But now where she was going to sleep was a moot question, because it looked as if she wasn't going to be getting any sleep for quite a while. That was assuming her next bed wasn't in a jail cell.

"Here," she said, going over to the painting. The two detectives ranged themselves slightly behind and on either side of her, in case she tried to do something stupid, like run. She didn't look at them as they studied the painting. She knew exactly what they were seeing, and what they were thinking.

"Ms. Sweeney." Detective Ritenour's tone was flat. "Would you like to tell us how you knew the details of the murder scene?"

"You won't believe me," she said helplessly.

"Try us."

"I didn't." She stood as still as a small animal with a wolf sniffing at the entrance to its lair. "I painted it in my sleep."

Fleeting *Yeah, sure* expressions went over their faces. "We'd like you to come down to the precinct with us. This painting will be taken as evidence . . ." Aquino's voice droned on, but Sweeney didn't listen. She tried to beat down the panic that threatened to choke her. They couldn't prove she killed Candra, because she hadn't done it. She tried to hang on to that thought.

"I painted it in my sleep," she repeated stubbornly. "I walk in my sleep sometimes, and when I wake up, I find that I've painted something. Wait—there's another painting I did, of a hot dog vendor who was killed several days ago. His name was Elijah Stokes. There was a witness who saw a man running away, so I couldn't have had anything to do with that murder." She hurried to the closet and took out the painting, carefully not looking at the face that had always worn the sweetest expression God had ever put on a human being, and now never would again.

Ritenour took that canvas and grimly examined it. "I'm not familiar with this case," he said. "We'll have to check it out."

They didn't believe anything she said. Belatedly she realized she might find herself charged as an accessory in Elijah Stokes's murder, if she didn't manage to do something. She had been deliciously warm all day, but now a faint chill raced up her back. Automatically she hugged her arms, rubbing them.

"This isn't the only weird thing that's been happening." They weren't listening, their minds closed off to any explanation she could give except the obvious: she had been at the scenes. Panic congealed into a cold lump and settled in the pit of her stomach. She had to keep trying anyway.

"Please get your shoes and purse," Detective Aquino requested.

She did, and a coat to go over her sweatshirt, though they gave her disbelieving glances. The high that day had been in the eighties, and the late afternoon was still warm. She couldn't feel any internal heat, though, just the spreading chill of terror. She tried to control it, tried to keep calm, because that was the only way she had of helping herself.

Aquino took her purse and looked through it, then gave it back to her and took her arm.

"Listen to me," she said in as calm a tone as she could manage. "When we get in the car, pay attention to the traffic signals."

"We always do," Ritenour said with heavy irony as they escorted her from the apartment.

"No, I mean to what happens." She was trembling like a leaf, her breath hitching. "You won't have to stop. The lights will turn green when we get close. They always do for me. And there'll be an empty parking space right in front of the station for you." She felt as if she were babbling, but she couldn't stop.

"If that's so," said Aquino politely, "then people would pay you a fortune just to ride around in their cars with them."

They put her in the backseat of a nondescript sedan. She noticed there weren't any door handles in back, but at least there wasn't a wire cage in front of her. The paintings were placed in the trunk. She forced herself to stillness, imposing a tiny bit of control on a world that was coming apart around her. Had she been officially arrested, or were they just taking her in for questioning? She didn't know the procedure, didn't know what came next. She should probably call a lawyer, she thought, but who she wanted to call was Richard. She needed him. But the cops had already had him in for questioning, and calling him would just drag him back into this mess.

The traffic light at the corner turned green. "Did you see that?" she asked. "It turned green."

"Yeah, they do that occasionally," Aquino said sarcastically.

The next one turned green, too. And the next one. Sweeney sat very quietly, not pointing out the obvious again. They would notice every light now.

The traffic cleared from in front of them, cars switching lanes, turning down other streets. The sedan didn't have to slow, but kept a steady pace. As the seventh traffic light turned green at their approach, Ritenour turned in his seat and gave her an unreadable look, but neither he nor Aquino remarked on the phenomena.

As they drove up to the precinct house, a car pulled out of a parking space directly in front of the building. She thought Aquino said, "Shit," under his breath, but she wasn't certain.

The precinct was boiling with humanity. Peeling green paint, metal desks and filing cabinets, shouts and curses and laughter all running together, armed men and women in blue uniforms: Sweeney's impression of all this was a blur. Soon she was sitting in a very uncomfortable chair in a dingy little room, thoughts roiling in her mind, but no bright ideas on how to prove herself popped out of the cauldron.

Chills roughened her skin, and she began shivering. She pulled her coat on and huddled in it. So it was shock, just as Richard thought, her body's reaction to something upsetting. Probably when she painted the scenes she was at least partially protected by sleep, but when she woke up, the reaction hit with a bang.

"Ms. Sweeney, where were you night before last?" Ritenour was staring at her, pale eyes hard, his tone cold.

"At home." Her teeth chattered. "The weird stuff started happening about a year ago. Little things. Traffic lights changing, the parking spaces, things like that. I didn't notice at first. Like you said, lights turn green all the time. Everyone catches a green light occasionally. And my plants began to bloom out of season."

"Ms. Sweeney." Ritenour's voice had gone as hard as his eyes. "Do I look like I care about your plants?"

No, he looked as if he had wanted to add a copulatory adjective in front of "plants."

She opened her mouth to tell him about the ghosts, then

shut it. That wouldn't help her case at all. "I began the painting several days ago; I don't know exactly when. I don't keep track of days. When I woke up, I found I had painted shoes. Two of them, a man's and a woman's. Every morning I'd find s-something new added." She clamped her teeth together to control their chattering.

"Would you like some coffee?" Aquino asked, and she nodded gratefully. He left the little room. Sweeney looked back to Ritenour.

"After a c-couple of days, I knew I was p-painting a murder scene, but I didn't know who—I hadn't gotten to the f-faces. Yesterday m-morning, when I got up, I saw I had painted C-Candra. I tried to c-call her, to warn her—at the gallery, but no one answered. Her home number is unlisted. S-so I called Richard's office, to get her number, and his assistant told me Candra was d-dead." She was shaking violently, teeth chattering. Her bones and muscles began to ache. Her hands, resting on the table, had turned a transparent bluish white, as if she had no blood in her body.

"If all that's so, why didn't you tell us about it this morning?" Despite himself, Ritenour was interested. People came forward all the time claiming to have special, prior knowledge of crimes, calling themselves psychic and looking to get their names in the news. In his experience, they were usually the perps. People were weird.

"I knew you wouldn't believe m-me."

No shit, he started to say, but controlled himself. What in hell was wrong with her? She acted like they had her in a freezer, huddling in that damn coat when it had to be at least seventy-five degrees in here. She wasn't faking, though; even her lips were blue.

He frowned and left the room without explanation. Aquino

was just coming back with the coffee. "Something's going on with her," Ritenour said to his partner. "She's freezing cold. I'm beginning to think we might have to get the medics to treat her for hypothermia." He was only half-joking.

"Shit." A medical condition would bring the questioning to a halt. Of course, all she had to do was ask to see a lawyer and they wouldn't be able to ask her any more questions unless the lawyer was present, but for some reason she hadn't done that. "Maybe the coffee will warm her up."

They reentered the room. She was sitting exactly as Ritenour had left her. Aquino put the coffee down in front of her. She tried to lift the cup, but her hands were shaking so violently the hot liquid slopped over on her fingers.

"We got any drinking straws around here?" Ritenour muttered. Aquino shrugged. They both watched as she wrapped her hands around the polystyrene cup and leaned forward, awkwardly trying to sip the coffee with the cup still sitting on the table. Aquino was a real hard-ass, but, glancing at him, Ritenour saw that his partner was looking a little concerned.

The coffee seemed to help her a little. After a couple of sips she was able to lift the cup without sloshing the coffee all over her.

Ritenour began again. "Ms. Sweeney, were you aware that Mr. and Mrs. Worth had signed a prenuptial agreement?"

"No," she said, bewildered. "Why would I be?"

"You're involved with Mr. Worth. A man's financial situation would normally be of interest to a woman, especially if she thought he stood to lose half of everything in a divorce."

"I—We—" Sweeney stammered. "We've just begun seeing each other. We haven't—"

"You're involved enough that you spent last night with him," Aquino said. "Money's the reason behind a lot of things people do."

"But Candra had agreed to sign the papers." Sweeney looked up at them. "I knew she wasn't happy about the settlement because she wanted me to get Richard to increase the amount, so even though I don't know the exact amount of the settlement, it c-couldn't have been half of everything he has."

That at least was logical. She could see them acknowledge the point.

Ritenour rubbed his jaw. He wore an interesting wristwatch, the kind that let you check the local time in Timbuktu, with all sorts of buttons and gadgets. Sweeney stared at it, an idea glimmering.

"What time is it?"

Ritenour glanced at the watch. "Six forty-three."

"I can prove I'm—" She couldn't say *psychic.* She shrank from it herself, and she could tell they automatically rejected anything connected with the word. "You saw what happened with the traffic lights. You *saw.* And it happens every time. But there's another way I can show you I . . . know things ahead of time."

"Yeah? How?" They looked skeptical, but at least they hadn't rejected the notion out of hand.

"Is there a television here? *Jeopardy!* will soon be on."

"So?" Aquino asked.

"So it isn't a rerun. There's no way I could already have seen it. Agreed?"

Ritenour shrugged. "Agreed."

"What if I can tell you everything that's going to happen before it does?" She drained the last of the coffee. She was still shivering, but at least her teeth had stopped chattering. "Will you at least admit then that there's a possibility I could have done the painting without having actually been at the scene?"

"You want to demonstrate your 'psychic abilities,' huh?"

Her temper flared. She was tired and cold and sick with worry, and almost at the end of her rope. "No, I don't," she snapped. "What I want is to go home and go to bed, but I'm afraid when I do, I'll get up in my sleep and paint something else. I'm tired of dealing with this. If you want to know who killed Candra, you'll give back that damn painting and let me finish it, maybe tonight."

They looked at her in silence. Defiantly she stared back. Then Aquino jerked his head toward the door and they left again. Sweeney leaned her head on her hands, wondering how much longer she could hold out.

Aquino and Ritenour stood outside the door. "Whaddaya think?" Aquino asked.

"What will it hurt? Let's watch *Jeopardy!*"

"What will that prove? That she's a good guesser?"

"Like she said, it'll prove whether or not it's at least possible she has some psychic ability. I'm not saying I believe in the crap. I'm saying . . . I'm saying this is interesting. We don't have to accept everything she tells us, but we do need to check it out. It isn't as if the painting is all we have to go on; the lab's working on the fiber analysis, and once we have that, we can tell for certain whether or not any of the fibers came from her apartment."

"So what you're saying is, you like *Jeopardy!* and want to watch it."

Ritenour shrugged. "I'm saying, it won't hurt anything to let her watch it. Let's see what she can do."

CHAPTER TWENTY

The three contestants filed out and took their places, with the voice-over giving their names and places of residence. Alex Trebek came out and announced that all three contestants were newcomers, as a five-time champion had retired on yesterday's show. "Number three," Sweeney said, holding another cup of coffee under her nose and inhaling the steam. "She'll win."

The two detectives merely glanced at her. They were seated on dilapidated office chairs with pieces of foam padding coming out of the cracked vinyl seats, in a small, messy, dingy room littered with coffee cups and soft drink cans. A coffee machine, candy machine, and soft drink machine took up a lot of space and underlaid the silence with an incessant humming. The television was a thirteen-incher, receiving only off its bunny ears, but the picture and audio were fairly clear.

They weren't the only three in the room. Cops being a naturally nosy bunch, whoever had a few minutes free found an excuse to see what was going on. Three uniforms and two more suits had joined them. When Aquino growled that this wasn't a damn circus, one of the suits shrugged and said, "Hey, we like *Jeopardy!* too."

Alex read off the categories. *"Inventors."*

"Cyrus McCormick," said Sweeney.

" *'Little' Movies,* and the quotation marks mean the word 'little' will appear in each answer."

" 'Little Women,' " Sweeney said.

"I coulda guessed that," said a uniformed officer.

"Then why didn't you?" asked someone else.

"Quiet!" Aquino barked.

"Colleges and Universities."

"Tulane," Sweeney said. She gripped the cup tighter. Doing this in her apartment wasn't the same thing as getting it right this time, when it was important. Maybe she *had* just been making lucky guesses.

"Business and Industry."

"Three-M."

"Math."

"Prime numbers."

"And finally, *Highways and Byways.*"

"I-Ten, and I-Ninety," said Sweeney, and waited tensely for the first contestant to make her choice.

"Math, for a hundred," said contestant number one.

Alex read the clue. "These numbers are evenly divisible by only the number one and themselves."

Number three was hot with the button, ringing in even though the other two were frantically pushing theirs, too. "What are prime numbers," she said.

Silence fell in the dingy little room in the police station. One by one other choices were made, and each time Sweeney gave the correct answer. Sometimes she barely had time to get the answer out before the clue popped up on-screen, but she always made it. Contestant number three was on a roll; even if she didn't ring first, she was always ready in case one of the other two stumbled. By the time the first commercial break rolled around, she had twice as much money as the other two combined.

"I think we've seen enough," said Aquino, getting to his feet.

"Maybe you have," replied one of the other detectives. "I want to see the rest of the show."

Shakily Sweeney rose and followed Aquino out of the room, with Ritenour right behind her.

"All right." Aquino growled when they were once again in the interrogation room. "So you can do that. And that thing with the traffic lights. I'm impressed, but I ain't convinced. Convince me."

She stared helplessly at him. "Convince you, how? I can barely believe it myself, and I'm living it. I can't tell you what's going to happen tomorrow, and I can't read your mind. I paint in my sleep and I see ghosts—oh, damn," she finished weakly, seeing those looks they were giving her again. She hadn't meant to mention the ghosts. There was no way to prove she saw them, because she was the only one who did. If she hadn't been so tired, she would have had better self-control.

"Ghosts," repeated Ritenour.

"Forget I said that."

"Uh-huh. I'm going to forget to eat for the next week, too."

She wished he hadn't mentioned eating. She had been try-ing to ignore her hunger, which was just one more discomfort added on to being cold and exhausted. She made a dismissive gesture. "No one else sees them, so it doesn't matter. They don't bother anyone; most of the time they don't even say hi. Although Elijah Stokes did tell me his sons' names so I could send a sketch to them."

"Elijah Stokes."

"The hot dog vendor who was killed. The other painting. Have you checked on that yet?"

"I'll see what I can find. Some other precinct probably han-dled it. Where was he killed?" asked Ritenour.

"I don't know, but one of his sons could tell you. Their names were . . ." She searched her memory. "Daniel . . . no, David. David and Jacob Stokes. They're both attorneys."

Ritenour left the room. She leaned back in the uncomfort-able chair and closed her eyes, rubbing her forehead where a headache was beginning to form.

"Does anyone else know about that painting?" Aquino asked, and she opened her eyes to find his shrewd gaze on her. "Besides Mr. Stengel."

"Ste—? Oh, Kai." She had heard his last name only a couple of times, and most of the time it escaped her.

"What about Mr. Worth? He's been in your apartment. Has he seen the painting?"

Not mentioning Richard was one thing; lying to a cop was something else entirely.

"Yes," she said, her voice so weary it was almost inaudible. "He's known about it from the beginning."

Aquino's eyebrows rose. "From the beginning . . . as in sev-eral days ago?"

"That's right."

"I wonder why he didn't see fit to mention this to us yesterday."

"He didn't want to implicate me. He knew this would happen," she whispered. "He said that when I finished the painting and we knew who the murderer is, or at least have a description, he would somehow point you in the right direction."

"Big of him," said Aquino furiously. "I don't like civilians deciding for me how I should do my job."

Sweeney slapped her hand down on the table, suddenly as furious as he. "Just what would you have said, Detective, if Richard had come to you and said, 'Oh, by the way, the woman I'm seeing has some psychic ability and she's doing a painting of the murder'? Would you have believed him, any more than you believe me?"

He put both hands on the table and leaned toward her, aggressiveness in every line of his burly body. "It isn't my job to believe everything I'm told."

"No, but it is your job to recognize the truth when it's staring you in the face!" She leaned forward, too, bringing her nose as close as possible to his.

To her surprise, he raised his eyebrows. "As far as that goes," he said mildly, "I'm inclined to believe you."

Talk about taking the wind out of her sails. Sweeney sat back, feeling herself go flat without the puff of indignation. "You do?"

"You proved the possibility to me," he said. "I didn't think you could, but you proved everything you said. Traffic lights turn green, parking spaces open up, and you could make a killing playing *Jeopardy!* What you did is way beyond the law of averages. So if you can do all that, then . . ." He shrugged. "The painting is possible."

She couldn't think of anything to say. For a second she thought she might cry, but the urge went away. She was too tired to make the effort.

"Tell me something. Why didn't you call a lawyer?"

"I would have, if you actually arrested me. I haven't been arrested, have I?"

"No, but if it hadn't been for that *Jeopardy!* thing . . . probably."

"I would like to make a call, though."

"You want a lawyer now?"

"No," she said. "I want to call Richard."

"I think I'll place the call myself," he said.

While they were waiting for Richard, Ritenour returned with a copy of the investigative report on Elijah Stokes's murder, complete with a diagram of the scene. The clothing description matched that in Sweeney's painting, as did the head wound, and the body's location and position. A nineteen-year-old punk had been arrested, and blood splatters matching Elijah Stokes's blood type had been found on a shirt under the kid's bed.

The painting was eerily accurate, and there was no way Sweeney could have come by the knowledge other than the way she described.

Richard didn't arrive making angry comments had loud demands; he was too smart for that. Nor did he bring in a high-powered lawyer with him, though Sweeney had no doubt he could have one there on a moment's notice. He was dressed in a suit and tie, which at that hour made her think he must have been with Candra's parents, making the final arrangements or perhaps even receiving friends who came to offer their condolences.

He shook hands with both detectives, but the entire time

his gaze was on Sweeney, and when he saw how she was bundled in her coat, he made no effort to hide his worry. She had stood when she saw him, and now he stepped toward her, unobtrusively opening his suit jacket. When he folded her in his arms, she was wrapped inside the warmth of the garment, her cold hands sliding around to rest on his back at waist level. She buried her face in the curve of his shoulder, so relieved by his warmth and presence, the knowledge she was no longer alone, that she almost sagged against him.

"You should have called," he murmured.

"And you should have told us about the painting yesterday," Aquino pointed out.

"I would have, if I had thought it would spare her this."

"Do you verify you saw the painting in progress, days before Mrs. Worth was murdered?"

"Yes. I saw it from the first, when she had completed only two shoes." He glanced up at the detectives. "I wasn't at the scene, and you still have what Candra was wearing that night, so you'll have to tell me if the clothing Sweeney painted was accurate. The dress was black, full-skirted, and the shoes were black pumps with little gold balls set in the heels. Right?"

"Right."

He had just verified everything she had told them, Sweeney realized. He hadn't been to her apartment since Candra's death, so there was no way he could have seen the painting after the murder. What he had just described had been painted prior to the murder. They knew he hadn't seen the clothing anywhere else.

"Okay, okay," Aquino said, rubbing his bloodshot eyes. "Unless you two conspired to commit murder, for God only knows what reason, since you have no motive that I've been able to find, Ms. Sweeney is clear."

"What about the painting?" Richard asked. "Do you want her to finish it?" She felt his arms tighten around her as he asked the question, and knew he worried about what she went through but couldn't see any other option.

"By all means," Ritenour said, after an agreeing nod from Aquino. "The painting is in no way admissible as evidence, but we do have some trace evidence that would provide the link, if we can identify the guy."

"What if neither of us recognizes him?" Sweeney asked.

"With a good physical description, we should be able to match him to the surveillance tape, which shows the date and time. By matching the time to the guard's signature log, we'd have him cold."

Richard looked thoughtful. "I might recognize someone, if I saw the tape."

"We didn't," Aquino said. "We've managed to get photos of most of the guys on the list—"

"What list?" asked Sweeney.

They ignored her. "—but the guard didn't recognize any of them, and we couldn't match any of them to the tape. We're still tracking down the people who did register as visitors, but so far they've all checked out."

"The painting's our best bet right now," Ritenour said.

Richard nodded. "I'll stay with her tonight. I don't want her to be alone. Kai has probably spread the news about the painting all over town, and whoever killed Candra could already know about it. Not only that, I can call you immediately if she finishes the face."

Something in Richard's voice must have alerted the detectives. "Mr. Worth," said Aquino, "if you're thinking about any heroics, I have to tell you I don't think that's such a good idea. If by any chance Ms. Sweeney should be in any danger, you should concentrate on getting her to safety and leaving the apprehension of a criminal to us."

"Taking care of her is my prime consideration," said Richard, and Sweeney wondered if they noticed he hadn't necessarily agreed with them.

Edward was driving that night. "We're taking Ms. Sweeney home."

"Very good, sir."

The detectives had given both paintings back to her, and Edward stored them up front with him. The paintings startled him enough that he actually looked taken aback for a moment, then his expression smoothed out and he handled them as matter-of-factly as if they had been landscapes.

When they were seated, Richard reached for Sweeney's hand and twined his fingers with hers. "You're cold," he said.

"I was scared." She squeezed his hand. "This wasn't as bad as the other episodes. As long as they kept the coffee coming, I managed."

"If you had called me immediately, a lot of this could have been avoided."

"On the other hand, once they witnessed my prowess at *Jeopardy!*, they were a lot more inclined to believe me."

He gave her a puzzled look. *"Jeopardy!?"*

"One of my new skills. I'll show you someday."

Their entwined hands were resting on her right thigh. His knuckles rubbed lightly back and forth. "Candra's parents and some of their friends are at the house," he said. "We've settled on the arrangements for the service—they want her buried close to where they live—but they're ready to go back to the hotel. I'll have Edward drive them, and I'll grab a change of clothes then take a taxi to your place."

If she were noble, she thought, she would tell him she knew he had a lot to do and she would be perfectly all right by herself. She must not be the least bit noble, because she was tired of facing the nights by herself and she wanted him with her.

Besides, Richard's comment that Candra's killer could now know about the painting hadn't gone unnoticed. Part of her couldn't believe she was in any danger, but the logical part of her pointed out it would be smarter not to take any unnecessary chances. She slept very soundly; she might not hear anyone breaking into the apartment, unless they crashed, movie-style, through the window beside her bed. After being awake all the night before, she was so exhausted now even a crashing window might not wake her.

As if he followed her thoughts, the way he so often did, Richard said, "Did you get any sleep today?"

"No. Did you?"

"I caught a couple of hours after lunch."

She envied him both the nap and his stamina; he looked untouched by fatigue, as alert as he always was.

"You can sleep tonight," he promised softly.

She squeezed his hand and pitched her voice low enough that Edward couldn't hear. "Not *all* night, I hope."

"I think I can guarantee that." He squeezed her hand in return, and Sweeney sat in contented silence for the rest of the drive.

A tiny Italian restaurant was located across the street and several doors down from Sweeney's apartment building. The restaurant was popular in the neighborhood, with a steady stream of nearby residents stopping by for takeout. Kai managed to snag a table by the window, seating himself so he could see anyone entering the apartment building.

Letting himself get involved in the plan to kill Candra had been partly impulse, because she'd been such a bitch and was planning to fire him anyway. The biggest consideration, however, had been the money. A hundred thousand dollars wasn't a lot of money to some people, and it was a hell of a lot less than the million Candra had asked for in blackmail, but it would mean the difference between several years more spent taking penny-ante jobs and supplementing his income with infrequent modeling gigs for sleazy underwear catalogs, which usually included having to fuck some bony, middle-aged hag who thought she was hot because she wielded a lot of power over young men who needed the jobs she provided.

With a hundred thou, he could quit work, finish his art classes, and begin making a name for himself with his paintings. Kai had no doubt he was talented. He knew his stuff was a lot better than most of the crap he had helped sell at the gallery, and now he would be backed by a very influential name that would get him displayed in the most prestigious gallery in the city. He wasn't going to start low and gradually increase his prices; he was going to ask a small fucking fortune right from the beginning; there were a lot of rich fools who would buy paintings carrying a high sticker just because they liked the idea that not everyone could afford to buy them.

Everything would be perfect, if it weren't for that damn painting of Sweeney's.

He regretted that. He liked Sweeney. She was funny and honest, and she had never looked at him as if he were nothing but a piece of meat. She was also genuinely talented, with a knack for realism that meant any portrait she painted would be a faithful re-creation of the subject. Too bad she'd turned out to be a fucking psychic, too.

So he waited, watching for her to come home. Unlike a certain other party, who wasn't the most realistic person he'd ever met, he didn't expect the cops to book her on the basis of that painting. They weren't idiots; without physical evidence at the scene to back it up, they'd have a hard time convincing any D.A. to take the case to court. On the other hand, if she managed to convince them she was for real, they would be checking with her every day to see if she had finished the damn thing yet. Just getting rid of the painting wouldn't be enough; its existence didn't matter, just whether or not the other face was revealed. Sweeney would recognize it instantly, and then all hell would break loose.

That couldn't be allowed to happen.

Getting into her apartment had been easy. He had watched until the cops arrived; then after they took her away, he waited for his chance and slipped in with a crowd of people returning home from work, while the dumb-ass super was busy watching some dumb-ass game show and seldom looked up.

He took his time checking out the building. There wasn't a hallway window on Sweeney's floor that opened onto the fire escape, but there was such an access on the floor below hers. After ascertaining that, he took the elevator to the floor above Sweeney's, just in case anyone noticed at what floor he got off, then bounded down the stairs to her floor.

Getting into her apartment hadn't been easy, because she had locked both dead bolts. He listened at her neighbor's door, and when he didn't hear any noise from inside, he risked ringing the doorbell. Nothing, and these people hadn't bothered with the dead bolt, trusting in the doorknob lock, which took him about ten seconds to open.

He slipped inside, and stood listening for a moment to make certain no one was in the shower or something like that. Reassured that the apartment was empty, though it might not be for much longer, he turned the flimsy little lock on the doorknob just in case the tenant showed up before Kai did what needed doing.

He had gone to a tiny bedroom on the side adjoining Sweeney's apartment and climbed out the window onto the fire escape. Crouching beside one of the huge windows in her studio, he used a glass cutter to cut a hole in the window right next to the lock. Just in case anyone noticed him, he pretended to do some work in the fire escape, checking the joints and shit like that.

The lock on the window was stuck. Using his knife, he jimmied it open. Then he lowered the fire escape ladder down to the next level and left it. Someone might notice, but since it didn't go down to street level no one would be very alarmed.

Once everything was set, he slipped back into the neighboring apartment and left as unobtrusively as he had entered. Then all he had to do was wait for Sweeney to come home.

He flirted with the waitress in the little restaurant, pretended to read a newspaper, dawdled over his pasta, and then ordered a dessert and coffee. His patience was rewarded a little after nine, when Richard Worth's Mercedes rolled to a smooth stop outside the apartment building and both Sweeney and Richard got out. Richard took two canvases from the front seat and went inside with Sweeney. A few minutes later, he came out alone, and without the canvases.

Kai paid his bill and left the waitress with both a good tip and a slow, wicked smile that did more for her self-esteem than a good haircut. Then he crossed the street and walked around the block until he could see the big corner windows of Sweeney's studio. The lights came on in there, but the angle was too acute for him to see what she was doing. Then the lights went out again; she wasn't working on the painting. That was good.

It was still too early for her to go to bed, but he decided to get back into the building while he could. He had to wait about twenty minutes before a young couple entered the building, and he caught the door before it could close. The super glanced around when he heard the buzzer, but saw the young couple, and turned back to his television without seeing Kai.

Everything went smooth as silk. He went up to the roof and sat patiently, watching the lights and the traffic, listening to the car horns honking and the sirens blaring, distant voices carrying up to him. The city was never silent, never still. He loved the energy of it. The longer he waited, the less likely he was to run into trouble. People would be sleeping in their beds, peaceful and secure, and if anyone happened to wake up when he lowered the sections of fire escape ladders between the floors, so he could work his way down to the street, they would get to the window too late to see him.

They would sure as hell be too late to help Sweeney.

CHAPTER TWENTY-ONE

Sweeney was so tired she could barely think, but a hot shower revived her enough that she was able to concentrate on feeding herself. After hot soup and half a peanut butter sandwich, she felt almost human—almost. Only the fact that she was waiting for Richard to return kept her awake. She thought about relaxing on the couch until he arrived, but knew if she did she would be down for the count and might not even hear the doorbell.

She wandered into the studio, not bothering to turn on any lights. With the huge windows, enough light from streetlights, neon signs, and other buildings poured into the room to make it easy to negotiate the clutter. She strolled around the room, pausing before some canvases, touching others, like a mother putting her children to bed at night. She stopped in front of the painting of Candra, positioned on an easel, and stared at it for a long time. She tried to get a sense of the killer; what had he been thinking, standing over Candra like that? What kind of man was he, to gloat over a woman's violent death?

She had intuitively known other things about the painting, such as how the shoes should look, but she felt as if she were hitting a brick wall when she tried to grasp the essence of the killer. Something was there, on the other side of the wall, but she couldn't reach it.

Perhaps she would never finish the painting, she thought. Perhaps she could trance-paint only those people she knew, whose images were already in her memory bank. If the killer was a stranger, he might forever remain so.

Richard returned in little more than an hour. He dropped a small bag on the floor and turned to lock the door. Sweeney stood motionless, staring at him. He had changed from his suit into jeans and a black T-shirt, and Sweeney instantly forgot about being tired as she took in every detail. *This* was how she had always seen him in her mind's eye, without the disguise of an expensive suit. The short tight sleeves clung to his muscled arms, his jaw was shadowed with beard stubble, and he was the toughest, sexiest-looking man she had ever seen.

"That's it," she muttered, a little distracted as she framed the sketch in her mind. "I need to paint you just like this."

She looked around as if searching for her sketch pad. She had actually taken two steps toward the studio when he hooked an arm around her from behind and lifted her off her feet, drawing her back against him. "Not tonight, sweetie. It's bedtime for you." He began carrying her toward the bedroom.

Maybe it was because his mouth was so close to her ear.

Maybe something finally clicked in her brain. She twisted her head to stare up at him. "You called me 'sweetie,' " she accused.

He lifted his eyebrows. "Of course. What did you think I was calling you?"

"My name. Sweeney."

He planted a quick kiss on her sulky mouth. "I told you, I refuse to call the woman I'm sleeping with by her last name. That goes double for the woman I love. If you don't like 'sweetie,' we'll think of something else."

He said it so smoothly, and she was so tired, that it almost slipped by. "I guess 'sweetie' is okay," she began to mumble, then went rigid in his arms. He almost dropped her. He stopped, set her down, then turned her so she was facing him and wrapped both arms around her, lifting her again.

She put her hands on his shoulders to brace herself. "Did you say you love me, or was that just something to throw into the conversation?"

"No, I definitely said it."

This was a defining moment in her life. After thirty-one years of living she had finally fallen in love, and not with any ordinary guy. No, she had fallen head over heels for a tough, sexy rich guy, and he had just told her he loved her. No one else in her life had ever said those words to her. She felt as if they should be doing something romantic and dramatic, like drinking champagne and shooting off fireworks, to mark the moment.

"Oh," she said, and blinked sleepily at him. "I love you, too."

"I know," he said, and gently kissed her. He set her on her feet beside the bed and undressed her as if she were a child. She wished she had a sexy nightgown to put on for him, but all she owned was flannel pajamas. With him in bed beside her, she wouldn't need the pajamas to keep her warm.

He put her between the sheets and stripped off his own clothes, then got into bed beside her. She wished she had a king-size bed, so he would be more comfortable. Hers was a queen, but she suspected his feet hung off the end.

They turned toward each other like a magnet and steel, the force irresistible. He stroked her breasts, making her nipples tingle and her breath shorten. "You need to sleep," he muttered, but he was rock hard.

She closed her hand around his erection, stroking him with the same slow touch he was using on her breasts. "I need you more," she said.

He put on a condom and rolled on top of her. Sweeney spread her legs, taking him between them. He prodded the entrance to her body, his shaft thick and hot.

Sweeney didn't wait, couldn't wait. She clasped her legs around his and lifted her hips so that he slipped inside her.

Pleasure seemed to spread smoothly through her body, without the sharpness and urgency of the night before. His strokes were slow and deep, as if he wanted to savor every inch of her. She found the rhythm and joined him in it, and despite the lack of urgency, it seemed only moments before the heat and friction grew to intolerable levels. She clung to him, her nails digging into his back, small cries breaking from her throat with each move he made into her. He hooked his arms under her legs, bending over her with his weight braced on his hands, holding her legs spread wide so that he had full access to her and she could control neither the speed nor the depth of his thrusts. She felt as if he went straight into the heart of her, and she climaxed on the third deep stroke. He held himself there and shuddered violently as his own release took him apart.

Sweeney dozed, but roused a little when he carefully withdrew from her and rolled out of bed.

"Where are you going?" she murmured, reaching out to caress his back.

"To the bathroom, to get my bag, and to turn out the lights," he replied, and the answer seemed so prosaic she chuckled, turning her face into the pillow as lassitude claimed her again.

Still, she wasn't quite asleep when he returned. She went into his arms, shivering a little at the wash of cool air on her bare shoulders despite the heat that surrounded her everywhere below. "Let me wear your T-shirt," she said sleepily, and he leaned over the side of the bed to pluck it from the floor.

She sat up and pulled it on, then settled back into his arms. "Okay, now I can sleep."

"It's about time," he grumbled, but she heard the amusement and physical satisfaction underlying his tone, and she went to sleep feeling more secure than she ever had before.

She came awake with a jolt, heart hammering, every muscle tense.

She couldn't have been asleep long. She had the sense that very little time had passed, certainly no more than an hour. Something had wakened her, something that made her skin prickle, her reaction much as it would have been had she slept in a cave thousands of years ago and woke to the sound of a tiger prowling at the cave entrance. She listened intently, wondering if the comparison was apt. Was someone in the apartment?

Her mind replayed the undefined, unfamiliar noise. She hadn't imagined it. It hadn't been loud, nothing more than a scrape, a whisper of a sound. Like a footstep. Like a window sliding up. Either of those, or both. Coming from the studio.

She shook Richard and felt his instant alertness. "I heard something," she whispered.

He moved like oiled silk, rolling naked, soundlessly, out of bed. As he stooped down, he motioned for her to join him, holding a finger to his lips to indicate silence, both gestures plainly visible in the colorless light coming through the window.

She tried to imitate how he moved, without any jumps or jerks that would make noise. She got out of bed without any betraying squeaks from the mattress, only the whisper of the sheet marking her departure. His T-shirt, which had been bunched around her waist, settled down over her hips but did nothing to protect her from the cool night air washing around her bare legs. She noticed the chill and then promptly forgot it, her attention riveted on the open door of the bedroom, expecting at any moment to see a dark, menacing form come through it.

Richard stooped down to the small bag he had brought, never looking away from the door as he reached inside the bag. When he straightened, light glinted dully on the big weapon in his right hand. With his left, he reached out and tucked her behind him.

Gripping her wrist to make sure she stayed with him, and behind him, he glided soundlessly to a position behind the door, but not so close that it would hit him if someone shoved it completely open. Then they waited.

She couldn't hear him breathing, but her own breath seemed to echo in her ears and surely her heart was pounding hard enough to be audible. Carefully she breathed through her mouth, to eliminate even that small sound. And she listened.

She could hear the clock ticking in the living room. She heard the distant wail of a siren. She didn't hear a repeat of that scraping sound.

But Richard didn't relax, didn't move from his alert stance. He was closer to the door, his body blocking her; did he hear something she couldn't?

Then she felt, sensed, someone just on the other side of the doorway, not stepping into the bedroom but looking into it.

The door opened back toward the wall against which the bed was positioned. Because of that, he couldn't see the complete bed, just the foot of it, unless he came further into the doorway. Sweeney was acutely aware of the empty bed. Would he look at it and know they had heard him and were somewhere in the apartment, or would he assume no one was at home and she simply didn't make her bed? Would he stroll into the bedroom, or—

The door crashed back against the wall, the sound exploding in the dark silence.

Richard dropped, already moving before the door hit the wall, his grip on her wrist dragging her down with him. An explosion deafened her, blinded her. Another one, nearer, came so close on the heels of the first one the sounds almost blended into one. A strange percussion hit her, a small burst of air blasted against her skin.

Gun shots.

Her realization was immediate, but by that time there was nothing but the tinny ringing in her ears and the sharp smell of cordite burning her nostrils.

Her hearing and sight began to clear. She saw him now, flopping in the doorway. She heard him, a guttural, inhuman groan. The air fluttered out of his lungs like a balloon going flat, and then she smelled him.

She gagged, but fought back the bile that rose in her throat. "Are you all right?" Richard demanded, his voice harsh with urgency as he spun on his bare heel to face her.

"Yes," she managed to croak. He stood from his crouched position and went to the bed, switching on the bedside lamp.

She squinted, almost blinded again. Before her eyes

adjusted to the light, Richard was on the phone, his gaze locked on the body sprawled in the doorway. "This is Richard Worth," he said quietly, to whoever was on the other end of the line. "Kai Stengel just broke into Sweeney's apartment and tried to kill us."

Kai?

Stunned, Sweeney blinked several times and looked at the body, then wished she hadn't. Kai sprawled facedown in the bedroom doorway, his head turned toward her and his eyes open, set in the emptiness of death. There was a small, almost neat pool of blood under him, but the doorframe and the wall behind him were splattered with blood and gore.

"Don't bother," said Richard. "I shot him. He's dead."

As he replaced the receiver on the hook, Sweeney rose shakily to her feet and turned to him, instinctively wanting to go into his arms. She froze. Dark red rivulets streaked down his arm and chest, streaming from the top of his left shoulder.

"Oh, my God, you're shot!"

He glanced down at his shoulder. "Just a little," he said calmly, catching her as she launched herself at him.

She fought free of his grasp and pushed him down to sit on the edge of the bed. "You can't be just a little shot," she said fiercely. "It's like being pregnant; you either are or you aren't. Stay here."

She whirled and ran. Her first aid supplies were in the bathroom vanity cabinet. She had to step over Kai's body to get out of the room, but she hesitated only a fraction of a second. Richard was bleeding, and the urgent need to take care of him overrode everything else. She was careful where she put her feet, but she didn't slow down.

When she returned, laden with her first aid kit and a towel and washcloth, Richard had pulled on his jeans and was stepping into his shoes. "I told you to sit down!" she all but roared at him.

"No, you didn't. You told me to stay here. I'm here."

His mild tone infuriated her. But he sat down on the bed again and let her press a gauze pad to the top of his shoulder. "It's just a burn; it won't even need stitches."

He sounded so remote that she gave him a sharp glance. His face was expressionless, his eyes cool and watchful as he looked at Kai. She remembered that he had been an army ranger, and suddenly she knew that he had killed before, that this was the way he operated in a firefight.

After a moment she lifted the pad and saw that he was right; the wound across the top of his shoulder was a raw streak that sullenly oozed blood. Sirens wailed, coming closer and closer; they sounded as if they were right outside, then the noise abruptly stopped. Sweeney picked up the wet washcloth and began cleaning the wound. Richard took the cloth away from her. "I'll do it," he said, and slipped his free hand under the T-shirt to pat her bare butt. "You'd better get some clothes on, unless you want the cops to see this pretty ass of yours."

She scowled at him, but went to the closet and took out a pair of jeans, pulling them on without bothering to put on underwear. She was just in time; it took the first responding cops only a minute to get inside the building and up to her apartment. Richard made his escape while she was zipping and snapping, stepping past Kai to get to the front door before the thunderous pounding broke it down.

Four uniformed cops poured into the apartment. Sweeney had a glimpse of avid expressions on the faces of her neighboring tenants as they milled in the hall outside her door, then Richard pulled her into the kitchen, removing both of them from the scene so the cops could do their work.

The next few hours were a tumult. Detective Ritenour arrived hard on the heels of the uniformed cops, beating the

EMTs by a couple of minutes. He was dressed, but his shirt was wrinkled and his tie hung crookedly. Richard had called the detectives instead of 911. More uniformed cops arrived, and the emergency medical team, and Detective Aquino. Her apartment was full of people. Radios crackled. More people arrived.

Richard kept her in the kitchen, seated with her back to the door so she couldn't see any of what went on behind her. Two of the medical team looked at the wound on his shoulder and applied an antibiotic salve and a bandage. He finished cleaning himself up at the sink, scrubbing away the blood with a wet paper towel, and refused any further medical treatment.

Aquino and Ritenour took their statements. They found the window in her studio where Kai had entered. There was no question about Richard firing in self-defense.

"I think we'll find he killed Mrs. Worth," said Aquino. "When he saw the painting Ms. Sweeney was doing, it must have been a real shock to him. Took him by surprise, otherwise he would have tried to do away with you then," he said, looking at Sweeney. "Then I guess he thought he could pin the whole thing on you by telling us about the painting."

"But how did he know you didn't arrest me?" she asked, bewildered.

Aquino shrugged. Ritenour answered. "He could have called the precinct, or maybe he was watching. How doesn't matter. He obviously came here tonight intending to kill you, only you heard him raise the window, and you weren't alone."

Aquino said sourly to Richard, "It's illegal to own a handgun without a license in the city of New York."

Richard shrugged, not a flicker of discomfort from his wounded shoulder showing on his face. "I have a license," he said.

Aquino looked even more sour. "It figures. You did a damn

good job. That was a clean hit to the heart. You've had training, haven't you?"

"Military," Richard replied. "Army."

"Yeah?" Ritenour said. "What unit? I was in the army."

"Rangers."

Sweeney saw their expressions change, and they sat back in their chairs.

"The bastard didn't have a chance," Ritenour said softly.

CHAPTER
TWENTY-TWO

"You're at the end of your rope," Richard said roughly, tilting her face up. She was paper white, as much from fatigue as stress and shock; her eyes were dull and circled by shadows so dark they looked like bruises. "Get some clothes; I'm taking you home with me."

Aquino got to his feet. "I'll take care of that. She don't want to go into the bedroom. Is there anything in particular you want?"

She shook her head. Normally she would never have allowed a stranger to paw through her clothes, but right now she didn't care. He was right; she didn't want to go into the bedroom. She might never go into it again. "There's a satchel on the top shelf in the closet. Just throw some things in it."

"You'll need to sign a statement," Ritenour said to Richard, "but that can wait a few hours. Get some sleep if you can." He paused. "The media will be all over this, you know."

"Yeah, I know." Richard rubbed his jaw. "Is there any way we can keep the painting out of the news?"

So Sweeney wouldn't be a tabloid sensation, he meant.

"Maybe. I don't see any need to mention it. The reporters will probably play up the lover angle, make it sound like some sort of lovers' quarrel."

Candra's parents had already been hurt enough by her death, but now the sensationalism would double, and her relationship with Kai would be analyzed and dissected in public. "I wonder why he killed her," Ritenour said, almost to himself. "We may never know."

"If he did," said Sweeney, speaking through a blur of exhaustion.

Both men gave her sharp looks, Richard's lingering longer than Ritenour's. "What makes you say that?" asked the detective. "If he didn't kill Mrs. Worth, then he had no reason to worry about the painting, and no reason other than that to try to kill you."

She shrugged. She didn't know why she had said it. She tried to imagine Kai's face in the painting, but that brick wall was still there, refusing to allow the image to form.

A few minutes later Aquino returned with the bag. "One of the policewomen packed it," he said, as if he wanted her to know he hadn't been handling her underwear. "I thought a woman would know better what another woman needed."

"Thank you," she said. She reached out to take it, but

Richard's hand was there first. If the weight of the bag bothered his shoulder, he didn't show any sign of it.

"No sense in calling a taxi. One of the patrolmen can drop you off at your house."

Richard nodded and cupped Sweeney's elbow. "I'll call you later in the morning."

"Make it real late," Aquino replied, and yawned. "I'm going to try to get some sleep. My advice is take the phone off the hook and get as much sleep as you can."

"I need the painting," Sweeney said as Richard began steering her toward the door.

"Sweetheart, there's no need—"

"I need the painting," she repeated, digging in her heels and dragging him to a halt. She couldn't think straight; she was swaying on her feet, but she knew she couldn't leave the painting behind.

"There are reporters outside—"

"I'll wrap it in a cloth." Tugging free, she trudged into the studio and took the painting down from the easel. She always kept lengths of cheesecloth for cleaning up and for covering the paintings, and she wrapped the painting in that. Richard was right beside her every step she took, watching her worriedly, but she was too tired to reassure him. She had just enough strength to do what was necessary, and getting the painting was necessary.

A policeman escorted them through the crowd of onlookers and reporters who clogged the hall. Flashbulbs went off in her face and a tangle of questions were hurled at them, but she made no effort to sort out individual words, nor did Richard answer. He was recognized; someone called him by name. He didn't respond, keeping all his attention on her and on getting out of there. He did swear under his breath, but she was the only one who heard him.

The policeman managed to evade the couple of reporters who tried to follow them and dropped Richard and Sweeney off at Richard's town house without incident. She clutched the painting and stared at the steps, wondering if she would be able to make it up them, much less the full flight of stairs inside.

"Come on, sweetie." Richard's voice was gentle, cajoling.

"I'm not a baby," she said, scowling at him. "I'm all right."

"Of course you are."

Now he was soothing her. She hated being soothed. And she was pretty certain she could have made it up the steps without his help. She didn't want to seem ungrateful, however, so she leaned against him as they climbed the steps.

He unlocked the door and let them in, then reset the alarm system. "Just leave the painting here."

"No, I want it upstairs."

Evidently he decided that trying to argue with her would take a lot more time than going along with her. He dropped the bag at the foot of the stairs and lifted her in his arms, painting and all.

"Your shoulder!" she protested, trying to wiggle out of his arms.

"Be still, before you hurt me."

She froze, blinking up at him with big owl eyes and not moving a muscle as he climbed the stairs. If she hadn't looked so utterly exhausted, he would have laughed.

He put her on the bed, and she was asleep before he got her shoes off.

He peeled her out of the jeans but left her in his T-shirt. By the time he'd removed his own clothes and got her under the covers, he was ready to collapse beside her. Getting in on the other side of the bed, he cradled her against his right side and determinedly shut out the ache in his left shoulder, concentrating instead on the joy of having her alive, in his arms and in his bed.

The sun was up and shining brightly when Sweeney woke him with her restless movements. He opened one eye and looked at the clock. Seven-thirty. "Go back to sleep," he muttered. She didn't reply, just kept rolling her head and pushing at the covers. A chill went through him as he realized she *was* asleep.

She slipped out of bed, moving so smoothly she was out of his grasp before he could react. She stood beside the bed, her eyes open but strangely blank. She seemed bewildered, as if she wanted to go somewhere but didn't know how to get there.

Richard got out of bed and put his arms around her, shaking her gently to wake her. "Sweetie. Wake up, honey. You don't need to paint today. Come back to bed."

It was a long time before she responded, blinking and looking up at him with bleary eyes. "What?" she mumbled.

"You were sleepwalking." He kept his tone calm and got her back into bed. She immediately dropped into a deep sleep again, lying still in his arms. He allowed himself to doze, but didn't relax his guard. She was in an unfamiliar place and might fall down the stairs if she began wandering around in her sleep. He woke every time she turned over, bringing her back into his arms and keeping her safe.

Because he didn't want to leave her alone in bed, he woke her at ten-thirty. She managed to glare at him through only one eye, but to his relief she was fully alert. "You had better be waking me to have sex, because otherwise there's no excuse," she growled.

His eyes glinted, giving her maybe half a second of warning before he turned her on her back and mounted her. "I was only kid—" she began, then gasped as he pushed into her with a hard thrust that took him to the hilt. She half-screamed, and her nipples pinched into tight little buds. Her swift arousal turned him on even more, his erection hardening to the point of pain.

"Jesus," he ground out, his voice hoarse almost beyond sound. He thrust a few more times and began coming, his body arching and shuddering as he spurted into her. She cried out again and her inner muscles clamped convulsively around his cock, milking him with her orgasm.

He felt like a human wreck afterward, lying sprawled on his back, incapable of moving. He couldn't remember ever before coming that fast or that hard, not even as a teenager, when he had still thought of sex as a race to the finish line. She stirred before he did, pushing a tangled curl out of her eyes and sitting up.

"That wasn't fair," she accused, but her voice was husky with satisfaction. "Do it again, and do it right this time."

"In your dreams," he managed to growl, delighting her into a laugh. "Well, maybe tonight."

"It's a date." She bounced out of bed, moving him to a sour mental observation about being the one who had done all the work. She pulled off his T-shirt and headed for the bathroom, and the view of that curvy butt was enough to get him out of bed and into the shower with her.

He put on a suit and tie, knowing he would face a battery of reporters at the police station. They hadn't been bothered so far, only because his private number was unlisted, but he figured it wouldn't take some enterprising reporter much longer to get it. The phone downstairs in the office was probably ringing nonstop.

He buzzed Tabitha and found that he had guessed exactly right. "Tell them I'll be giving a statement at the precinct in two hours, and that you don't know anything else."

"I don't," she said, disgruntled.

"And take a long lunch," he added.

"Now you're talking."

He called Edward and asked him to bring the car around, and then he kissed Sweeney, who had put on her usual jeans-and-sweatshirt combination and was sitting cross-legged on the bed watching him. "I'll have the cell phone with me," he said.

"The number's at my apartment."

He scribbled it down again. "If the phone rings, don't answer it. If I call, I'll let it ring once, then I'll hang up and call right back."

"Got it."

"I hope this won't take long, but I'll be back as soon as I can."

"Why are you so worried?" she asked. "Kai's dead." It didn't seem real. The terror of the night felt as if it had happened to someone else.

He gave her a long, searching look. "Maybe because of what you said, about *if* he did it. I don't want to take any chances until the lab tests on the trace evidence are in."

She thought of that wall in her mind and of the blank space on the painting where the killer's face would be, if she ever finished it. "I'll be careful," she promised.

He had been gone almost an hour when his assistant called on the intercom. "We're going out to lunch. Would you like me to bring back something for you?"

"No, I'll rustle up something in the kitchen."

"Too bad Richard gave Violet the day off; she makes the most wonderful omelettes you've ever tasted. But he was supposed to be out of town today, and she had made plans to visit her son in Chicago. When all of this came up and he had to cancel, he insisted she go on."

"I'll find something," Sweeney said. She had been feeding herself for most of her life.

She made toast and scrambled an egg, though the simple meal took much longer than usual to prepare in an unfamiliar kitchen. She had to search for everything, including the toaster and coffeemaker, which weren't sitting out on the counter where all toasters and coffeemakers were supposed to sit.

Eventually she found all the necessities, and after the simple meal, found herself at loose ends. If she had been at home, she would have been working, but here she had nothing to do. She explored the house, poking her head into every door and ending up back in the bedroom. She felt much better than she had the day before, but she still hadn't had nearly enough sleep and was considering a nap when her gaze fell on the wrapped canvas, sitting propped on the chair.

She was reluctant to unwrap it, after all that had happened. She didn't want to gaze on that scene of violence again. But some nameless compulsion drove her, and she pulled the cheesecloth away.

Nothing had changed. The blank space still taunted her inability to finish the painting. She was never without a supply of charcoal pencils, so she dug one out of her purse and made a few preliminary lines on the canvas, trying to block in Kai's head. Her fingers felt clumsy, and the lines looked all wrong. Kai's hair had been thick and glossy, almost Asian in texture but with just a hint of wave. She tried to capture that look, but the lines that emerged were far too smooth and the style was all wrong—

She stepped back, staring at the painting. The charcoal lines looked rough in comparison with the precision of the oil paint, but the image was clear. The hair was smooth and pale, curving under into a chic bob. There was something familiar about it, something nagging at her, but she couldn't place what it was.

Abruptly she stiffened, staring at the canvas. She whirled and went to the phone, punching in Richard's cell phone number.

He answered immediately. There was a lot of noise in the background, and she wondered if she had caught him in the middle of his press statement. "It's a woman," she said shakily.

"*What?*" he demanded.

"It's a woman. I've done the hair—just a rough sketch, but I can tell. And . . . I've seen this hairstyle before."

"Goddamn it," he swore. "I never thought—I have to tell Aquino; he's only looked at the men on the surveillance tape. Keep the door locked and don't let anyone in until I get home."

"I won't," she started to say, but a hint of sound startled her, cut her off.

"Sweeney!"

"I think I heard something," she said. "Something downstairs."

"Are the doors locked?"

"Yes, of course."

"Where are Tabitha and Martin?"

"Gone to lunch."

"Son of a bitch." The urgency in his voice sizzled through the telephone line. "Honey, lock the bedroom door. Shove furniture against it; anything to buy some time, do you understand?"

"Yes."

"Don't hang up the phone. Keep the line open. I'm on my way."

She laid the receiver down and went to the door. She wasn't certain she had heard anything, and she would feel like a fool if the house was empty or if the sound she thought she had heard was Tabitha or Martin returning from lunch. No one was in sight; the hallway was empty, and from where she stood she could tell no one was on the stairs.

She tiptoed to the railing to look down into the foyer. Nothing.

Then she heard a faint rasping sound, coming from downstairs, perhaps in the kitchen.

She pictured the knife in the gloved hand, in the figure standing over Candra, and she knew beyond a doubt what that sound was: one of the big knives being drawn from the butcher block in the kitchen.

A blond head came into view below.

It was Margo McMillan.

Sweeney jerked back, shock numbing her to her toes. She stumbled toward the bedroom door, not caring how much noise she made, and slammed the door shut. The lock turned easily. She dragged a chair over and wedged it under the door handle, but it seemed shaky and she wasn't certain it would hold against any force. How much force could Margo exert? She was thin, but perhaps she was stronger than she looked, and interior doors weren't equipped to withstand the kind of force exterior doors were.

"Damn damn damn," she breathed, and ran to the phone. "Richard!"

"I'm here." He sounded breathless, and a siren almost drowned him out. He was in a squad car, she thought, she hoped.

"It's Margo." Her teeth suddenly chattered as a chill swept her. "M-Margo McMillan. She's here."

"She's inside the house?" he asked sharply.

"Yes. She has one of the kitchen knives. The door is locked, but—"

"If necessary, go into the bathroom and lock that door, too.

Get some towels and wrap them around your arms. Use anything you can to hinder her. Throw towels on her, and try to get them around the knife so she can't use it. Spray deodorant in her face. There are weapons in the bathroom, baby; all you have to do is use them."

"I understand," she said, whispering, unable to speak louder, though he probably couldn't hear her over the siren.

The door handle rattled. She jumped and put down the phone to go stand by the bathroom door.

Something scratched the lock. Margo was picking the lock.

The bathroom lock wouldn't be any more substantial than the bedroom lock. Sweeney ran into the bathroom and grabbed an armful of towels, as well as the can of spray deodorant. Doing as Richard had said, she wrapped a thick towel around each arm. She knew why. She was supposed to use her wrapped arms to deflect the knife. She remembered the wounds on Candra's arms.

The door opened, shoving the chair aside. Margo didn't say anything, just entered the room in a rush, the knife gleaming in her hand.

Sweeney grabbed a thick towel and lunged at the woman, throwing all her weight at her in an effort to knock her off balance. Margo screamed as the towel entangled her arm, but she struck anyway, and the knife bit through the thick fabric. Sweeney felt the kiss of it burn on her left triceps.

She didn't know how to fight. She had never fought anyone in her life. But she twisted, getting inside the arc of the knife, and hammered her fist into Margo's nose. Blood spurted, and she saw the look of shock in Margo's infuriated eyes, as if she couldn't believe anyone would dare strike her. The whole thing struck Sweeney as so ridiculous that she hit her again, and again, digging her feet against the thick carpet and pushing, using all her strength and weight to push Margo backwards.

"Bitch!" Margo shrieked, trying to wrench the knife free.

Sweeney saw the stair railing behind Margo and pushed harder, pushing, driving for the edge. The knife bit through the towel wrapped around her left arm, and the searing pain ignited a firestorm of rage. She heard herself screaming, over and over, and she pushed harder. A startled look crossed Margo's bloody face, just for a second; then the resistance of her body fell out from under Sweeney and she tumbled over the railing to land on the slate tiles below.

Panting, Sweeney dropped to her hands and knees next to the railing, heart hammering, and for a moment she thought she would faint. Blood streamed in rivulets down her left arm, soaking the towel. She would need stitches, she thought, absurdly irritated by the thought. She had never had stitches before. It would probably hurt. Her lower lip trembled at the thought.

That small tremble made her realize she was close to hysteria. She took several deep breaths, trying to focus, though it was incredibly difficult to think. The deep breaths helped, and she sat on the floor. She couldn't bring herself to look over the railing; Margo had landed with a sickening, squashy sort of thud. Slate tiles weren't forgiving of bones and flesh.

Richard. His name spread through her brain, the thought of him galvanizing her into action, pouring energy back into her legs. She scrambled to her feet and ran—stumbled, actually—into the bedroom to snatch up the receiver.

She fumbled with it, banging it against her cheekbone. "Damn it," she mumbled, and even thought she didn't have it pressed to her ear yet, she heard Richard's roar.

"Sweeney!"

"I'm okay," she said hastily. "Well, almost. Margo fell over the stair railing. I haven't looked yet."

"Don't," he said, sounding strangled. "My God—" He broke

off, and even over the sound of the siren coming through his cell phone, she heard his labored breathing. "We'll be there in about five minutes. Other patrol cars are on their way. Are you hurt?"

"A little. A couple of cuts on my arm, nothing serious." *I don't think.* She hadn't looked at the cut on her triceps or the one on her forearm, where the knife had sliced through the towel. She didn't intend to unwrap that towel, either; she didn't want to see the damage. She knew it hurt, and that was enough. "I'm going to hang up now, okay? I think I need to vomit." She didn't wait for an answer, just hung up, and then put her head between her knees, taking deep breaths and fighting the nausea that threatened to overwhelm her.

The sound was so low she wasn't certain she heard it. Her head came up, blood leaping through her veins as she prepared to fight again, but no one was there. She blinked, bewildered, then heard it again: a low moan, from downstairs.

Gingerly Sweeney crept out of the bedroom to the stairs and looked over the railing. Margo lay on her stomach, her left leg bent at an impossible angle under her torso, jagged edges of bone showing white through the torn flesh. Her arms . . . oh, God, she must have tried to brace herself. Margo moved feebly, trying to roll over, and another of those low moans echoed through the house.

Her legs trembling, Sweeney went down the stairs. No matter what, she couldn't leave Margo in that condition without trying to offer aid, though she had no idea what she could do for injuries so severe.

She knelt beside Margo, and to her shock the woman focused dazed eyes on her. "I fell," Margo whispered.

"Don't talk. People are coming—"

"I want to . . . tell you. So someone knows." She coughed, and blood dribbled from her mouth onto the floor. "Candra . . .

Candra was blackmailing . . . Carson. I . . . I had to stop her. Kai had a . . . key . . . to her apartment. I . . . rented an apartment in the . . . building, and waited for her." She winced and coughed again. "Couldn't . . . find the . . . tape, or pictures. I wore Carson's clothes . . . so if anything surfaced, he . . . would be blamed. Her blood . . . on his shoes. Then you . . . painting—"

Sweeney understood. "Kai saw the painting and told you."

"He was . . . so beautiful," Margo whispered, her gaze losing its focus and growing more distant. "I . . . loved him. Silly. Old enough . . . to be his mother. Because of Carson . . . he's dead. Tell them . . . Tell them about Carson. Find . . . the pictures." Her lips twitched in a ghastly, bitter smile. "Nail . . . his ass."

"You can tell them yourself," Sweeney said urgently, but Margo's eyes were already fixed, her expression fading, and her last breath sighed out of her lungs, never to be replaced.

A distant siren got louder and louder as it neared. Numbly Sweeney got to her feet and went to open the door as two patrol cars squealed to a stop in front of the house.

She was sitting on the bottom step of the stairs when Richard and Detectives Aquino and Ritenour burst in a few moments later. Richard's face was paper white, his skin drawn brutally tight across his cheekbones. His gaze went straight to her. He didn't even glance at Margo. With a rigidly controlled stride, he crossed to the stairs and, without a word, bent and lifted her into his arms, holding her to his chest.

"I'm taking her to a hospital," he said hoarsely. His entire big body was trembling.

Aquino said, "The medics will be here in just a minute—"

Richard ignored him and carried Sweeney outside. She blinked like a mole at the bright sunshine. Evidently Edward had followed hard in the wake of the detectives' car, because the Mercedes was parked right behind it. He got into the backseat with Sweeney, holding her on his lap, and barked instructions at Edward.

Her voice shaking, Sweeney began telling him what Margo had said, just before she died. He stopped her with two fingers laid across her mouth. "I don't care," he said fiercely. "Just—just shut up and let me hold you. God, I was so scared—" His voice broke and he buried his face in her hair.

He stayed with her the entire time her arm was being stitched. The cut in her forearm was the worst, requiring twenty-six stitches, but neither cut was deep enough to have damaged nerves or tendons. "Because of the towels," she told him, her eyes wide and her lips trembling now that shock had set in. "If you hadn't told me about the towels—"

"I'll give you a prescription for pain medication," the doctor said, easing off her stool. She smiled at Sweeney. "Go to your regular doctor in a week to get the stitches removed." Then she went on to her next casualty, and Richard scooped Sweeney onto his lap again.

"I love you," he said, his voice still shaken. "I was so afraid I was going to lose you. Will you marry me?"

That question rattled her almost as much as Margo's attack. "M-marry?" she stuttered.

"Marry." He framed her face with his hands, searching her features with dark eyes stark and naked, letting her see every emotion. "I know you're wary; I understand that. But I would never try to get in the way of your painting; you're too talented for anyone to try to stifle. I've made some tentative plans to liquidate and get out of the market, buy a ranch somewhere, but if you—"

"Where?" she asked, interrupting.

"I haven't really looked yet; either the South or Southwest.

As I was saying, if you prefer living in the city, I'll forget about the ranch and—"

"As long as it's somewhere warmer I don't care," she interrupted again. "Though a palm tree or two would be nice."

He went still, looking down at her. She looked back at him, then said, "Tick-tick-tick."

"What's that?"

"That's my biological clock. I think it's about to alarm."

His face changed, filling with such heat and passion for a moment she thought she might be ravished right there in the hospital. "Are you certain?" he asked, and he sounded shaken all over again.

"I'm terrified," she admitted, her own voice shaking now that she had time to think about what she had just said. "I mean, I might be as lousy a mother as my mother was. But I want—" She swallowed. "I want you, and I want your children."

He laughed softly. "Then, sweetie, we're all yours."

Epilogue

A Year Later

Richard looked up from the book he was reading. "What time of day were you born?" he asked curiously.

Surprised, she gave him a questioning glance. "What are you reading?" she asked suspiciously.

"Just answer the question."

"I don't know exactly. I think I remember Mom saying I was born a little after sundown, whatever time sundown was. Why?"

He smiled and held up the book. She read the title: *Ghosts and Other Spirits*. "So?"

He looked down at the page and softly quoted, " *'And there are those who are born on the twilight of certain days who shall be blessed with magic, and have the ability to see spirits.'*